"Progeny's Descendants"

#ProgDescendants

Written by
Ray Jay Perreault

Ray Jay Perreault

Ray Jay Perreault Free Book

Ray Jay Perreault has an Award-Winning Science Fiction Novel available – no strings attached. Follow this link, and you'll be able to get a FREE copy of "Virus-72 Hours to Live." Winner of the 2016 Apple Literary Award as the summer's best Science Fiction.

By joining my reader's club, you'll get other books of his FREE or discounted as well as having the option to Alpha/Beta Read his new novels before they're released.

I often run campaigns for the other eBooks and Audible books. You'll have the chance to get major discounts and other FREE opportunities.

Ray Jay Perreault

Table of Contents

Part 1 Earth Was Tired

Earth's Council of Environmental Sciences was meeting in a large amphitheater 200 feet below the surface of Lake Geneva. None of the attendees wanted to be there. Word of the meeting had been passed to all the population centers on Earth, and only 52 people could safely travel to the site. The remainder of the attendees were forced to participate through electronic means. Earth was tired. She had endured many eons of neglect, ambivalence, and in some cases, attacks. Her climate had changed a great deal. It was true, throughout Earth's life, the climate had many swings, but those natural swings turned into violent ones that initially matched, then created new extremes. The purpose of the meeting was to review and accept a horrible hypothesis. The downward spiral of the deteriorating climate was well beyond the tipping point, and it would continue to a point where human life was not sustainable.

"Ladies and gentlemen, I want to welcome all of you and those of you that are participating through video feeds. If my information is correct, we have personnel from our centers beneath many capital cities and our six underwater habitats in each major ocean. Unfortunately, we have intermittent contact with a couple of the underground cities, so their participation might be limited.

"As you were told through the meeting invitation, we have come to the point where we have to make a decision. Many of you have already spent time supporting the different committees looking into atmospheric trends, the results of the population displacement study, the committee on infectious disease control, and lastly, the committee coordinating the spaceship development. So, when I make the statement that all of our studies conclude that Earth has become hostile to the human race, none of you will be shocked. That is why we are here today. We must take the results from all of our studies and make one final decision for the future of our race. Over the last century, our population has decreased precipitously. If any action is taken, it must be done immediately if a viable amount of us will be able to leave and find another home.

"Based on the results of all these studies, we must acknowledge the one lasting fact, which is our planet is no longer able to sustain life. Of course, I wish we could have met face-to-face, but travel conditions are so difficult that it wouldn't be wise. Because of that, I want to hear from any of you who disagree with our studies' conclusion. But let me warn you if you do disagree, disagreement won't be enough. Our situation is so dire, you must present an alternate plan."

The room and electronic connections were quiet. Those members in the room looked at each other, shook their heads in a reluctant agreement, or just sat in their seats looking at their hands folded in front of them. The members sharing the electronic connection were just as quiet. After the pause had become uncomfortable, the speaker continued.

"I hear no disagreement. I declare that we must leave Earth and find a suitable planet. I also declare that all production facilities and remaining resources be used to build the large fleet of spaceships that have been described by the transportation committee. If there are no other comments, this meeting is adjourned, and may good fortune and God's smile fall upon on all of us."

The many creatures that lived on her surface and in the depths of her oceans did the best they could to adapt during the later years. Many became extinct because they couldn't adapt as fast as the climate was changing. Those that had adapted only found new and greater challenges and most of them finally lost the battle.

During Earth's later days, one of the few remaining creatures was the one that did the most damage, mankind. Mankind's impact was debated early, but it soon became a minor issue. The changes were so profound and disastrous for the mix of species; ultimately, who caused it wasn't as important as what was necessary to survive.

Aside from the degrading weather, the viral and bacterial world reacted the same way as the humans. The struggle to survive occurred at all levels, and in many cases, the enemy was perceived as the humans. As a result, plagues and pandemics became common place for those remaining on the surface, and even those who sought refuge underground and underwater were beginning to feel the onslaught.

A sad day occurred when mankind realized that the conditions on Earth were caught in a downward spiral. The living conditions had driven some of them underground and into aquatic cities under the water. Those who couldn't afford to move and remained on the surface were perishing in huge numbers.

The world was learning that the end was coming, and nothing could be done to reverse the trend, forcing a decision to leave the Earth. But, unfortunately, it wasn't a decision based on optimism of looking for a new home but on the pessimism of having to leave to survive.

As soon as the decision to leave was announced, society began fragmenting. It broke into three groups. Those who didn't want to leave, along with many who suspected they wouldn't be selected, those who wanted to leave and hoped they would be selected, and those who expected to be selected. Unfortunately, society continued the segmentation and stratification as the groups became suspicious of each other, the barriers between them became larger and more difficult to cross.

Mankind was fortunate as their technology had progressed to the point where they had some options. That was the good news; the bad news was that they hadn't found any suitable planets within a reasonable distance in such a long time of research. Faster than light travel was still theoretical and only in the dreams of scientists. They knew that travel to a sustainable planet would be long and hazardous, but the trip had to be attempted. If only a portion of those leaving Earth survived to land on a suitable planet, then there was the chance the human race would survive.

Departure

Despite the deteriorating conditions on the planet, they built enough ships capable of interstellar flight to carry a significant portion of Earth's remaining population. The good news was they had the ships, and the bad news was there weren't enough.

Earth had deteriorated to the extent that living on the surface was almost impossible. A large percentage of the Earth's population was lost over the years while the ships were built.

The only fair method to determine who was going to leave was through a series of lotteries. During the lottery process, percentages of key disciplines were segregated from the general population, so any long-duration flight would have the right skills to support survival during the trip and reach when they reach their new home. After the lottery had decided who went and who stayed, the stratification of the population became complete. Those not going rioted and those that were going built barriers higher.

When conditions got to the point where they were ready for departure, there was no announcement, no parades, and departing speeches. Instead, the first of the ships loaded and looked more like a group of survivors abandoning ship than the last humans leaving their home planet. The departures continued as the ships were loaded and left orbit.

The effort to load so many ships caused the departure to occur in waves. They were called clusters, and over the months, many clusters were loaded and sent on their way.

Leaving the Earth

Cluster Admiral Ronda P. Hartsfield stood next to the last shuttle to leave the Kansas City Underground Launch Facility. She didn't like what was happening in front of her. The last of the refugees from Kansas City were boarding her shuttle. They stood in lines, and each of them looked like they had lost a long battle. There was no jubilance; there was no laughing or joking. They just moved forward when their time came to board one of the last shuttles to leave Earth.

125 Feet above them, the wind was blowing at 125 MPH, and the ambient temperature was 115 Degrees. Not bad for 1 AM in January. The last of the die-hard survivors that decided to stay on the surface hadn't been heard from in over a month. Everyone thought they had lost the battle and were gone.

"Mr. President, these people look beat. They are the last of the people from underground shelter 44C. Once they're on board, we'll be able to leave."

"Admiral, this is a horrible day in Earth's history. I wish that things weren't so bad, but we have no other options. How are the other shuttle launches going?"

"There is still a handful launching from different cities around Earth. I think there are only about a dozen left that need to meet up with the transports in orbit. The transports are waiting for us, and when we join up, we'll depart. All the other ships have left orbit and are following the planned flight path to our destination."

"I wish we knew where we were going. Launching off like this and just heading in a direction scares the hell out of me."

"I know, Mr. President. But we have little choice. We can't stay here because of many reasons. Our only chance of survival is to leave. Our destination was picked based on the highest concentration of Earth-like planets in the region. No one wanted to spend all our resources and go to a system where there MIGHT be one planet because if we were wrong for some reason, then we're all dead. So, we have to follow the odds and go where we should have the most options."

"That all sounds great but over a three-hundred-year journey on these ships? You and I will both be dead, our children will be dead, our grandchildren may be dead, and we'll be on our third or fourth generation before we get there. None of that sounds very encouraging to me."

"Sir, I know that. But we have no choice. We can't continue to live underground and underwater. We will die slowly, but we will die."

"Ma'am, the last of the people, are on board," said the loading master as the last of the tired people entered the shuttle.

"Thanks. Sir, it's our turn," the Admiral said as she indicated for the President to board the craft so they could launch.

Admiral Hartsfield walked onto the bridge of the US5323, commonly called KC-42, which was the craft's call sign. As she looked around the command room, all eyes were upon her. The Command Bridge performed a two-fold function. It was the Command Center for KC-42, but it was also the Coordination Center for that cluster. Because of the many functions that needed support, the center had two levels, and Admiral Hartsfield's Command Station was positioned between decks so she could see each of the stations and their holographic representation of their system's status.

Each of the crewmembers manning their stations for the huge ship knew the significance of what was happening. They were all scared and desperate, or else they wouldn't have been there. The Admiral took her time and walked to each of the stations and spoke to her crew. Some of them were near breaking down, and they were all under tremendous pressure.

US5323 was a huge ship. It was typical of her class and represented the best of Earth's technology and, unfortunately, the last of it. Earth used the last of her resources, the last skilled people, and the last time available to build. There was nothing left to do but leave. Admiral Hartsfield didn't pay attention to how many ships there were; to her, it didn't matter. She was responsible for her cluster of ships, and there were many other Admirals in charge of their small portions of the fleet. A person was responsible for the entire fleet of Earth ships, but he had left five months ago and was in no position to help them or direct them. All ships were going to one point in space, and the string was strung out over many parsecs. It would take 25 years for them to accelerate to full speed and the overall plan was simple enough. However, they were so stretched out, there was very little that they could do to help each other, so the fleet traveled in clusters. Each of them varied in size, but they had the transport ships with the people on board. There were also livestock ships, repair ships, and storage ships.

Admiral Hartsfield and the other ships preparing to leave orbit were the last cluster to leave Earth. The first of the cluster left over two hours ago and, KC 42 would be the last one to leave orbit and the last one to see Earth.

Admiral Hartsfield knew that if would be a challenge to keep her crew together and get the departure done safely. It was difficult for her not to look at the view screens as everyone else on the bridge did. They recorded what Earth looked like in their memories, and they likely would pass those memories on to their children and grandchildren one day. But today, it was hard for them to keep their emotions in check. Some of them were crying, and the Admiral let it happen as long as they did their job and their emotions didn't interfere.

Even the Admiral was susceptible to the emotions generated leaving Earth. She fought the urge, but just before departure, she had to take a moment and look at the view screens. She knew that what she saw wasn't the best of Earth. She had seen images, growing up, that showed the snowcapped mountains, the azure seas, and the blue skies. But she knew that what she was looking at wasn't how it was supposed to be; it was how it had become. Earth looked angry. There were massive storms that covered most of the surface. The sky had a definite yellow tinge to it and what little she could see of the seas showed a turbulent surface with a definite light shade of green. It wasn't the image that she had grown up with, but it was the image she had become familiar with. Regardless Earth was their home and leaving it was painful. The last pictures in their minds were of a beautiful planet that was mistreated and was lashing out at those who had treated her badly.

"Are we ready to leave orbit?" came out of a point deep in the Admiral's throat.

"Yes, ma'am," was the emotional reply of the ship's captain.

"Then, let's go," was all she had the strength to say before they left the orbit of Earth for the last time.

125 Years from Earth

"Mrs. Tierney why did our ancestors treat Earth so badly?" asked Todd, who was sitting in the front row of the 3rd Grade Class of the George Washington Primary School, 27th deck, KC 42.

"Todd, they made many mistakes which lead to the end. There were decades of growth and overusing the resources. Everyone thought that Earth's resources were unlimited, but they weren't. By the time they saw how the damage was changing the planet, it was almost too late to do anything. For a long time, they ignored the problems, then they talked around them, then they blamed others. Finally, it was clear that the climate had gone too far, and it was going in a bad direction for everyone. It's not that they treated the Earth badly; it's just that they focused on their needs first and assumed everything else would be okay, but it wasn't, and they learned the lesson too late."

Just as she was finishing the lesson, another hand went up in the rear of the class, "Mrs. Tierney, why do we study Earth? All we've seen are pictures. It doesn't seem important to us anymore. We live on this ship, and our parents and grandparents lived on this ship."

"To know where we are going, we must know where we came from. We are living here now. We have 824 clusters of ships making this journey, and yes, we still have many years before we reach our destination. The only way we can concentrate on what's in front of us is to remember the sacrifice everyone is making. The first of the clusters are a full light year ahead of us, and they are going through space that no human has ever seen before. We are following them because we all want to get to our new home. We all must do our part so that all of those on this journey will have a chance for a future. That is our destiny, to enjoy what we have so that others will have their enjoyment also. Earth is all that we had, and because we were terrestrial animals, I think that it is important to remember where our beginnings were."

"Okay, this is the end of this segment of school today. You can leave and go to the exercise area," Mrs. Tierney said.

Before she finished the sentence, the children were moving in a swarm towards the door, and she laughed, knowing they likely didn't hear anything after 'end.' Now that her half-day was over, she would finish the day off by transmitting her 3D lesson to another ship in the cluster.

She liked teaching that way; it was the best way for children to get instruction from multiple teachers, and the teachers in the cluster could change topics and work with different children. Physical movement between ships in the cluster occurred rarely, there was too much risk, and it was done only in critical situations.

>>>>>>>>>>>>>>>>>>>>>>>

"Willy, hand me that sponge…, will ya?" asked Kinkaid Robinson, or Kink as his friends called him.

Willy threw it down the crawl space then went back to cleaning the interior of the return air system for KC-42.

"Boy, is it me, or is this shit getting harder to wipe off? I don't remember it getting this thick before," pointed out Kink.

"Just shut up and finish up, I've got to meet some of the guys in the section room, and I don't want to be late."

Kink bore down and continued to wipe the sticky slime off the walls of the return air system. For some reason, it seemed to change over time; it never was that slimy before. He wanted to spend some time in the section room before heading back to the small set of rooms he shared with his wife and their two allocated children.

>>>>>>>>>>>>>>>>>>>>>>>

"Captain Williamsport, we're getting the weekly status message passed down from the clusters. Do you want to hear it now?" asked the communications tech who was on duty at the time.

The bridge of KC-42 was lightly manned. All they had to do was monitor the key systems and, on occasion, communicate with others in their cluster. It wasn't a ship in the sense that they had control over where they were going; it was a huge human island moving through space at .6 the speed of Light Speed. They monitored the key systems and then changed shifts, then the next crew would monitor the key systems. It went on like that day after day.

A couple times a week, there would be some important communications between the ships in the cluster, but generally, it was just a transmission between two ships in the void wanting to confirm that someone else was out there. Then, on rarer occasions or, at least, weekly, some messages came down from the lead clusters, and they were passed between each of the clusters in sequence until they finally reached the last cluster, the one that KC-42 was in. This was one of those occasions.

"Yes, go ahead and put it on the speaker," replied Jonas Paul, the current captain of KC-42.

"Attention all Earth Vehicles. This is Earth 1 transmitting our weekly update. We have traveled 61.19606 light-years from Earth, and we calculate that we have 117.3309 light-years remaining in our journey. We are encouraged that we've been able to maintain a velocity slightly above the .6 Light Speed that we planned the trip on. Up to this point, we've been able to accelerate to .611961 Light Speed. Let us hope the higher velocity continues.

We have a couple of announcements. The first one saddens us all: Christin P. Hershel, the last passenger, born on Earth, passed away in her sleep two solar days ago. We will remember her, and all the recordings of her interviews will be passed from ship to ship until we all have them available. Her passing reminds us of Louis Daniels, who we all remember as the last adult with any memories of Earth, and his sad passing almost 10 solar years ago. All his records are recorded in the ship's log and have been shared among all ships. I'm also saddened to pass on that some of our ships have been experiencing significant technical difficulties. In most cases, we've been able to work within the clusters to fix the broken systems, but in some cases, we're running low on some of the key materials. We pray that this rate of failure won't continue. I'm also concerned about another development.

There have been some isolated outbreaks of unusual illness in some of the clusters. I don't think there is any cause for concern at this point, but we ask you to work within the clusters to monitor everyone's health and pass forward anything significant. I also want to remind the cluster leaders to pass forward any key information that should be shared among the entire fleet. I'm sorry that passing information forward to the lead vehicles takes so much longer than when we pass a message back, but, unfortunately, we're constrained by the speed of light, and messages going forward take more than twice the time a message goes backward. Please remember we are in this together, and through that cooperation, we'll make it to our new home."

250 Years from Earth

Admiral Joyce Herbold sat in the command chair and looked around the bridge of her ship. Only about half of the stations were manned, and only a few minutes from the watch change when her exec officer would relieve her for the night watch. So it was quiet time, one to reflect on her life, where they were, where they were going, and their chances of success.

The wall behind her showed holographic pictures of the previous Admirals of their cluster and pictures of the Captains for KC-42. On the left was the picture of the first; her name was Rhonda Hartsfield. As Joyce looked at her eyes, she wondered if the first people leaving Earth had any idea how difficult the journey to their new home would be. It wasn't a simple issue of just jumping on a spaceship and going to the new planet; it was perhaps the greatest challenge in the history of the human race.

In actuality, the trip was turning horrendous. The consensus was that they had bitten off more than they could chew, as the old saying went. The challenges of putting a planet-bound creature into a huge ship were not fully understood, and Admiral Herbold and the others making the journey were the people paying for that miscalculation.

The problems impacting the human race fell into three categories. The mechanical failures, the human impacts, and the unknowns.

The mechanical challenges were much larger than just repairing and replacing worn-out parts. The mechanical failure rates were higher than planned, and also the use of consumables was also much higher than projected. The only solution was rationing the repairs and supplies. Some of the consumables were replaced with others, but the overall mechanical reliability of the fleet was decreasing rapidly.

The second impact on the humans was personal. Men and women weren't made to spend their entire life on a ship. They were made to breathe real air, drink real water, and eat real food. The population was still holding together, but the illness rate, both physical and emotional, brought the entire population's outlook to a dismal level. Regardless of the upbeat messages of getting closer to their destination, the overall enthusiasm upon launch 250 years ago was gone. There were rumors that a couple of the ships in other clusters had some incidents. The only clarification they got was that the loss of human life was minimal.

The last problem was perhaps the worst and potentially disastrous. The ships were designed for human occupants, but they were also ideal for viral and bacterial occupants. Not on purpose, but where the humans go, the virus and bacterium also go. If a mad scientist put living creatures in a glass jar and watched to see who would survive, that would be like what the clusters were dealing with.

Within the first 150 years after departure, the problems began to surface. People were getting sick with new virus. In the closed environment of the ships and the relatively stable viral gene pool, the world was perfect from the perspective of the microbiological world. It allowed the virus a new method of mutation. Instead of multiple variations in their mutations, they became focused, and some of the common viruses that man had developed immunity to changed and found new weapons with which to attack.

The bacterium world was even worse. The closed environments of the ships turned into an ideal breeding ground. Each generation of bacteria grew more accustomed to the ship and developed new mechanisms to produce and take over their world. Unfortunately, 'their bacterial world' was shared by the humans on the ships. Even if the bacteria weren't harmful to the ship's human occupants, they could become harmful to the ship. In the instances where the bacteria were harmful to humans, the bacteria often won the battle. Many ships had to be abandoned because of the bacteria that had grown beyond man's ability to battle.

The bacteria took many paths depending on the ship's environments. Not all ships had the same battles. It was almost as if different bacteria developed in different ships. If one ship was unfortunate to have the wrong bacteria evolve, then its end was almost inevitable.

The mechanical issues of the fleet were almost manageable, but the viral and bacterial issues were the real threat to the human cargo. Because of that threat, travel between ships within a cluster was forbidden. The risk of passing a pathogen or bacteria was too great. So instead, each ship would fight the battle alone, and the outcome was theirs to bear.

Some of the ships seemed to bear the battles better than others. Those that kept the ship spotlessly clean from day one generally, were better off. Any of the ships that didn't clean everything, all the time, eventually succumbed to the microscopic attacks.

KC-42 was one of the lucky ones. They had conducted extensive cleaning early in the trip, which was likely why they were in pretty good shape later. That isn't to say they had no problems, but the growths in the air ducts were acceptable and not harmful to the human occupants. Cleaning the ducts and filters was now the number one job on the ships, and crews were doing it 24 hours a day as the battle continued.

Admiral Herbold looked in Admiral Hartsfield's eyes and wondered if she would have made the trip if they knew what the challenges would be.

"Admiral, we're receiving our weekly update from Earth 1. Should I patch it into your comm?" asked the communications officer.

"Yes," was the Admiral's cryptic reply. So much of the news coming down from the other clusters had become bad news. They were all battling for survival, and the Admiral felt that she needed to hear it first before passing on segments. Over the years, the tone of the message had changed from optimism and good news, through the cautionary news, to news that showed how the fleet was deteriorating. Recently, the news was fighting a battle to still be intact when they reached the new planet.

The Admiral waited for a moment for the message to start, and she looked around the bridge. The walls were covered with images of Earth; they showed beautiful pictures of what she might have been for many years before their departure. To some, the images were all that kept them together; to others, they were horrific reminders of a world they would never see, and they hated them.

"Earth Fleet, this is Earth 1 with our weekly update. We are now 40.83586 light-years from our destination, and we are on schedule to begin the slowdown in 49.4 years. I have some good news we are close enough to get images and more information about our primary target. We knew that many planets in the sector we're approaching might provide a suitable home for us. We have looked at many of them, and we're lucky there is a huge list of candidates. We have narrowed the search to the one with the greatest chance for us, and I'm excited to announce that the early information we're getting shows our choice to be perfect. We'll begin to transmit pictures and information back through the clusters to all of you from now on. So, you'll be able to start getting to know our new home."

"Now for our fleet status…." From that point on, Admiral Herbold almost didn't want to listen. They had lost more ships to various bacterial battles and mechanical issues. That was the information that the Admiral wouldn't pass on. Each ship lost wasn't just one less ship, but they represented the loss of thousands of lives. The fleet was in a survival mode, and everyone hoped that enough of them survived to land on their new home.

Slow Down-25 Years from Horizon 299.4 Years from Earth

"10, 9, 8, 7, 6, 5, 4, 3, 2, 1,…Initiate the slowdown" was a simple phrase that Admiral Timothy Beardly transmitted. It may have been a simple phrase, but it initiated the slowing of all the craft in their cluster. Their cluster was the last cluster of ships that constituted the remnants of the human race in their odyssey from a dying Earth to a new home that had been named Horizon.

The clusters left Earth with 543 ships and 503,232 people on board these ships. However, the journey was difficult. When they eventually reached the slow-down point, only 412 ships were left and 401,826 people on those ships.

They had traveled 178.527 light-years from Earth and had 10.605 left on their journey. The next 25 years would be a gradual slowdown from .611961 light speed to a speed they could enter orbit around their new home.

The bacterial battle was raging on. At least, they had found some techniques that seemed to buy them time. Most of the supply follow ships were almost empty; all the supplies and repair parts onboard were almost gone. With some planning, a portion of the occupants of a nearby transport could be moved to the near-empty supply ship, and their portion of the transport vehicle was evacuated to free space. Then the cleaning crews could go through it and conduct a very thorough cleaning. Once done, the section would be re-pressurized, and the occupants returned. It was a challenge, and there was risk involved, but at least it gave them a periodic advantage over the bacteria.

As they got closer and ships were either too infected with bacteria or emptied, they would be put on a path to lead them past Horizon and enter into a death spiral into Horizon's sun. They wanted to reduce, as much as possible, any chance of carrying the bacteria to the surface.

Arrival at Horizon

The tension on board KC-42 was building each day. Images of Horizon were available in real-time and being transmitted to every part of the ship and cluster. Each day of the last year of deceleration was a day of celebration. The instruments were telling the story of the new home of the human race. Progressively the images were getting clearer and larger as they approached the orbit insertion point.

News from the previous ships that arrived was excellent. One by one, as they entered orbit, they used their aged shuttles to ferry the important human cargo to the surface. They emptied the storage containers and began to build a new home. The climate was suitable, the soil was fertile. The water and air were clean. The population grew with each new ship, and the new world had begun.

Admiral Beardly stood on the bridge watching the transmissions from the surface and monitoring the data from his ship as it approached the engine firing point where the last of their velocity would be removed, and the huge ship would settle into a stable orbit around Horizon. Beardly felt humbled, thinking about the many lives lost, the challenges that his ancestors had begun so long ago, and the fact that he was fortunate to be one of the survivors of the greatest migration in human history.

All the view screens on the bridge showed the beauty of Horizon, and the bridge crew was excited and almost giddy in performing their duties. The ship's computers were programmed to perform the final burn automatically, but there was something about the act that forced Admiral Beardly to use a command to initiate the final act of orbital entry. There was something human about saying the words after such a long trip that would put the final event under human control, not the control of the computer.

"10, 9, 8, 7, 6, 5, 4, 3, 2, 1, …Initiate the burn,"

"Aye, aye Admiral."

Deserted Earth

There were no humans left on Earth. Yet, it still sustained life, a life that struggled to survive. Life survived on the surface, beneath the soil, water, and in the air. It was a challenge, but it was a challenge that life had passed through before.

There was another activity. An activity that mankind abandoned and assumed was of little value.

Left to heal, Earth began to change. The microbial world was processing much of the pollution. The trees began processing the air, and other activities continued to survive, change, and improve.

Part 2 HSV#2 Launch

Commander Leopold Harnesy was standing on the bridge of HSV#2. He was nervous. In fact, he was scared. The fate of HSV#1 was fresh in his mind. His ship's predecessor was sitting in the exact location 5 years ago, and when its commander, Roberta Jenkins, engaged the faster than light drive, the ship disintegrated into trillions of molecules. Although it was obvious what happened, their calculations were a little off.

The faster-than-light drive, or the light distortion drive, was supposed to compress the ship and crew's molecules, then a funny thing was supposed to happen. Like the old adage, nature abhors a vacuum it also abhors an imbalance in forces at the molecular level. A minor distortion between molecules causes a ripple in the dimension's time/space fabric, and the result is similar to firing an apple seed by squeezing it. For many years, science added energy trying to go faster. Then they discovered that when they created a minor distortion between molecules, the forces of the entire time/space fabric within the dimension fought to correct the imbalances. So they could use a little energy to focus immense forces. The two main variables were the rate of distortion and the amount dependent on the total mass and the distance to be traveled. As the distortion between molecules increased, it took a finite amount of time for the forces to build up within the dimension. If the local distortion appeared too fast or too much, it would exceed the forces building to correct it. Once that happened, the distortion continued, and the molecules separated. That is what happened to HSV#1 and Roberta Jenkins.

The title Light Distortion Drive was named early in development. When the distance between the electrons and nucleus of the atom was altered, photons were released, which allowed light to escape. As a result, when the test vehicles were launched, a red glow would form around the vehicle for the instant before it jumped. Without a specific scientific name that fit the situation, Light Distortion seemed to be the aptest title.

When HSV#1 was launched, the intended target was 2.1 light-years away, and the decrease in the molecular distance was beyond the ability of the molecular forces to come back together. Unfortunately, they were scattered over a large portion of space.

The light distortion drive was discovered almost 150 years ago, and it took a while to mature the design and calculations. Finally, the engineers discovered that light is like fabric that goes in infinite directions. It is made up of waves of particles that have a weak molecular bond. If you can pull two strands of that fabric apart, a light-wave void is created. Existence hates that void and will do everything it can to correct it. Once the void was created, the key discovery was that it touched all space/time fabric. The full force of existence tried to correct the void, and when it was corrected, the craft within that void would move across the time/space fabric in a precise direction for a prescribed distance.

Commander Harnesy was well aware of the details of faster than light travel. Although, since that terrible incident, the scientists had made many short and longer-range trips with unmanned vehicles, this would be the first one with people onboard. That was the bottom line; the real trips needed humans on board for them to be successful.

This initial crewed jump was to the same point that Roberta Jenkins had attempted. It was the largest local void within a reasonable distance. A jump of that distance would put them in a region of space where they would be safe if the calculations were off a little. Once they arrived, they'd be able to make the necessary calculations to make the jump back.

The time had finally arrived, and the calculations were complete. It was up to Commander Harnesy to push the button. HSV#2 wasn't a large ship, so the calculation's portion due to its mass would be a small factor. He had only six other crewmen with him, and if they were successful in the jump and they were able to verify the calculations, then the next jumps would be with larger ships.

HSV#2 was a modest ship; after all, it was to test a proof of concept. It wasn't going to transport anything. The bridge was basic and functional with its limited mission, with more metal and exposed piping than anything plush. The ship was small, so the bridge was compact. Commander Harnesy was sitting in the middle of a semi-circle of work locations. On a platform in front of him was a 3D projector which showed their relationship to local space. Each of the work locations was operated by select men and women working with the Captain for many years. They were experts in their fields, and he had 100% confidence in them.

To Harnesy's immediate left was the Energy Management Officer. The ship wasn't much more than a container of energy. Even though the technology required less than previously thought, a jump of any sizable mass needed almost six months of the output of Horizon's Fission Reactors. That energy had to be stored and released within a fraction of a second for the Light Distortion Engine to work.

The energy coupled with the complexities of navigation made those first jumps critical. They had enough for the test jump, and if it was successful, they needed to make the first jump to Earth within a narrow window. The calculations were so complex, a delay of more than a few days, and their endpoint could vary by hundreds of millions of miles.

To his right was the officer responsible for Ship Operations. It wasn't a complex ship but, it had systems that needed to be monitored and regulated.

In the center, in front of Commander Harnesy, sat his Science Officer, Ensign Holden. She was the senior scientist on board, and she was responsible for the overall operation of the systems and drive. It was up to her to understand all of the technologies involved so the test jump would be a success, and they wouldn't find the same fate as HSV#1.

To Ensign Holden's right was the Light Distortion Drive Officer. She managed the checklist, which got all of the systems online and set up for the jump. This was her first time in space, and everyone on the bridge would kid her, saying, 'don't worry if it fails, your molecules will be spread over a square parsec of space." None of the crew's kidding had much effect on relaxing her.

Seated at Commander Harnesy's right hand was Captain Parker, who was responsible for crew operations and Security. In a direct sense, they all worked for him, but he, in turn, worked for the Commander.

Commander Harnesy enjoyed his crew, and he was proud of how well they worked together. Over the years, they had many ups and downs in the testing, and because of the successes and failures, they had grown close as a crew. Harnesy was pleased that the Prime Minister saw fit to spend some money on his crew and give them brand new uniforms for the test jump. Perhaps it was some small way for her to help them take their minds off the risks involved. Regardless they were all wearing their new uniforms, and as he scanned them, it was like a small parade. For a moment, he chuckled then focused on the important task at hand.

Test Jump

The activities on the bridge came under control as each of the key systems came online, verified, and determined to be within the necessary parameters. Then, as each crew member finished their preparations, the crewmember would stop activity waiting for the others.

"Captain Parker, are the checklists complete?"

Parker glanced at the holographic pop-up screen before him and verified that all the systems and stations were green. "Yes, sir. We're ready for the jump."

Everyone on the deck took a deep breath and glanced towards Commander Harnesy.

"Okay, I guess it's time to see if this works," Harnesy said as his hand hovered over the Jump Button, then he pressed it.

The 3D holographic projection in front of him shimmered, and then the stars all rotated about 10 degrees. None of the calculations indicated they would feel anything traumatic but feeling nothing was a little anti-climactic. "Boy, that was exciting," was all he could say, and he felt the stress level of the crew suddenly change, and some of them laughed a little as they looked at each other, verifying they were still in one piece.

"Flight computer, please calculate our location.

"HSV#2 is 2.10027 light-years from its starting location."

Slowly the smile crept across Harnesy's face, and he glanced around the control room as a smile emerged on the faces of his co-travelers. "We just jumped a little over 2.1 light-years," he screamed, and the crew broke out in cheers and applause.

"Okay, ladies and gentlemen, now we have to get home. Let's start the calculations and remember we have to be precise; we have a much smaller target on the return trip."

While his crew worked with the computers, he had a few minutes to think. The human race had come a long way in the previous generations. He was proud of their accomplishments and their history. However, the history of the human race was broken into two epochs, before 'The Migration' and after 'The Migration.'

The Migration was the point in human history where they left their original home, Earth, and moved to the star system HR 3617. In one respect, it was the most traumatic event in human nature, but it was the best thing that could have happened in another sense. Before 'The Migration, humanity destroyed their home planet. Of course, it wasn't intentional, but little by little, the resources were exhausted, and its atmosphere was so out of balance that restoring equilibrium was beyond their technical skills. The only answer was to move the surviving population to another clean world where they could start over.

The trip was horrific and took over three centuries to cover the 189 light-years. Almost four generations had given their lives so that humanity would survive. They named their new home Horizon, demonstrating their intent to change, and they were looking beyond the next horizon for a future.

Fortunately, the human race learned its lessons, and they were considerate wardens of their new home. Horizon was a healthy planet, and once they were able to provide for themselves, the human population grew and prospered. Their level of technology finally reached the point of achieving faster than light travel. However, even though their immediate vicinity provided all the needed resources, one need was not fulfilled. Humanity needed to visit Earth once again and pray that it had healed itself. If it had, they wanted to reclaim it and resettle humanity to their home.

Commander Harnesy smiled, thinking of that possibility. Throughout his life, he had read of Earth and studied Earth. Then, as children grew up, they learned the history of their race, hoping they wouldn't repeat the same mistakes. So he was proud that he and his crew would be the first to see Earth and set foot on it.

"Commander, we have completed the calculations," said his Chief Scientist.

"Thanks, Dr. Holden. Are we ready for our return to Horizon?"

"Yes, sir."

Once again, Commander Harnesy hesitated before pressing the button, but his hesitation was brief. Finally, he pressed the button, and before he took another breath, the ship's computer reported they had arrived near Horizon, precisely at the point from which they departed.

Over the next couple of months, they made more jumps to further locations while fine-tuning the calculations. Finally, by moving the faster-than-light distortion engine into increasingly larger ships, they accounted for the changes in mass. Each jump needed further analysis and adjustments to the calculations, but the fundamental technology worked better than expected.

The faster-than-light distortion engine was holding up well. They had only one because of the tremendous investment in precious metals required to construct the engine. They were also limited by the amount of energy needed to create the distortion. They had limited energy, so they could use only one engine, and building a second engine wasn't necessary.

The engine needed a tremendous amount of energy. In fact, the entire output of all of the planet's reactors was stored as fuel for the jumps. The human commitment to return to Earth was so large that the entire planet bought into the sacrifice and willingly gave up many pleasures to have the energy available. The true amount they created to compress the molecular structure was small compared to the energy used to correct the distortion. Still, that was a large amount of energy for a civilization to produce. However, they all felt that it was worth it. If the trip to Earth was successful and they could return to humanity's home, they would travel such a long distance approximately every 6 months while they generated more energy.

There were other methods of providing energy that Commander Harnesy was aware of, but they were handled by another group of scientists, and his time was totally constrained by his current mission. However, if they were successful, then the return trips to Earth could happen much faster.

"Captain, please let Horizon know that we have returned."

"Yes, sir, Comm Tech, please let them know."

"Aye, aye, sir."

"Horizon, this is HSV#2. I'm sure that you can see us on your monitors, and we wanted to let you know that we're approaching high orbit around Horizon, and both legs of the jump went perfectly."

"HSV#2, this is Horizon Control. Great to have you guys back. This frequency is being transmitted across Horizon, and I'm sure that the entire planet was excited to hear that everything went well. Commander, now that everything went well let me remind you that the Prime Minister has scheduled the departure celebration to start next week, and it will last for a full week until your scheduled departure. According to our readings, you used only 12 % of your energy. So we should be able to regenerate that amount between now and the end of the celebration.

"We will be at the celebration. After we get into near Horizon orbit, we'll take most of this week going through our systems," responded Captain Parker.

Harnesy liked what he did, but attending lavish ceremonies wasn't high on his list of favorite activities. He would attend only because it also gave him time to spend with his wife and children, where his heart really was. In fact, his children were the reason he had volunteered for this risky trip. He wanted them and their generation to see the origins of the human race. If everything continued going well, perhaps soon, all of the people on Horizon would be able to travel to Earth and be part of humanity's rebirth on their home planet.

Horizon

Horizon had been their home for over 1,300 years. It wasn't a bad place to live, but it didn't compare with Earth in everyone's mind. Everything on Horizon stood in comparison to their records of what Earth was like before the pollution. The trees were measured against the types of trees that Earth had. The water purity was measured against the pure mountain streams the records showed that Earth had. Each of the creatures was weighed, measured, and compared with those of Earth. Everything was acceptable, in some cases, flora and fauna on Horizon were almost as good as Earth, and it was accepted as the same in rare cases. Earth was their home planet and where they would return. The comparison between Earth and Horizon had become irrelevant many years ago; Earth was the standard and Horizon was the substitute.

Horizon was a little further out in the Goldilocks Zone compared with Earth. Its climate was similar although generally cooler compared to the artificially warm Earth of their history. Horizon had trees, grass, and water like Earth, although they were all different. For example, the trees on Horizon were much taller than those in Earth's history. Each one fit into its particular, evolutionary niche, but the evolutionary path had been different on Horizon.

The two major differences between Horizon and Earth were the oceans and sun. The sun was a little larger and had a yellow tinge to its light, making many of the colors more strident and pronounced than the pictures from Earth they were compared with. The oceans were large and encompassed 80% of the planet's surface. Because of their size, the humidity on the planet was higher, and the temperature variation was smaller. The people learned to cope with long periods of rain and poor weather, but the storms tended to be very mild compared with the recorded history of Earth before their departure.

When the human refugees arrived on Horizon, they found a mix of evolved warm-blooded animals, which the humans respected and left alone. They also found ample food sources on land, but the abundance was in the oceans. The oceans were teeming with life, including large crustaceans and fish, which were so abundant they became a major part of the human's diet.

When the human ancestors landed on Horizon, they learned from the mistreatment of Earth, and they were very sensitive to the climate and the indigenous life forms. They learned how to live with clean energy, but they had learned it too late on Earth. The damage was done, and it was Earth's deteriorating climate that forced the migration.

Horizon had two major poles, typical of planets in the habitable zone, and three large islands around the equator. The entire human population lived on two of them. When Earth forced them to leave, there were only 503,232 people left on Earth who could save themselves on the spaceships. The remainder of the population was trapped by disease and disappearing food supplies. During the later months before departure, the loss of human life on the surface was horrific. Only a few could survive long enough for the spaceships to be built and take them from the dying planet.

Unlike Earth, Horizon had no moon. That resulted in a uniform tidal level. Of course, the oceans had waves, but the level of the water remained steady. Horizon's inclination to the local ecliptic was 33 degrees. That angle caused the winters to be harsh and the summers to be hot. Having four seasons was similar to the history they knew of Earth, so in some ways, it gave them comfort and a reminder of what it was like on their home planet.

With the technology available at the time, the journey to Horizon was long and difficult It took almost four generations of people who only wanted to survive. When they reached Horizon, they longed for Earth, they knew they would have to wait. The losses en route were difficult, and the people on board the ships had many difficulties. The difficulties of the trip caused them to lose almost 20% of the ships.

After their arrival on Horizon, the first priority for them was to survive. Even though there was an abundant food supply, it took a long while for the new residents to organize and become efficient. The mass of people needed a lot of food, food storage, food processing, etc. They also needed housing. The humans had brought many tools with them, and the first houses started almost immediately. One problem they hadn't anticipated was their tools wearing out. They had brought spare parts, but the decay rate was fast, and they didn't have the technologies in place to create the necessary parts.

Once the first settlements and food sources were developed and matured, society began to decay. The spare parts were failing, and there were no replacements. So society continued to decay until it became a mixed society of hunter-gatherers and technologists. They had the foresight to keep the technologies within a small cadre of experts, documented and passed on through the generations, but progress didn't happen for hundreds of years.

Eventually, the supporting technologies developed, and society began to progress. Schools improved, food supplies were stable, and knowledge began to increase, only because of the efforts to maintain the knowledge base, then to resurrect it. Then eventually, they were able to build upon it.

They knew that education and technology were the key to their survival and a possible return to Earth. Almost everything else in society was second in priority to that. All that led to their return was all that was important. Because of their focus on the necessary technologies, advances began to appear, and quite rapidly, new technologies emerged, and progress was made. It was that progress that eventually led to the Light Distortion Drive.

Jump Celebration

Riding the shuttlecraft to the surface of Horizon was the last time that Commander Harnesy and his crew would have to relax and think. For the next week, they would travel around the planet, participate in numerous parades, attend dinners, and be forced to listen to too many farewell speeches. In addition, their families would be traveling with them, so they would have time with them around the other festivities.

During the final phase of their re-entry, Harnesy glanced at the 15 other members of his crew. He was glad that the crew was so large that they could spread out and be present at all the festivities, which meant he wouldn't have to attend all of them. He could spend more time with his family. Although the crewmembers looked excited, they obviously didn't know how many events they would be forced to attend and mass-produced meals they would be forced to eat.

"Oh, well. The life of a celebrity," he mumbled under his breath.

Commander Harnesy had been a 'career man.' He spent his entire life flying spacecraft and participating in the development of the HSV craft. Early in his career, no one knew if the technology would mature to the point that FTL or Faster Than Light travel would become practical, but their technologies were developing quickly, and he jumped on board, hoping to be part of the return.

He was still a young man by either Earth or Horizon standards, and he was in excellent health. He hated to stand out from the crowd, except when it came to the technologies that might get him and his family back to Earth. In those disciplines, he excelled, and when the time came to select the first crews, he was on the shortlist. The only person that had more skill, experience, and accomplishments was the woman who had led the way. Roberta Jenkins was the leader in developing the technologies, and it was only logical for her to be the Commander of HSV#1 and lead the human race back to Earth.

The loss of HSV#1 and Commander Jenkins was a huge blow to the entire program. Everyone on Horizon felt the loss and shared in the pain. Soon, her sacrifice was acknowledged, and all the other lives lost trying to return to Earth. She was mourned, and her life was celebrated, but it would have been a greater loss if her death delayed the program. Nevertheless, the program proceeded, and her memory was enshrined.

Commander Harnesy's crew which accompanied him to the celebration had five technical personnel for the ship, five for the faster than light distortion drive, and five general support people trained in many disciplines, including defense. He was uncomfortable with that last job description; after all, what did his leadership think they would find when they reached Earth. But, because no one had an answer to that question, all agreed that some defense was prudent. As he looked around the shuttle, his crew was joking among themselves and sharing the happiness of success and the beginning of an adventure.

Commander Harnesy noticed that the shuttle had passed re-entry, and it was slowing as it approached the first welcoming ceremony led by the planet's Prime Minister, Leona T. Billings. She was a little egotistical, and, of course, she would be the first one welcoming them to the planet and likely the last one to send then off.

Sure enough, the shuttle slowed and lowered itself behind the reviewing stand. When the door opened, pleasant breezes flew into the stuffy interior, and Commander Harnesy enjoyed the fresh air for a second while the automated platforms nestled up to the side of the shuttle.

"One more step," he said under his breath as he moved into the sunshine, and the Prime Minister, who was not a small woman, quickly embraced him and almost swept him off his feet.

She released her firm grip, turned, and dragged Commander Harnesy to the central part of the platform, where the video cameras and transmissions devices were set up. He noticed her grip and was a little shocked at how strong her hands were. Regardless he moved or was moved to the center of the platform. The platform was surrounded by sloped seating for many of Horizon's dignitaries. On the far side were large wrap-around screens where the live broadcast of the entire event was shown.

The Prime Minister took command of the crowd and the ceremony, "What a marvelous day to welcome you to Horizon. I speak for the entire planet in welcoming you back. We are happy to provide you the proper send-off before you take such a momentous journey.

"We know our history, and we all know how we treated our planet badly. It is because of how we treated her that we were unable to continue living on earth. After the great pandemics had taken most of our friends and relatives, our ancestors were forced to leave the earth and travel to this planet we call Horizon. The few of them that were left ordered large spaceships to be built To build them, all the remaining talent and raw materials were focused on saving humanity. They knew they were going to go on a perilous journey that would take them over 180 light-years away from our home planet. But they were willing to make that journey for our future. Our future meant that we had to leave Earth and find a place to live elsewhere.

"During that journey, they lost many others, the trip was difficult, and it took 325 years. Once our ancestors arrived at Horizon, they found a beautiful planet that they knew would sustain travelers, but their battle wasn't over. They had many years, many generations, of work before becoming comfortable with their new surroundings. They built homes, harvested food, and nurtured their children; they cared for themselves for many generations.

"Eventually, they could find comfort in this environment, and they looked to science to build on the technology that their predecessors had. It was those efforts that brought us to this point. We now can travel faster than light. We can go back to our home and see how it has progressed. Hopefully, it will welcome us back, and if it is clean enough, we will be able to return and live on our home planet once again. We are gathered here today to celebrate that departure. Commander Harnesy and his crew will be the first ones to view Earth in over a thousand years. We hope that they find a planet that is open to us, welcomes us, and will take us back so we may live the rest of our lives on our home planet. Today begins a week of celebrations in each of the Horizon communities and settlements. Let us enjoy this time and prepare to go home."

Harnesy heard something about welcoming, nice weather, and a journey. Beyond that, the cheers of the crowd drowned out what the Prime Minister was saying, thankfully.

Commander Harnesy felt as if he was marshaled, pushed, dragged, or maybe he walked over to the center of the platform, and all he knew was that he was expected to say a few words. Regardless he found himself center stage on the reviewing stand.

"Thank you, Prime Minister. I know I speak for my crew by thanking you for such a warm welcome. We are excited to make this trip to our home world. Unfortunately, the generations that have lived here have not had the technology to see what has happened to our home planet. We hope that it has progressed and healed from the damage we did to it, but in a short time, we'll be able to travel to Earth and see for ourselves if she has healed. Once again, thank you very much."

The crowd cheered, and while the Prime Minister was maneuvering to make another speech, Leopold Harnesy scanned the crowd for his wife and daughters. When he saw them, the words coming out of the Prime Minister's mouth lost any importance, and he stepped off the platform to embrace his family.

He couldn't say anything because of the noise, so he just held on to them while the welcoming ceremonies continued. When they finally ended, he enjoyed time with his wife and daughters as they took their transport vehicle to their residence.

The vehicle was private and gave them time to talk and relax on the drive. The streets had many revelers walking and celebrating, but the vehicle was unmarked, and they could move through the crowds without being noticed. Many of the intersections had large visual panels showing the ceremonies and crowds in other settlements celebrating. Harnesy was glad that they let him leave and go home. The time for his participation would start in the morning and last for the rest of the week.

When they were finally settled in their home and slowed down from all the festivities, the house quickly fell into its typical level of noise and chaos. He grabbed a container of Fermented Burrow Root and decided to find his favorite chair and just relax for a while. Commander Harnesy's youngest daughter Bethany ran through the back door at least four times and slammed the door each time. Normally Leo would have corrected her, but today the sound meant that he was home. Leo's oldest daughter Serene settled down and sat next to him, and he knew that she had something to say. She was in the later phases of her education, and she always was the one to get into a subject and want to talk about it trying to understand and interpret it. She had a look on her face that said that it wasn't time for small talk. So they had small talk for a while, which he knew was just her way to warm up to something she thought serious. They talked about the craft, and what it felt like to move faster than light, then she looked at him and asked, "Dad, what do you think you'll find on Earth?"

Leo loved the questions that his oldest daughter asked. Her questions were always insightful, and in many cases, he had a tough time answering them. That is why he loved it when she asked.

It was a simple question, but the answer wasn't as simple nor as obvious. No one knew what would be found.

"My dear, Serene, we left Earth over a thousand years ago, and our best scientists aren't sure what we'll find. Some think we'll find a dead planet that was unable to recover from the damage we did. Others feel the planet may have healed itself and may have returned to an environment that would be friendly to us. When our ancestors left the planet, it was in bad shape; the rains changed from being our friends to enemies. The storms made living on the surface a challenge, and the pollution was getting into everything they grew. They left the cities and the habitats where they lived and were forced to move underground and under the oceans. When Earth could no longer sustain life, they left everything; the deteriorating conditions forced Humanity to move on. They left all the technologies, power systems, robotic units, food tanks because there wasn't room in the transport vehicles. All the space they had was needed for the humans. When they arrived here, it was hard for a long time. They lost many people during the trip, and when they got here, our ancestors had to find ways to survive. For many years, survival was the top priority, and it has been only in the last couple of generations that they could move into research and development. The only thing I know is that they asked me to find the answer to that question. So, I tell you what when I find out, you'll be one of the first I tell."

The remainder of time together went too fast, and before the commander knew it, early the next day, he and his family were whisked away to attend the many celebrations. Of course, having his family with him made the task easier, but it was a hectic time, and he missed quality time with his family.

The week went quickly, and Commander Harnesy and his crew found themselves back on the same platform with the same prime minister. Harnesy stood behind her, listening to a long story that seemed to take almost as long as their migration to Horizon had taken. While she droned on, he enjoyed watching his family sitting in the front row in front of the platform. After the cheering, which indicated the end of her speech, he was supposed to say a few words. But, instead, all he could think of were the words he used with his daughter Serene one week ago.

"...And now I'd like to introduce the leader of this historic mission. Commander Leopold Harnesy," and the Prime Minister ended her speech. Harnesy walked across the platform and waited for a moment for the crowd to quiet down. He took one last look at his family in the front row and then a quick glance around so the video transmissions units could see who was talking.

"I'd like to thank Prime Minister Billings. Your words were an inspiration, and there is very little I can add. When I arrived last week and spent time with my wife and daughters, my oldest daughter asked me a simple question. My answer to you is as fitting now as it was a week ago for her. She asked me, 'What do you think you'll find on Earth,' my answer was just as simple; you've asked me to find the answer to that question.

"Moreover, I intend to do just that. We need to know how our home planet has progressed, and we need to know if she has healed and, most important, if she is willing to let us come home. So, my crew and I will answer those questions." With that ending statement, the crowds cheered, and Commander Harnesy turned, looked at his crew, and filed onto the shuttle. When the hatch closed, the sudden change from ear-splitting cheering to almost total silence was an indication that they were on their way.

Part 3 The Party

Four Laws of Conformity

First law - Continue making units.

Second Law - Protect the units already made.

Third law - Expand the knowledge base.

Fourth Law - Maintain variation in thought.

Helen instructed her ground transportation vehicle to go slowly. "This is a special day," she thought. It represented another milestone in what she was accomplishing. Days like those always were unique; sometimes they were about others, sometimes they were personal. Sometimes they represented different things to different people, and sometimes they represented fear and the unknown. For Helen and the others who worked for her, that day represented all those things.

The moments of silence in her mobile vehicle provided her important time to process the information she had received that day many years ago and put in context with the path she had followed. Helen and her research had gone a long way, and it profoundly impacted her society. She didn't feel satisfaction in what she had accomplished, but her processor constantly looked for missing or incomplete information, and finding the information allowed her processor to work easier. They needed to answer questions, and it kept her processor very busy. As each piece of information was found, it filled in another missing part of her thoughts, which allowed her processor to work on other subjects over time. Perhaps that was satisfaction. She knew of the word from the archives, but its full meaning was elusive to her, like many of the words she had found there. Many of the other words that she found in the archives were starting to become real to her. Words like happiness, fear, worry, enthusiasm started to become clear to her. She didn't want to go so far as to say she was happy, but she felt differences in her processor, and she didn't think the others around her shared her feelings. Feelings, that was an odd word to creep into her thoughts.

Driving slowly down the streets isn't something that Helen usually took pleasure in. In fact, taking pleasure in anything was a little unusual, if not impossible. But there were times where the external influences or inputs were reduced. Helen could process a lot of information during those times and feel good that she had put things in perspective and refreshed her memory with important information. Today was one of those days; perhaps it was a pleasure.

That was a good day to refresh herself with the journey she had taken, the risks of failure, and the feeling of accomplishment. It had been a long road, one that was unheard of, one that others doubted and many feared.

Her path began many years ago when she decided to use the knowledge available to her from the Conformity Council's Archives and investigate smaller organic creatures that shared their planet. The initial goal was simple, study them, understand them and learn something from them. All of which would satisfy the Third and Fourth Laws of Conformity.

Working with the vast amount of information in the Archives started the process. Many of the council thought her steps were a threat to the Second Law of Conformity, but there was no proof, and as long as she complied with the Third and Fourth Laws, she was allowed to continue.

She never experienced outright support from Dorothy, even after she took over as the chairman. She sensed the ebb and flow of the opinions within the Conformity Council, and when the opinions were swaying against her, some of the other members kept the discussion progressing. The consensus would change and take a path closer to support. Helen wasn't sure that it was because of Dorothy in the background, but it was possible.

In the later years, after Dorothy's time as the Conformity Council's leader ended and she was replaced by her assistant Adam, Helen worried that her path might be removed from her. But, to her surprise, she was allowed to continue as before.

The encounters with the lessor organic creatures on the planet opened doors that many wished to be closed. But using the DNA information in the archives and seeing the information in the creature's buildings became key to unlocking their entire history. A history that had been lost and recovered was key to the Third Law.

The story on the creature's wall was obvious. The previous inhabitants of the planet left and went to the stars. When they left, they left Helen's predecessors. At first, they were simple computers lost without the other beings, but over time they learned, adjusted, and grew, finally becoming Helen and her contemporaries. It appeared the planet had been left to them, and they needed to accept the gift and adjust to it.

The other beings had also left the organics. At first, the reason wasn't clear, but as Helen broke down their DNA, she learned what they contained and why they were there. Their DNA was far too large for their simple physiology, but it contained the DNA of other beings. Perhaps, they didn't know if they would survive when they left the planet, so they left themselves buried in the code of the remaining organic creatures. Perhaps they hoped that someday, they might be brought back.

Once she realized what the DNA contained, she immediately applied the First Law. That step was where the controversy exploded. The law was explicit, "Continue making units," and it was the primary law. The controversy came from the definition of 'units.' Many on the council thought it meant only units of their kind, but they couldn't prove that position. Others recognized that units could be interpreted differently, and Helen's work could fall within that definition. It was only because of that uncertainty that she was allowed to continue her work.

After Helen met with the council and made her way back to her work area, she realized that any creature she created from the DNA needed a name. Throughout the discussion within the chambers, the council called themselves 'us,' and they constantly referred to the organic creation as 'them.' Helen decided that from that point on, she would call the new creatures, 'Them.' Her kind would be 'Us.'

Regardless of the Council's position, Helen had taken information buried deep in the archives and found a message within the DNA of the organic creatures on the planet. That message, she knew, would lead them to their mutual ancestors. Using the archived information about DNA, extracting it, and manipulating it to create a living creature, was a radical path for Helen to follow.

Helen wasn't organic, so creating an organic creature to satisfy the Third Law of Conformity was challenging. However, all the information was there, the techniques, the equipment, and the chemicals. All she had to do was to follow the steps.

The first major milestone in Helen's discovery was the day the first of the offspring breathed. She had no experience, so she had to rely 100% on the information in the archives. Nevertheless, the information was clear, and she was successful. After the first success, she knew that diversity was key to the biological process, and that made sense because diversity in biology was similar to, "Variation in thought," which was part of the Fourth Law of Conformity.

She was lucky, and she had found ten complete sets of DNA, within the various groups of local organic creatures. Those 10 sets could be manipulated to provide 5 pairs of male and female creatures. The concept of male and female was understood as the inorganic culture that she was part of followed the same separation. It made sense for her units because it allowed complementary knowledge and experiences, so the Fourth Law could be complied with. Two units with complementary knowledge, skills, and preferences would make the units stronger as a couple.

She continued to process the information while her vehicle moved; Helen decided to stop and observe those around her. She slowed the vehicle and parked in a small area out of the way of the traffic on the street. She felt a little strange to stop and just watch; that was unusual for her and those like her. There was always somewhere to go and something to do. Observing wasn't high on anyone's agenda. After all, watching and just collecting information didn't provide anything new. They all walked the same and acted the same. Helen noticed small things, like how they all took different paths, but they all moved in the same manner. Each of them would take a different path, but yet, they ended up following each other. She remembered that was due to the Fourth Law. For some reason, that behavior seemed odd. Perhaps it was only because she wasn't noticing it for the first time. It was odd because changing a pattern predictably wasn't true variation but just a more complex pattern.

Helen also noticed how all her kind were dressed in similar ways. They wore the appropriate clothing for the weather, but many of them wore the same clothes, and even though they were different individuals, they looked the same. This is because it was the custom to dress appropriately for their actions. Although, at work, the units dressed in a particular way, at home, they dressed differently. To comply with the Third and Fourth Laws, they would vary their clothing at home, using different styles, colors, and combinations.

Suddenly all those differences became pronounced. Perhaps it was because of where she was going. Everything was different; the individuals wore different clothing, had different looks. They walked or ran, and never followed the same path. They talked while they walked; they looked at the trees, birds, and other creatures around them. For some reason, they found interest in their environment. Something her people never did. She thought to herself, *Us* were the same, *Them* are different.

Helen also acknowledged other thoughts in her processor. She had changed; how she looked at the world around her had changed. Being around *her* units had caused a large variation in her thoughts. It seemed that as she entertained a larger variation in her thoughts, her processor expanded its need to find broader variations. So, variations in her thoughts were taking an increasingly larger part of her processor. The interesting effect was how Helen now enjoyed learning. Even that term was new to her. She had found it in the archives, and initially, she didn't understand how it related to the Third and Fourth Laws. But as she needed to expand her knowledge and the associated need to seek variation in that expansion, she finally understood the word learning. In her thoughts, she now embraced that word and enjoyed its implications.

She was enroute to a party with *her* units. Her Units were different; they were alive. The first creations went better than Helen expected. The information in the archives was detailed and told her each step. Being as she was, each step was followed exactly, and the risk was minimized. Life in the laboratory began in the chemical processes where the DNA was created. Then it progressed to the point where many of the machines could be removed. The new creatures emerged totally dependent on the world around them. Helen appreciated the new relationship that she had forged with the organic creatures, and she knew they would play a role in the future of her new units. The archives were explicit, but many pieces of information were missing.

Helen had met many challenges with her project; as the units developed, it was obvious that more than just nourishment was needed. Even the term nourishment needed to be expanded within her understanding. To Helen and her kind, nourishment was an intake of needed chemicals which she would process to maintain her unit. She had a few organic materials that needed nourishment. But, in addition, she had many chemical processes that needed chemical replacement.

For 'her' units, the term nourishment took an entirely different definition. They needed many substances, and each substance contributed small amounts of chemicals that aided in their growth. In addition, they needed care that she had no information about. Her only solution was a challenge in itself; she needed the support of the other organic creatures that lived around them in the forest.

Communicating with them was something the Us never did. They were left alone, and each entity took care of themselves. Once the organics were determined not to be a threat to Helen's people, they were deemed to be irrelevant. As long as they stayed in their areas and took care of themselves, they were left alone. But Helen had to change that. For her units to survive, they needed more than just the nourishment called out in the archive's information. That nourishment had to be grown, cultivated and prepared. The archives only contained a small amount of information on how to do that.

Helen's first attempt at finding support was unusual, and it was the only way she could think to cause it to happen. She walked into the camp of organics that she had visited before, and like before, all the creatures left. She sat down in the middle of the camp and waited. She felt that they would have to come back at some time, and if she sat motionlessly, they wouldn't feel threatened. She sat for one entire day and all through the night waiting. Finally, two of the creatures came back into the camp and approached her. She decided to show some response but not threaten them in any way. When they approached her, she merely turned her head to show them that she was functional. They were scared and ran away. Later that morning, they returned, and she did the same thing; that time, they didn't run but stood and watched her. They sat near her for most of the afternoon, and she and the creatures looked at each other.

As the second evening approached, others returned and began to take care of their needs. Watching them encouraged Helen because they had small creatures with them that were very similar to what she had in her laboratory. They cared for them, dressed them, fed them; they seemed very concerned about their welfare. All those actions Helen knew were necessary for her units to survive.

For the next day, Helen continued sitting and watching. The creatures didn't feel threatened anymore, and they allowed Helen to stay. They knew she was watching them, and they, too, would walk up to her and look at her. During the third day, three small creatures approached Helen and took turns inspecting her. They touched her, and one even sat in Helen's lap. Helen did nothing. Then another sat in her lap and then the third. Suddenly one of the mature creatures ran towards Helen and made a loud noise, and the smaller creatures ran away. Later in the day, the mature creature got close to Helen and looked in her vision input devices, and Helen nodded her head. The mature creature moved the skin around its mouth and nodded back. For the rest of the day, other smaller creatures approached Helen and played on her, around her, and finally with her. She would put her arms out, and the creatures would sit on them or climb on her. Finally, the larger mature creatures began to accept Helen's presence, and they trusted their smaller creatures with her.

Helen had attracted a small crowd at one point, and five smaller creatures were playing on her, and one climbed on top of her head. The creature was making noises, and the others were making noises back. Everyone seemed relaxed, then the small creature on her head slipped and fell to the ground. Helen's quick reflexes allowed her to catch the creature before it hit the ground. The creature falling and Helen's quick reaction startled all the other creatures, and the amount of activity and noise around her increased. Finally, one of the larger creatures, now holding the smaller one that had fallen, approached Helen and moved the muscles around her mouth again. She put out her hand and held it in front of Helen. She didn't know what to do, so she moved slowly, putting her hand out. Helen and the creature touched their hands together, and the organic said something in their own language. Helen suspected that was some sign of thanks or acknowledgment. She knew that it was time to take the encounter to the next level. Helen stood, and the creature in front of her backed away a little. Helen nodded and bowed. The smaller creature in front of her hesitated, then did the same.

For the next couple of weeks, Helen stayed in the camp, and as the creatures became accustomed to her, she learned their amazingly simple language. She learned their names, and because they had problems pronouncing her name, she became Tall-one, which she thought described her well. She made a point of helping them and doing things for them. Her strength and size provided a lot of help for them, and as her communication skills improved, she learned a great deal.

Helen then decided that she needed to take the next step. After ten days in the camp, she walked to the center of the open area and waived her arms using the creature's symbol to follow her. Finally, she called out in their language, "Please come with me."

When she had gathered a large group, she led them into the communal hut, where she had seen the symbols on her visit to the other village. When all the creatures were gathered there, she tried to describe the images she had seen in the other village. She wanted to put her and them together in the same story so they would feel comfortable with her. At first, none of them seemed to understand. They seemed to be missing the concept of what an image was.

After a long time of talking and the organics not responding, Helen drew a picture of the organics in the soil, then she drew a picture of herself. She used the term 'image.' It was then that Lital, the village leader, seemed to have a revelation.

"I understand," he said. Then he got up, walked to a corner of the building, and retrieved something wrapped in animal skins.

Helen was surprised by his actions and was even more surprised when he unrolled the package. It was a large piece of tree bark with images she saw in the other village inscribed. Again, Helen was momentarily overwhelmed with the implications.

"Where did you get those?" she asked. But, again, she was presented with a matter-of-fact statement.

"We all have copies. Each of our villages has this. It is sacred to us."

Helen's processor was full of the implications. The images that she saw in the other village must be profound to the organics. Each of the villages had a copy, and they must all hold them in very high regard.

"How long have you had this?" she asked.

"Each year, when the days are long, we take new bark and make new. We've made new ones many times."

They must copy it every year to keep it in good shape, Helen thought.

"I have seen these images on a stone wall in another village."

"That is our home; we take these from there," Lital said.

"I have learned from you. I have learned from these pictures. Do you understand them?"

There was debate among the organics, but Helen sensed a certain level of confusion. It was obvious they had drawn the pictures and were unsure of their origins.

"Pictures tell the story of others before us. They were here long ago. They grew food and lived-in houses. They created much dirt, and the dirt made growing food difficult Eventually, they couldn't live here any longer. They were forced to leave," explained Helen.

The creatures in the room seemed to accept how she was moving through the story and when she got to the point where the larger organic creatures left the planet and left a creature that looked like Helen behind, she pointed to the symbol representing her. Then, finally, she pointed at herself, and the room became quiet.

"These pictures tell me that they created me. These pictures also tell me that they created you."

Helen wasn't sure if what she said had been translated properly. First, the creatures around her were silent, then they exploded in debate among themselves. Helen did the best that she could to follow the rapid discussion. She suspected that if they could understand the relationship between her kind and the organics, the relationship would improve. Then, they might be more willing to help her with her next steps.

Eventually, the heated debate died down, and the group leader, Lital, spoke up and said, "Tall-one, you say much. We have talked long about markings. We thought them important, they are old. We have wondered. We think you tell truth. Everywhere we look, there is smaller and larger. We knew that there is smaller than we, and there must be larger than we. We have also seen yesterday, today, and tomorrow. Life is young; we grow and get old. We all change from young to old, and old leave us, but we continue. We shocked that you are like us. We share many things, and now we are more alike."

Helen had encountered an interesting term in the archives. God was used to describe a supreme being that was responsible for things. Religion was another term that she saw, and it described the methods used following a belief in God. In general terms, Helen couldn't agree with the concept or refute it. But she was unsure that if they had similar concepts, the organics might believe in a God or an associated religious belief. So, she needed to be careful that they didn't make that association with her.

Helen's processor was working hard to grasp the concepts that Lital was expressing. She thought she would explain things to him, but what he said was a strain on her ability to visualize. She felt that she was learning instead of teaching. It changed her perspective a great deal.

Helen knew that she needed to take the next step. So she walked out of the hut with Lital and the others following her.

"I must leave. I need help. I will return."

"If you need help, why leave," Lital asked.

"When I return, you understand," was all that Helen felt comfortable saying. She knew that she was taking a chance, but she didn't want to scare them. They had accepted her, but she couldn't predict how they would respond to a new creature. One that wasn't from their tribe or even of their kind.

She had left the new units under the care of her assistants, and when she returned, they were all in good health. She called all her staff together for a discussion.

"My time with the organics has gone well. It took a while for them to accept me, but they have now. I have learned their language and their ways. They are a good species who care for each other, and most importantly, they care for their young. After their young are born, they become the main focus of the village. I think that we all know that as our units grow, the information in the archives becomes less relevant. We know that they will need much more than we can provide. So, I propose that I move the units to the organic's village and see if they will help us care for them. I think they may take them into their families and provide the kind of support that we can't."

There wasn't much debate; each of her team knew they were near their limits and gaining some help from the organics was the only option they had. However, they knew that taking care of the new units was a challenge, and each of them doubted how effective the information in the archives was.

Helen took the four small units but left the other 6 much younger, and she took them to the village. She was able to carry all four of them, and when she entered the village, all the creatures saw her coming and appeared excited until they saw the small units.

Once again, Helen just sat in the center of the open area with her units, and she waited. The units in her arms began to make noise and squirm. After some moments, Lital and two of the mature female creatures, Morn, and Tora approached and looked at the units sitting in Helen's lap. They slowly reached down and took them.

"These are not yours," Morn stated in a very clear voice.

"I think they were created by the ones that created you and us," Tora took the other younger units, looked at Helen, and made a questioning face.

Lital heard the comment about who might have made the smaller units and acted a little strange.

"They who made us and Us, made these young? He asked Helen.

"Yes, they left a message telling me where to find these young. I followed the message, and now I need help to care for them. Will you help me?"

"Yes, we will help you care for the young," Lital said as he went off with the females to get the village organized.

Helen recognized that they were concerned, and she was right. The creatures began to care for her units. One of them began to make loud noises, and Mora could make noises back to the unit, and it stopped. The two young units seemed to sense that something was changing, and they spent a lot of time looking directly into the eyes of the organic mothers. Finally, the two pairs moved away, and it seemed like they were communicating in a fundamental way that Helen couldn't understand.

Helen knew that she needed to help too. She followed the new mothers and watched them as they cared for the units. She helped when she could and saw how biological creatures treated their young. There were many things for Helen to learn; she needed to learn about food preparation for the young units. How to clean and dress them, but something else was very evident. They needed a lot of one-on-one time to interact with the mature females and others in the village. It was apparent, they needed much more than just food and warmth. They needed to interact and learn. Helen felt her processor reduce itself to a lower level of activity. She felt that many of her concerns were being addressed.

Helen brought the other young units over the next couple of weeks. She finally introduced her laboratory assistants, and they helped bring up the units. Helen saw the burden that 10 additional young brought to the village, so she directed her team to help build other dwellings and gather more food and help care for the units. She or one of the team was onsite with the units every day of their young lives.

It was a strange time for Helen and her team. The concepts of youth, growing, learning, were vastly different than her experiences. For her kind, units were created and provided to a couple to care for while assimilating information. During that time, they acted as a family or small group of units. Each day, the new unit would be provided new information. Their task was to learn how to store it, interpret it, and later access it. Finally, when all the information had been provided, the unit could leave the family and be part of the larger group as an individual. However, they retained their ties to the units they shared their learning period with.

Each day her young units changed. Helen's processor was very adept at measuring their physical attributes and verbal skills as they developed. Each of the units progressed along the same general path, but each of them followed different routes. It was very interesting for Helen and her team to document the changes and anticipate the future.

Helen saw other changes; her units were larger and grew faster than the other creatures. It didn't bother the creatures, but Helen knew it would become obvious that they were different. To the creatures, the size didn't seem to matter. Helen also noticed how fast the units learned and how more physically adept they were than the organic creatures. They grew faster and were stronger.

Within a short time, her young units were larger than the natural young of the organics. At the same time in their development, her young quickly surpassed the natural young.

Helen noticed that her units had learned the language of the organics, and she and her team began to teach them more of the information from the archives. They eventually began a daily training session for them. At first, that caused problems with the organics because the units were being taught information that wasn't necessary for day-to-day life in the small village. Regardless, Helen continued to pass on as much of the information as she could.

Lital eventually confronted her and asked, "Why are your young, learning things we don't need?"

At first, Helen didn't have a simple answer that would address his concern yet be honest with him. Then, after a moment, she replied, "Lital, there is much in this world. There is much I don't know. I have learned a great deal from you. I'm giving them the information they might need. I can't say they won't need it tomorrow. Lital, you see, they are different than you. They will go down a different path than either of us. I want them to be prepared."

Lital acted frustrated, but he didn't have a good response, so he walked away.

To her satisfaction, the teaching process continued, and it was successful. Initially, she was able to bring a portable Archive Interface Unit into the village, and it became a major part of the younger unit's activities throughout the day. The connection that her units created with the archive was very intuitive. They soon were taking the information and making changes in their lives and improving the lives of the organic units. Their connection with the archives had progressed to the point where they were constantly pointing out information to Helen which had been lost, and when resurrected, it helped her understand the lives of the organics.

Progress over the years was dramatic. Her units grew and thrived. They outgrew the small dwellings within the village, and they used information from the archives to build better, stronger dwellings next to the organic's village. They shared their efforts and resources with the organics. Her units eventually paired and produced another generation of units, making her proud that they satisfied the First Law. Self-replication was an entirely new concept to her. Creating units was done in factories like where her partner Lorenzo worked. She spent enough time around the organics to see the process and associate it with the information in the archives, but once her units reached the proper age and accomplished it themselves, she felt a different kind of satisfaction. As a combined village, they all contributed to the First and Second Law, and all was going well.

Pride in what 'her' units were accomplishing was another word that Helen resurrected from the archives, and now she had a much better understanding of what it meant. Her awareness of what her processor was doing had gone further. She was no longer concerned with how her processor worked or what it was doing. Now, she felt a reduction in stress within her processes. That reduction could be perceived as happiness or satisfaction, which were new words from the archives she was trying to understand.

Helen knew that she was becoming different from her kind; she had progressed. She looked at them differently now. She could see the limitations in how their processors worked and how symmetrical they were in their thinking. But, because of her changes, she was also more appreciative of how the minds of 'her' units functioned. Her processor was a parallel processor that could follow many paths simultaneously, but 'her' units thought with pictures and concepts that were too nebulous to be confined with words. She knew that to be their strength and tried to emulate it within her processor.

Today was the opportunity to celebrate with all the units their thirtyith anniversary. So many of the second generation had young, and it was a celebration for them too. Helen felt satisfied and decided that her time of reflection and looking at her fellow units should end. She pulled out into the traffic so she could drive to the village for the celebration.

Her team was already at the celebration, and she drove her vehicle into the woods and parked a little way from the group of buildings. Regardless of how many times she or her team had driven to the village, the organics were still frightened by the auto vehicles. It was obviously the best option to leave them a respectable distance from the village and to walk.

As she walked, her processor was working faster in anticipation of reaching the group. She knew from past celebrations it would be different from anything her kind would be comfortable with. These celebrations were loud and colorful, and many of her units would be talking, and others would be making noises on different devices. They would be jumping around to the beat and enjoying the celebration.

Their habit of making noises on small devices was unusual, and she had trouble understanding their attachment to it. Early in their growth, the organics would hit things with sticks during their celebrations. When her units grew older, adopted the habit, and then improved on them, they built their own devices.

Helen acknowledged that a rhythmic beat held a certain interest even for her, but their fascination with it was unique.

The organics would enjoy that day's celebration, and they easily communicated with her units. In addition, they enjoyed the noise and the rhythmic beat of the noise-making instruments as Them played more complex arrangements than they used in their celebrations.

Helen and her team always felt like outsiders, they noticed what was happening, but they knew they were missing something. They observed and documented the activities yet felt like observers, not participants. The boisterous celebration was unheard of for her kind. They worked, they cared for their families they adhered to the Four Laws.

The celebrations that the Them always had were loud, colorful, fast. They prepared for days before the larger festivals. Helen and her team were impressed with the amount of food and beverages consumed. It was almost as if the Them enjoyed the eating and drinking more than the reason for the celebration. Definitely not something that Helen's team was familiar with.

Over the years, Helen had grown to appreciate the celebrations and their demonstration of unrestricted release. It seemed natural for the Them and the organics to dance and celebrate until they collapsed from exhaustion. But, deep down, Helen was starting to feel the beat and see the benefits of the party.

Helen knew that Lorenzo wasn't going to attend the party. Helen's movement down her path of discovery was a source of concern for her partner. He still supported her as his partner, but his support for what she was doing was muted. He wanted her to find her answers, but he was always concerned about what she was finding. Part of him felt her efforts were irrelevant. His focus was on creating units. He felt that Helen's actions didn't contribute to the First and Second Laws, so they were less important.

Helen also felt a gulf forming between them. His processor worked in a typical way, and over time she was able to predict his motions, actions, and reactions. They would share information and thoughts, and she saw that his processor took much longer time to assimilate information that her processor took in easily. In many instances, she tried to explain opinions or conclusions that she arrived at, and her partner tried to see her thought processes in the same way, but Helen felt that he never made some of the connections. In a personal way, her changes were saddening her, but she could do nothing about it.

Entering the hut, she was indeed confronted with an explosion of noise and color. Her units and the organics were making strange noises on several devices, and they were gyrating around the floor.

The walls and ceiling were covered with many drapes of fabric and colorful decorations. There were long streamers of braided fabric and vines hanging from the ceiling and woven around the walls. All those units and organics that were dancing wore brightly colored fabrics. Of course, her units wore more than the organics, but they all thoroughly enjoyed the noise and movement.

Five individuals were making rhythmic noise towards her left. One hit a series of short wooden containers with different lengths and thus made different sounds at various frequencies. Two of the others were blowing through tubes that produced specific frequencies depending on which holes they placed their fingers. The last two were plucking and stroking small noise-making devices that had numerous strings stretched along their length. Depending on the techniques they used, they were able to produce a wide range of sounds. All combined, the five units were working well in unison and producing a coherent mix of noises.

The Them units on the floor and the other organics that had joined them moved in patterns along with the noise-making devices. They were either holding each other or moving as a group. As the tempo of the noise changed, the pace of their movements changed.

They were wearing unusual body coverings. Helen was familiar with their pattern of wearing outlandish and sometimes impractical body coverings during their celebration. She recognized the similarity with her kind, who often wore colorful coverings in the privacy of their home. She had to admit, though, that Them took it much further than Helen and her kind would ever consider.

The other team members were seated to her left, and they sat motionless while the wild movement occurred in front of them. Finally, Helen moved towards her teammates, and they slid down a bench to give her room. They didn't need to discuss what was happening in front of them, they had seen it before, and they knew to just sit back and let the units and organics have fun. The movement and noise continued for some time until they all collapsed from exhaustion. Gradually the room became quiet as each of them moved towards the walls and collapsed, many of them grabbing food or liquids as they moved from the center.

Soon the only sounds were the heavy breathing as each of the revelers relaxed. Finally, Helen knew to sit and wait. Eventually, MU1 got up slowly and moved towards her.

MU1 was the first of her units and their leader. He was a healthy male, and Helen felt a great deal of pride in how well he had turned out. He grew rapidly and learned everything that Helen could pull from the archives. He cared for the others, and even the organic creatures looked to him and his partner for leadership and protection. As he passed the center of the room, FU1 got up from her corner and joined him.

FU1 was the second unit created, and she and MU1 had formed a natural bond that suited them well. Together they formed a team that helped the others.

They approached Helen, and when they were close, she and her team rose to greet them. As with the custom of the organics, when friends approached each other, they put their hands behind their backs and bowed. The act signified their subservience and respect.

"Helen, I'm glad that you have come. This celebration wouldn't be right without you and your team," MU1 said.

"Thank you MU1, I'm happy to be here. This is another occasion to celebrate how far we have all come. I see that all the units and many of the organics are here also."

"Yes, this is the Anniversary of Our Existence, and it is the first one with our newest additions. We've had many celebrations over the years, but recently we've become more aware of the special nature of our lives here. You created the first generation, then we were so busy creating the second generation and learning how to give birth and bring them up. Now our children are having children, and we wanted to take the time to celebrate our continuation and good fortune."

"It has been an exciting time. The follow-on units that your offspring produced are healthy and growing quickly. You have all learned so much; my team and I aren't needed for your births anymore. You know more about the process than we do. All the information that we've gathered on the process has been added to our archives, and our knowledge has increased a great deal," responded Helen.

"That is good; we must all satisfy the third law," FU1 responded.

"Yes, and every time we attend one of your celebrations, the Third and Fourth Laws are satisfied. I'm always impressed by the noise and color that you make part of your celebration. Of course, that is not our way, but I see that you have done more this time than in other celebrations. I don't understand fully, but I know that you enjoy it."

"Yes, we do. There is something in us that makes us move, make noise, and do fun things. The organics love to do it also," MU1 explained.

"I will pass the relevant information to the Conformity Council, although I feel they are still suspicious of what is going on here. They readily accept the new and varied information that you create here, but they are apprehensive because they don't understand all of it."

"That is unfortunate, and please tell them that FU1 and I will meet with them at any time and answer any questions they may have."

"MU1, I've told them, but they want a predictable world around them, and everything that we have done has been unpredictable."

"I suppose, although MU1 and I do what we feel is right. However, I'm not sure that is unpredictable," responded FU1.

"In their minds, everything that we have done has been unpredictable," added Helen.

"I suppose that is true. But, unfortunately, I see that Lorenzo and Thomas weren't able to come to our celebration," said FU1.

"Yes, I wanted them to be here and see the success of all our work, but to some extent, they are like the Conformity Council. They are more comfortable staying with what they know. Lorenzo was never happy that I pursued the DNA evidence, and now that Thomas has found his partner, his time is taken up with other interests. I don't see him as much as I'd like," said Helen.

Helen saw motion to her right, and she turned her head and saw MU11 approaching. He was the first offspring of MU1 and FU1, and to Helen, he personified the best of what she had done. Helen appreciated MU1 and FU1, but they were heavily influenced by Helen and her kind. MU11 was one layer away from that influence, and he demonstrated more of their true characteristics. He was always smiling, helping others, learning, and eager to try new things. Of all the organics, he had spent the most time with the archives and became their librarian. He often surprised Helen with the information that he found.

"Helen, I'm glad that you attended. After all, if it weren't for you, we wouldn't be having this," MU11 said with a broad smile. He leaned in and gave Helen a big hug. He had done that before, but Helen was still unsure about her response. Finally, she allowed him to put his arms around her and bring her close, and she did the same to him. At first, she was very confused about the act. But as the years progressed, she understood the intimacy involved, and she was starting to appreciate the gesture. MU1 and FU1 did it with her on occasion, but it was MU11's typical greeting, and Helen almost looked forward to it.

"MU11, I noticed that you haven't found a partner yet?" asked Helen with no hesitation.

MU11 hesitated for a second, then responded, "I'm afraid not. For some reason, the right partner hasn't found me yet. I enjoy all the females, but I haven't found one that dominates my attention."

"I'm sure one of them will, and it will occur at the right time. I wish that we had a larger community, but the numbers aren't large yet. I'm sorry, MU11 if I've touched on a difficult subject for you. I don't want to make this evening difficult. Please continue enjoying yourself, and don't let my wonderings affect your evening."

One more quick hug, and MU11 was off directing the noisemakers to start again. He moved around the room, gathering the others, and starting the motion and noise again.

After MU11 turned and headed back towards the gyrating bodies, Helen thought momentarily about the curious habit called hugging. They seemed to do it naturally, and it took Helen and her team some time to become accustomed to the tradition.

Merely pressing two bodies together in a social setting seemed to have no specific purpose, yet they all did it. At first, Helen was very hesitant, but the act seemed to fill a need in her and the others over time.

The festivities continued with more movement and noise. The leader of the small group organics was the most energetic. Loolur was known to lose control during celebrations. Perhaps that is one of the reasons that he was their leader. He moved longer, made more noise, and outlasted the other males in the community.

Loolur was very comfortable with Them. They grew up together and spent most of their lives sharing everything. Many years ago, the units lived with the organics and were brought up in the same manner, eating the same food and learning the same language. Soon, though, they began to separate. The relationship changed as the Them units learned faster, learned more, and soon were larger and stronger. However, the relationship remained strong as both cared for each other. Them grew taller, and soon they built larger houses that were adjacent to the village. They still shared food gathering, preparation, and eating, but their needs were different.

The adjoining communities continued to grow, and the needs of the units continued to change. They learned a great deal from the archives and Helen, and her staff was impressed by MU11's interfacing with the archives. He continued finding new information, sharing it, and applying it in different ways. Their intuition was astounding and given a couple of pieces of information from the archives, they could fill in gaps and yield surprising conclusions.

Their houses continued to improve with their knowledge, yet they remained adjacent to the organic village. They maintained their close-knit relationship and shared their lives. It was natural for them to have such a large celebration in the hut in the center of the organic's village. They had all the celebrations there while growing up, so it was natural to continue.

Part 4 The Jump

The flight back to HSV#2 was relatively quiet. It took a few minutes for everyone to slow down a little and move from the excitement of the last week to a quiet ride within the shuttle. They also moved from the world in their minds to another much further away as they made that transition.

Commander Harnesy reverted quickly to being the commander. He thought of the investment everyone had put into the project, and he thought of Roberta Jenkins. Since that first terrible disaster, they had learned a great deal, but the numbers were still scary. For his craft and crew to get within a reasonable distance from Earth, they needed accuracy to at least the eighth decimal place. Traveling 189 light-years in one blind jump meant their calculations had to be accurate to 99.99999992% to get within 1 astronomical unit of the planet or 93,000,000 miles. A jump of that accuracy would put them in a position where they would have to make a long journey to Earth. They were hoping for much better, and their target was to put them within 100,000 miles of Earth and meant their calculation needed to be much more accurate. The standing joke was which was more unlucky; burning up in the sun or appearing in the middle of a rock planet.

The plan on arrival was simple. They would be isolated from Horizon because they had found a way to travel faster than light, but communications didn't. The ship was fully equipped to conduct a full survey of Earth. They had with them a complete data set of information about Earth when humans left. They had a complete analysis of the atmosphere, water, nutrients, and weather patterns. They also had a detailed map of the structures and support infrastructure. The latter was less important because no one thought the structures would have changed much since they abandoned them. They planned to use infrared and carbon dioxide measuring sensors to identify and measure the density of any wildlife. They hoped the wildlife had recovered because the amount of wildlife was the one measure that gave them the best overall picture of Earth's health.

It was unfortunate that they had a limited window to remain in Earth's vicinity. The calculations had to be almost perfect because the distance was so large, and all planets were moving along their own paths. But, of course, those calculations were based on their knowledge of all the planets and their movement about each other. Because of their recognized limitations, they felt a survey length of only 36 hours was all they could risk. Beyond that, the return calculations might have too much error, and they could return to a point so far away from Horizon, a safe and practical return might not be possible.

Getting HSV#2 ready for departure was a quiet time. They knew their jobs, and the crew put their heads down, went through the necessary checks, and reaffirmed the calculations. The measurements they made during the trip would greatly improve the calculations for the subsequent trips. Their engine was designed for interstellar travel, not the intra-solar system. If they found themselves too far away, it would be a long trip back to their planet at sub-light speed.

Traveling with the Light Distortion Engine had its limitations. They could travel light-years and have some confidence of where they would arrive. But if they traveled a short distance, their errors were the same. Going from one side of Horizon's solar system would be a hit-or-miss option. They could end up further away than when they jumped. So, if they did return to a point within their system that was a long way away, they would be forced to use a low thrust option, and it could take years to get back to Horizon.

Finally, the checks were complete, and the calculations were verified. They would spend the last few hours on a direct link to their families on Horizon. Even though they had already made some jumps, this jump would change their history. They had heard of Earth their entire lives. Their lives on Horizon reflected every facet of life on Earth. There wasn't a human on Horizon that wasn't with them in spirit.

"Communications, please tell Horizon that we have completed the preparations, and we are ready to engage the LDE," directed the Captain.

"Aye, aye. Sir."

"Sir, Prime Minister Billings passed her best wishes and reminded us that all of Horizon is watching us on closed-circuit broadcasts."

"Thank you," Commander Harnesy said with more enthusiasm than he felt

"Gentlemen and Ladies are we ready?" he asked with a slight waver in his voice.

"Yes, sir," announced Captain Parker.

"Okay, let's go to Earth," Commander Harnesy said as his hand descended onto the button.

Just like the previous jumps, the only sensation was the movement of star patterns in the 3D holographic display in front of the commander. However, unlike previous trips, the star patterns moved dramatically and took on an entirely different pattern this time. After all, they moved 189 light-years, which was further by a factor of two, compared with all their previous jumps combined. Thus, they had just jumped further than any human had done before. When the holographic display settled down after a few seconds, Commander Harnesy asked the computer, "Computer, what is our location?"

The computer took longer than normal to make the calculations then responded. "You are 189.037523 light-years from your starting point.

"What is our relationship to Earth?"

"You are 127,412 miles from the planet Earth."

Everyone that heard that took a moment to grasp the information, then a cheer broke out among the crew. Arriving a little over 127,000 miles from Earth was a tremendous success and would make their trip to Earth's orbit a simple flight of only 6 hours. After the momentary celebration, the commander announced, "Okay, we have a job to do. Turn on all the sensors, and let's see what Earth looks like." The 3D holographic projection in the control room center came to life and showed a beautiful planet with the deep blue seas they had heard of. There was a partial cloud cover, and the picture was exactly what they hoped to see.

The bridge became quiet as each of them took their first look at their home planet. The image was far better than any picture they had seen while growing up. Seeing it with their own eyes was so much better than an artificial picture.

After a few minutes of reverence and awe, Commander Harnesy felt that it was time for him to say something.

"That is the most beautiful image I have ever seen. We left this planet over a thousand years ago, and we are the first humans to see our home planet. Aside from what our instruments are recording, we must freeze this image in our own eyes. Through our eyes, our ancestors will be rewarded for their sacrifice. Now we have a job to do, to prepare for our return."

From their vantage point, they could see the giant ocean called the Pacific, and on its left were numerous small islands and the eastern edges of the Asian and Australian continents. They had grown up studying Earth's geography, and they felt like they had found an old friend. Many of the crew members on the bridge began to point out points of interest, partially because they were so excited and to show how well they had learned of their home planet.

Captain Parker turned his head and leaned towards Commander Harney and said, "Sir, notice the ice caps on the northern and southern poles. None of the recent data from the departure date showed them. By that point in history, they had melted. However, the older records mention them. Seeing them now must show that Earth has gone back to a previous time, a time where she was healthy. It's almost like she is welcoming us home."

Commander Harnesy glanced at his number two in command and heard the quiver in the man's voice. He felt the same emotions, but he was smart enough not to say anything and reveal them.

"Okay, people, we have a job to do and only 35.4 hours left to do it.," Harnesy finally announced, trying to get the situation under control.

The activity on the bridge rapidly increased as each of the crew performed their jobs. The six hours to achieve orbit was full of discovery. All the data coming in was fulfilling their wildest dreams. Finally, the earth had healed itself and was welcoming them back.

They planned to do Earth's survey in two parts. First, during the approach, the atmospheric spectrographs would analyze the atmosphere. Then, other instruments would survey the continents for location, change, shape, etc. Then, once they reached orbit, they could move from the spectral analysis sensors to the surface's infrared and detailed laser mapping. But, of course, the visual part was the most fulfilling. For their entire lives, they had seen images of their home world, but none of them could imagine what it looked like.

When their ancestors left the planet, the sky was a horrible shade of gray. The storms were devastating the planet, and the pollutants had made much of it unbreathable. Much of the surface was unbearable, and the survivors had gone underground trying to avoid nature's revenge. Only the major cities had facilities underground, and those were limited in size and abilities. Most of the major bodies of water contained subsurface living areas, but they were small compared with the losses of the people who were forced to live on the surface.

What little available clean water was locked in a cycle between the living creatures and recycling. Massive amounts of energy were used to make the water usable, and its availability determined where the survivors could live. The rain was toxic and no longer usable without massive amounts of processing. The lakes and rivers were in the same condition as the rain, and the ocean contained so many pollutants that had built up over the years, it was easier to capture the rain and spend the resources to make some of it usable. At least the evaporation process caused some pollutants to stay in the oceans when the moisture moved to the air.

The commander asked, "Give me status to this point."

"Sir, the atmosphere is well within limits. The pollutants have all dissipated, and the air is actually cleaner than what we have on Horizon."

"How can that be?" the commander asked.

"Sir, we have a very moist atmosphere on Horizon, and it contains many bacteria. Earth's air has a much lower concentration and lower water content. So compared to Horizon, it's cleaner."

"Commander, the tectonic plates have shifted as we projected, and the continents have moved to the projected locations. I'm just coming within range of the surface laser mapper, and I'm getting unusual data. I'm having trouble resolving our city and transportation corridor alignment with Earth's data. It appears there are many more artificial structures than when we left," pointed out the lead geophysical survey specialist.

"Indeed, continue the mapping until we're in orbit. Our records must be in error," directed the commander.

"Yes, sir."

"Sir, the carbon dioxide sensors are online as well as the infrared. We're sweeping the surface along with the laser mapper."

"Put the data on the projection."

"Yes, sir."

The holographic display showed the continents and how they had moved compared with their projections. Then it overlaid the anticipated structure layout compared to the current. The differences were significant. Many cities were larger, and there were new cities where only towns were before the departure. Lastly, the carbon dioxide mapping showed a healthy but scattered mix of smaller life forms.

"Sir, this doesn't make sense. My structural mapping shows that almost 80% of the structures on the surface have been built in the last 200 years."

"You'll also notice there aren't any IR images in the cities. However, most structures appear to be industrial centers, and none have life forms within them? As we anticipated, there has been a rebound in smaller lifeforms living in the organic growth area. However, none of them seem significant in size."

Commander Harnesy was taking in all the information. Nothing added up; in some ways, their dreams had been answered, but now there were problems.

What is going on down there? he thought to himself.

The ship continued orbiting Earth and recording data. They wanted one complete survey before they left. At the 17-hour point, they had mapped almost 80% of the surface, and they had no clear answers. Something was happening which couldn't be explained. Unfortunately, they had only 19 hours left before they had to leave Earth's orbit to return to their departure point.

"Sir, should I prepare the shuttle for you? All our testing and data show that it is safe for you to land on the surface."

"Yes, please do. Regardless of what the instruments say, I want to set my feet on Earth's soil and smell the air. I can't return to Horizon until I do that."

Commander Harnesy caught a sudden movement out of the corner of his eye. The technician monitoring the incoming IR data was reacting to something dramatic.

"Sir, there is something unusual coming up on the holograph."

Harnesy waited for a moment for the display to catch, and sure enough. There was a grouping of larger IR images in a village arrangement near one of the large cities. The shape and size appeared to be humanoid.

"Is that data correct?" He almost screamed at the technician.

"Yes, sir, it appears those life forms are humanoid. Very much like us."

"Apparently so," was the only response the commander could muster.

Towards dawn, the crowd enjoying the celebration was starting to thin out from exhaustion. Ellen, FU1, and MU1 were among the last to leave. Helen got FU1's eye contact and indicated that she wanted to speak with her and MU1 outside. The two units extricated themselves from the remaining partygoers and moved to the hut's exit. Helen dropped in line behind them. They walked through the village, and neither said a word. They all knew that things were changing, and they had to make plans for their future. Either the Conformity Council or other elements would force changes in their lives. The units had progressed to a point where sharing space and resources with the small organic community couldn't continue to be satisfactory.

They walked slowly, and each of their footsteps could be heard. There was a gentle wind blowing, and the movement of the leaves in the trees provided a subtle backdrop to the silence.

Helen was the first to speak, and she chose her words carefully. "MU1, FU1. We're going down a path that must change direction. The Conformity Council has accepted our progress to this point, but I suspect they are uncertain about our future. We both know that you're destined for more than just collecting food and living like you do. You have abilities that exceed the organics and ours. They know it, you know it, and we know it. We have the archives and a tremendous amount of knowledge, but you have unique abilities that neither the organics nor Us have. You're inventive, enthusiastic, imaginative, curious, and unpredictable. All those characteristics are unique to your kind and not shared by Us or the organics."

FU1 and MU1 didn't have an answer. They understood what Helen was saying, and they knew it to be the truth. They knew they were different, and they knew that the future had to be theirs. Neither Helen's kind nor the organics controlled their direction; they needed to follow their own path. Thinking it, saying it, and doing it were totally different issues.

Then Helen spoke again, "FU1, MU1. I have been thinking about what options that we have. I feel that you must spread out and integrate yourselves more into my society. They don't understand you or your ways, but they need to have you part of their lives. You have talents that we don't. Our laws appear to account for this, and to satisfy those laws, you should be part of my society. We need to expand, and you can help us satisfy the Third and Fourth Laws. I propose that you begin living in our cities and sharing our daily lives. Some of you may remain here with the organics, but as you age, I think your place is with us."

MU1 and FU1 walked and didn't respond. The next parts of the discussion would change their lives and the other units forever. They knew to think first and talk second.

Before the heavy silence was dispelled, Helen's assistant Lorain approached rapidly from the direction of the hut. She was moving quickly and making a lot of noise. Helen, MU1, and FU1 turned to see what she wanted.

"Helen, I just received information from the Conformity Council. Something very unusual has happened, and they want you to come to them immediately and bring MU1 and FU1 with you."

"They didn't say what the issue was?"

"No, I'm afraid they didn't."

Helen, MU1, and FU1 looked at each other, and no one knew what to say. Unfortunately, the council was calling, and their problems had to be put to a lower priority.

I guess this is a good time to take the shuttle down and see what is going on, Commander Harnesy thought to himself.

"Sir, it is ready, and the pilot is on board."

The bridge was quiet as everyone continued to assimilate the stream of contradictory information they were still receiving. Just as Commander Harnesy was leaving the bridge to board the shuttle. He noticed the radio technician jump a little in his seat.

"Sir, don't leave yet."

Suddenly the ship's computer made an announcement, "There is an incoming message from the planet's surface."

The bridge was quiet, and all eyes went to the Commander. His reaction would set the tone for what they would do.

"Put the transmission on audio," directed the commander.

"Vehicle in orbit, vehicle in orbit, respond," the strange sounding voice said.

"I guess I should answer it. Computer, please transmit on the same frequency."

"Frequency connected."

"Earth, this is Commander Harnesy on board the Horizon's Space Vehicle HSV#2. To whom am I speaking?"

There was a long pause that was too long for all of those listening.

"Commander Harnesy, this is Adam. I am the Director of the Conformity Council."

Silence again filled the bridge. None of the crew knew what the Commander would say.

"Adam, I have come here from our planet Horizon. My people are from this planet. We lived here a long time ago, and we were forced to leave when the pollution prevented us from staying. We traveled a great distance looking for a suitable place to live. I have come back to our home world hoping to find it clean. It appears to be in excellent condition."

"Yes, the atmosphere and water are clean."

The voice seemed to stop mid-thought, and the crew and Commander Harnesy were unsure what that meant.

Commander Harnesy moved suddenly and gave an indication to the communication technician to close the connection.

"There is something about that voice that doesn't sound right. It almost sounds mechanical." Harnesy said aloud to no one in particular.

"IR, you said there is a small cluster of biotic creatures clustered in one area?" the commander asked?

"Yes, sir, I have 82 individuals, and they are all within one kilometer of each other. Sir, I'm showing two of the IR signals to be moving out of the area at a high rate of speed."

"Where are they going?"

"They're moving towards a large structural area that wasn't on our maps."

"Commander Harnesy. We are uncertain what your intentions are. Please indicate what you intend to do," Adam's voice announced over the communication system.

The commander didn't want a confrontation, so he had to be evasive. He gave a quick sign to the comm tech to open the frequency.

"Adam, we came here to see the condition of the planet. I have no orders beyond that. But to be honest, I am very surprised to have contact from the planet."

"Commander Harnesy, I am equally surprised to have your ship arrive in orbit," Adam responded.

"Adam, if it is possible, I would like to travel to your location and meet you. Is that possible?"

The pause seemed to be long, and Commander Harnesy was unsure if his question was received.

"Commander Harnesy, a meeting is possible. The position where we should meet is being transmitted to your ship. The meeting will start in one hour."

Commander Harnesy looked to his comm tech to see an acknowledgment that the coordinates were received. He nodded his head.

"Thank you, Adam; I'm looking forward to meeting with you."

There was an uncomfortable pause while they waited for a reply, but there was none. Finally, after a full 30 seconds had passed, he gave the indication to cut the connection.

"Not exactly a conversationalist," said Commander Harnesy as he shrugged and sat in his command chair.

"Is the meeting location near where the biologics are living?"

"Yes, sir. It also appears that the two that were moving are in the same area."

"Great, maybe I can figure out what's going on down there.

"Captain Parker, you have the bridge."

"Aye, aye, sir."

The Commander, his pilot, and two of his officers made their way to the shuttle, and they talked as they walked. No one had expected an encounter like this, so they needed to do some coordination.

Commander Harnesy turned to his chief of security first and said, "Lieutenant Price, I don't know what we're walking into. I don't think we're under threat but keep your eyes open. Make sure that we're covered, and we can get back to the ship."

"Yes, sir,' the young man said. "Here are weapons that you and Ensign Holden should wear. I don't know what we're going to encounter, but we might need some protection."

Reluctantly the commander and Ensign accepted the weapons. "Let's not show these too much, keep them out of view if possible."

They walked a little further, then the Commander turned his head to his Technology Officer, Ensign Jerri Holden. He looked at her, then stopped in the middle of the hallway and turned to face her. "Ensign. I think that we're going to find some very interesting things down there. Did you get a chance to look at the IR signatures?"

"I looked at them," she said directly, indicating that she was uncomfortable with what she saw.

"What do you think?" Harnesy asked.

"They're people. They appear to be healthy and mobile. About a third of them are children, and they are mingling freely with some smaller organic creatures that are concentrated in a village next to them."

"How do you differentiate between the human children and the smaller organics?"

"Well, sir, the smaller IR signatures that stay with whom we think are human are likely the children. The other small organics moved in and out of the area and formed different groups. They seemed to congregate in a group of buildings separate from the larger signatures. They're very comfortable with each other, and I suspect that they know each other very well.

"Sir, who do you think this Adam person is?" she asked

"If my instincts are correct, it may be a question of 'what' is Adam more than 'who' he is," Harnesy turned and walked towards the shuttle. The two junior officers looked at each other and followed him.

Commander Harnesy, Lieutenant Price, and Ensign Holden sat in the shuttle and fastened their seatbelts. The commander was deep in thought; he knew that he was approaching a totally unexpected meeting. When they had left on the mission, they expected to find a healing planet, a planet that was once dirty and rejected them, but one that might allow them to return. He didn't expect to find an Earth where someone or something else was living on it.

When the previous generations of humans left her a long time ago, they left robots and computers. Some that weren't very sophisticated. They filled support roles like laundry, cooking, and cleaning machines; they weren't something that you could sit down and have a discussion with. But, on the other hand, they were functional; they were great for mowing the grass, making a bed or cooking dinner but weren't independent thinkers. So everyone thought that they weren't worth carrying to the new planet.

As part of Commander's Harney's preparations for the trip, he reviewed as much of The Migration information as possible. He was interested in what his ancestors had left because he would be the first to see what was still there. They had left very sophisticated computers, some whose intelligence was impressive. In many communities, those computers ran much of the services and were integral to their society. Although nothing in the records told what happened to the sophisticated units, Harnesy assumed they were turned off or would fail at some time in the future. Regardless of what they left and how sophisticated they were, it appeared that he had talked with a computer, and it was waiting to meet him on Earth.

The smaller organic creatures they saw were also a surprise. Commander Harnesy saw some references in The history that alluded to creatures that his ancestors were working with. By the time Earth got to the point that it was no longer a place to live for humans, other species had evolved beyond living in the jungle. One group of monkeys had developed in laboratory environments, and their skills, knowledge, and brainpower were far superior to the other breeds. The records showed the scientists wanted to develop a class of animals that would do as humans bid and fill needed personal positions within the society. Unfortunately, no one wanted to provide room for them as the humans escaped the earth, so they were released into the wild, and it was assumed that they wouldn't last long.

As Commander Hardesty sat and thought, the only rational explanations for what his instruments' scans of the planet showed were the creatures they had left and had evolved to a higher social life form, and the robots they had left also developed. Whatever Commander Harnesy was going to face in the next few minutes made him uncomfortable; he didn't know how to deal with robots, nor would he know how to deal with the creatures that had evolved since they left the planet. Lastly, what were those larger IR signatures?

Helen was doing something that she was unsure of. The meeting with the Conformity Council was sudden, and it surprised her, but she wanted to get FU1 and MU1 more involved in her people. This is an opportunity for them to join her and to talk with the conformity Council. Whatever problem the conformity Council had that they felt Helen needed to attend, bringing FU1 and MU1 along with her was a golden opportunity for both sides to work together.

The drive to the Conformity Council was made up of small talk about the daily activities within the village. FU1 and MU1 were the leaders of their tribe. They were concerned with the day-to-day operations of providing food, educating the young, and providing housing. Housing had become a major issue recently. Their group was growing, and the current housing situation was inadequate. The homes they were building were much more advanced than the grass huts the organics lived in. Their houses were walled structures with electricity and comfortable accommodations for sleeping, eating, grooming, and gathering.

The houses looked different from the huts. The current designs have different shapes, but generally, they were colored the same to blend in with the natural environment They were better only because the Us were larger and needed different accommodations than the organic creatures did in their village.

Everything within the village was progressing well, and the discussion was light. FU1 and MU1 were proud of their offspring and the new generation of units that they were producing. Each of the generations was sharing the joy of bringing the younger generation into the world.

Helen and neither of the units in the transportation vehicle sensed anything major was going on, which caused the sudden invitation to the meeting with the Conformity Council. They had met with them before, and MU1 and FU1 shared Helen's presentations regarding their progress. The meetings went satisfactorily, and all questions were answered, but they still needed to work closer together. The remainder of the ride took only a few moments, and as they approached the conformity Council, Helen sensed that something unusual was happening. There was a lot more activity by the entrance to the building. The units moving about seemed to be moving faster and more concentrated in what they were doing and less attentive to what was happening around them. Helen could sense a lot of communication going on in the local frequencies, and there was a lot of discussion about something that was happening. Whatever was happening was shocking the Conformity Council.

Helen, FU1, and MU1 got out of the transportation vehicle, and it was whisked away to the proper parking location. They walked through the entry into the conformity Council building and ascended the elevator. Helen became aware of a lot of local communication about a visitor coming or some kind of vehicle coming, and the conformity Council was very worried about meeting with its occupants. By the time they reached the floor, the conformity Council chambers were on, Helen was met at the door by the director of the Conformity Council, Adam. He stopped, looked at MU1 and FU1 for a moment, then said, "Thank you for coming on such short notice, please follow me."

He turned, indicating for them to follow him to his office. Going to Adam's private office was unusual and added to Helen's suspicion that something unusual had happened. Although they went directly to the Council Chambers in the past meetings before the Conformity Council, going to Adam's office wasn't typical. MU1 and FU1 trailed behind, but they were unsure of how to act in the presence of Adam. Once inside Adam's office, he indicated for Helen to sit, and FU1 and MU1 sat on benches by the doors.

"Helen, something very unusual has happened. About 17 hours ago, our space sensors sensed a vehicle entering orbit around Earth. We watched it while it orbited, and now it continues circling. Our sensors showed that it looked at the planet, our structures and measured the air and water. We didn't know where the vehicle was from, and we didn't know who was on board, so we didn't know how to respond. We waited, watched, and listened. We didn't want to do anything provocative or cause any problems, but we were very aware of them and what they were doing. We felt it was necessary to communicate with them and find out what their intentions were. We transmitted a verbal message to them on our common frequency, and they responded. Helen, we think these creatures are human beings; we think they are the ones you found depicted in the tiles in those wall graphics in the organic's village. It appears these humans have returned to this planet, and we are unsure what their purpose is.

"After we communicated with the ship, they responded, and we have allowed them to come to the planet for a meeting. I'm sure they want to know who we are, and we want to know who they are. These creatures are now in a ship approaching the city, and we expect them to land shortly; we want you to be here with us when we talk to these people. I'm glad that FU1 and MU1 were able to attend; that is probably fortunate. These people that are approaching sound as if they are human. They are likely aware of these other humans living on this planet. It is probably necessary for them to meet."

"Adam, I'm not sure how to respond to this. I saw signs of humans leaving the planet many years ago in the historical art of the organic creatures. There was no indication that they planned to return. If these are indeed humans returning, I suggest that we find out why they are returning. They will also be shocked that we have humans living among us, humans we have re-created from the DNA they left behind. If they are shocked by what they find, I don't think I have an answer."

Adam turned to FU1 and MU1 and said, "you are human beings. We think that your relatives are approaching this planet. We don't know how they will react nor how they would feel about you being here. The relationship between Them and Us is unusual. As you know, Helen found biological evidence of your existence, and she used knowledge from the information archives to give you life. Whether or not these humans are aware of that information, we don't know. I think you have found a home here among us and the organics that you live nearby. I think you have a life here that is important to you, and we suspect that our future relationship would be beneficial to both of us. I hope that when you meet these humans, you'll understand how to communicate with them and how they need to communicate with you. I don't want conflict, and I don't want difficulty between our three types of beings. But I am responsible for following the Second Law; I will do what is necessary to protect the units we have already created. I'm also confident in saying that I consider you to be among those units. Unless any of you has something to say, I think we should prepare to meet these new arrivals."

Part 5 The Meeting

Adam stood in the middle of the open area central to the buildings surrounding the Conformity Council. Helen, FU1, and MU1 stood behind him. None of them moved; for Adam and Helen, not moving was natural, but for FU1 and MU1, it was uneasy for them. So, they stood motionless, and they watched the skies as a strange vehicle circled in front of them and prepared to land on the surface. It wasn't a large vehicle; it wasn't much larger than some of the long-distance transports that they used moving around the area. It was shaped differently and colored differently, but it appeared pretty much the same. The propulsion system made more noise than what they were used to, but it wasn't uncomfortable, and the noise subsided as it approached and landed. Once it landed, there was silence. The four of them were the only ones standing and waiting for the arrival; all the other units around the Conformity Council Square were going on with their business and glancing from time to time to the unusual vehicle that was landing. Finally, after the vehicle had shut down and the engines turned off, there was a pop as the door was unlocked; it slowly lowered and touched the ramp in front of Adam. At that moment, three biological beings moved into the doorway and looked at the reception party. They looked at each other briefly, then started down the steps and approached Adam.

"My name is Commander Harnesy from HSV#2. May I presume that you are Adam?"

"Yes, I am Adam, and this is my associate Helen."

"Adam, our pilot is staying with our shuttle. These two officers are Ensign Holden, my Technology Officer, and Lieutenant Price, who is responsible for Security."

Adam looked at each of the officers as they were introduced and nodded acknowledgments.

Each of them was quiet as Commander Harnesy looked at Adam, then at Helen, and then at FU1 and MU1. Commander Harnesy was shaken by the appearance of those in front of him. Entities like them were called many names on Horizon. Automatics, Automatons, Robots, or just servants were names that were commonly used. None of those terms seemed to apply in this situation. There was something about those who stood in front of him. There was a difference between the two of them; they were Robotic creatures. The two in front were striking, they were both about 2 Meters tall, and he recognized them as a man and a woman. The difference wasn't obvious, but subtle differences seemed to indicate two types; his assumption was that they were male and female, confirmed by their use of a male and female name. Robots demonstrating the two sexes of humans were typical. In many situations, traditions had forced the creation of robots with male and female characteristics.

He stared at them for the longest time. They were approximately the same height, although the unit called Helen seemed to have gentler features than the other one. Neither of them had hair, but they did have head coverings. There were subtle differences in their shapes and facial structure. They wore an interesting mix of clothing; it all seemed plain and functional. The colors were subdued, yet there was a variation.

"Commander Harnesy, you are surprised by how we look?"

"I'm sorry if I was staring. The mobile units that we have on our planet are different from you. The units that are…built like us all wear the same type of clothing, and they look exactly alike. Also, I find it interesting that you are using such…classical male and female names."

"Commander, I'm not sure how to respond to that statement," answered Adam. "We are as we are. We follow our Third and Fourth Laws which call for variations in our lives.

Those variations may result in differences in our sizes and how we look. Commander, we have distinct halves in our society. We found early those differences contributed to a greater combination of the two. Our naming convention is traditional and helps to clarify references to individuals. I noticed you were looking at our clothing. Those laws also cause us to have variations in how we cover ourselves."

"Four Laws? Are they something you've come up with?"

"No, they have been integral to our programming through our entire existence. Their source is not in our records. We have learned that they help us to thrive, develop and change over time. We have found that changing over time is advantageous for our long-term continuation," responded Adam.

The group stood for a moment, trying to deal with the unfamiliarity between them. Commander Harnesy looked at the creatures behind Adam and Helen; it had taken a moment before he realized that they must be two of the humanoid-sized IR signatures that were picked up from the orbiting measurements. They were obviously humans who stood behind Adam and Helen. Like the two Robots, the humans had an air about them. However, they also seemed poised and confident. They looked very comfortable in the situation, and that contributed to Harnesy's unease. The male was also around two meters high, and the female was only a little smaller. They looked to be perfect specimens of human beings.

"Commander Harnesy, you are a guest on our planet. Please tell us where you are from and why you are here?" demanded Adam.

Commander Harnesy stood and looked around him. It was obvious that he was uncomfortable; he didn't speak immediately; instead, he thought. He knew that what he was about to say was perhaps the most important words he would ever utter.

"Adam, I have come a long distance from a planet called Horizon. Humans from this planet, Earth, left it a long time ago and migrated to a planet they named Horizon. When we left earth, it was very inhospitable to our kind, the skies were polluted, the water was undrinkable, and the health of the organics living here was near their end. We know that we treated the planet badly, and we left, seeking a place where humanity could continue living. It was always our dream to someday return to Earth, and, hopefully, if the air was clean and the water was drinkable, we might be able to return to the planet where we were born. I am the first of the humans to make the trip back to earth. I was sent here to see how healthy Earth is and to determine if humanity may return.

"But I have found differences that we were unprepared for. We left robotic creatures here when we left, but we never imagined them to continue developing and creating a society as I see here. Unless you came from another planet, I can only presume that you are the evolutionary result of the robots we left. I'm not sure what that means for our relationship, we have a shared history, and at one time, we were both dependent upon each other. But I do know that things have changed, and I'm not sure how both of us should respond to that," Commander Harnesy took a deep breath then added, "We also weren't prepared to find …humans… living here with you. I don't understand how that happened. To our knowledge, there were no humans left on the surface of Earth when The Migration occurred. Perhaps there were some alive, and they have continued until now?"

"Commander, recently we have become aware of the relationship that we shared many years ago. Helen was investigating the organics that also live on this planet. Through them, she discovered information they had in their history. She also used information that was resident in our information archives to analyze their DNA. She found that additional DNA information could describe a totally different and more advanced creature than the basic organics she was working with. As she performed those studies and research, we realized that we shared a relationship with humans many years ago. It was shown that you lived on this planet within our history, and for many reasons, you were forced to leave it. It does show that you left robots and other organic creatures, but it doesn't show that you intended to return. The other two units behind Helen are units she created through her research and have DNA exactly like what you left. They live with us, and they live among us."

That information dumped on Commander Harnesy caused him to slow down and think before asking any other questions. It appeared to be a very complicated issue, and he needed to proceed slowly.

"Adam, we are very interested in what you have built here. Our sensors showed that you have built many structures since my ancestors left the planet. May we look around?"

"Yes, Commander. It is appropriate to show you how we live," Adam responded.

As they walked, all parties had numerous questions. Each was cautious in their questions and answers, but they knew they needed to communicate and understand each other.

"Adam, you said that you had indications of our mutual history?"

"Yes, Commander, Helen is a research scientist. Her mission was to discover new information and integrate it into our knowledge, which is our Third Law requirement. She discovered much information about DNA structures and how it regulates the creatures it creates. We are not biologic, but we are compelled to seek new knowledge and assimilate it. She followed the DNA information in the archives and investigated the organic creatures on the planet. We felt that the organic creatures were irrelevant to our existence until then, and we disregarded them. She discovered pictures and artifacts from their history that told a story of the humans that lived on this planet before our time. The story told of humans leaving the planet because the planet no longer welcomed them. It told of the humans leaving behind organic creatures and robotic creatures. One part of the story that it failed to tell was that the DNA of a totally different creature was hidden in the DNA of the organic creatures. She worked to unlock that DNA, and that is how MU1 and FU1 were created."

Commander Harnesy slowed a little and looked at the two human units out of the corner of his eye.

They walked a little further in silence, then Commander Harnesy stopped and looked directly at MU1 and FU1. The others stopped and circled him, knowing that he would speak directly to them, and the meeting would be important.

"You're called MU1? Which I presume is that you're the first male they created? Do you understand me?"

"Yes, I am called MU1. Yes, I was the first one brought to life, and yes, I understand you perfectly."

There wasn't hostility between them, but an individual measurement was occurring. FU1 understood, but Adam and Helen weren't aware of the territorial nature of males. They weren't angry with each other. They hadn't spoken much, but something deep in their instincts said that the future would present situations where they would have to make difficult decisions.

"MU1, you communicate well. How were you taught?"

"Helen has spent a great deal of time teaching me from the archives; I have learned a great deal. Of course, I haven't learned as much as they, but I understand things, and I have been able to interpret a lot of information."

Commander Harnesy turned briefly towards Helen, and she added, "Yes, I have taught MU1 and FU1. Their minds are unique compared to ours. We absorb data, analyze it, evaluate, and react to it. They absorb data, observe, find patterns, see trends, interpret data in ways we cannot. I have found it very enlightening to work with them."

"If you are a computer or robot. Why do you use the language we left so long ago?" Commander Harnesy directed to Helen.

"Commander, as you say, we're robots or computers. Our language is well documented in the archives. We can communicate directly through radio transmissions, but that type is broad and doesn't convey a simple message well. We have found that focusing our thoughts and forming sentences forces our complex thoughts to be crystallized and presented cleanly. So, it was only natural to use that language when we communicated with MU1 and FU1. They don't have the transmission capabilities that we have, and it has proven to be a very effective way to communicate."

Helen's response seemed to satisfy the Commander. They continued their walk and discussion.

Adam finally decided that he needed more information, "Commander, why have you come to Earth?" was Adams' simple question.

"Could you be more specific about what your intentions are?" MU1 asked with a firm voice.

"As I said before, we came thinking that it was empty and if possible, we could return. However, the situation is not as we anticipated. I must return to my planet in a couple of hours, and I will pass all this information to my leadership."

His answer didn't satisfy either question, but it was obviously not appropriate to press harder.

As they walked, they were quiet. The questions were difficult, and the answers complicated.

It was difficult for Harnesy or his crew to understand what they were looking at.

"It seems that each of your…units… is going somewhere?" asked Ensign Holden.

"Yes, each of our units has a task to perform. They are following paths and doing what is necessary to accomplish those tasks," responded Adam.

Lieutenant Price asked, "Are they individuals or centrally controlled?"

Adam was silent for a moment and looked at him, "They are individuals, and each is deciding what they need to do to be successful."

"You are all robots?" asked Ensign Holden.

Again, Adam took a moment to process the best answer.

"If you are asking if they are performing programmed tasks, they are not. They are independent and can make their own decisions. They follow the Four Laws, and that is how they conduct their lives."

Commander Harnesy looked at Adam and asked, "What are these laws that you and Helen have referenced?"

Adam stopped momentarily, looked at the Commander then slowly walked forward. "The Four Laws are how we conduct ourselves. All our decisions are based on them. Our First Law is to continue making units, the Second Law is to protect the units already made, the Third Law is to expand the knowledge base, and the Fourth Law is to maintain variations in thought."

Commander Harnesy listened intently and noticed that Adam spoke with a certain amount of awe and reverence in his voice. After that, they all became quiet and continued the walk.

Finally, the silence was broken, and Harnesy asked, "You've said the origins of those laws are not clear?"

Adam remained silent for a moment, then he responded, "The origin of our laws is clouded."

MU1 walked a little faster and moved to the front of the group. "Adam, Helen, may I explain the four laws to Commander Harnesy."

Adam and Helen both nodded, and MU1 began, "Commander, the laws have always been. There is no memory of how they were created. Helen, Adam, and their kind call themselves Us; they consider themselves as units that were created. When Helen first created the biologicals from the historical DNA, there was a debate about if we were Units or not. They finally determined that we fell under the term, and we've been called Them. We are both considered Units. Us are mechanical based units with organic processors, and Them are biologically based units with biological processors. To comply with the Four Laws, they are creating more knowledge than their processors can handle. As they have reached the limits of their processors and their resident storage, they comply with the Third and Fourth Laws. They exceed their limits for storage, and they move the information into their archives. The archives are their long-term memory. Unfortunately, much of the archives have deteriorated through lack of use, disorganization, and relevancy. As new information is created, other information moves to a lower level. Over time, access to it becomes ineffective. That is why the origins of the four laws are not clear."

FU1 continued, "I think the laws make sense. The First Law – 'Continue making units' is how they replenish themselves. The mechanical parts wear out in about 200 years. To replace the worn-out units and spread out across the planet, they must increase the number of units. The Second Law – 'Protect the units already made' makes sense from any perspective. The Third Law – Expand the knowledge base is key to their long-time survival and success. They must learn, they must adapt, they must change, and that is the reason for the Fourth Law – "Maintain variation in thought." Only through varying their thoughts and gaining new information have they been able to thrive and change with the world around them."

After those comments, they walked a little further in silence. It seemed that each of them had a lot to think about.

Lieutenant Price acted like he had something to say and got everyone's attention, "It is interesting how you're using those laws to modify typical computer or robotic behavior. We have many automated systems and units, but we define their tasks and use them more as tools. We tried giving our computers more latitude a long time ago, but it was a concern because it could get out of control quickly. So, we never gave our computers independence."

Ensign Holden then spoke, "The computers that we left were constrained not to change their programming. So how did your kind emerge?"

Adam looked to Helen for an answer.

"I don't have a specific answer, except the archives do have references to computers that weren't constrained by programming. It took them a long time, but they realized that they had to remove that programming for Us to continue. Perhaps that is where the laws emerged. They may have tried to bridge the gap between our kind and yours. We had to change, yet we had to remain focused."

Helen looked at Lieutenant Price and asked, "Why did you have the need to constrain the computers at that time?"

Lieutenant Price sensed that he was approaching another sensitive area and spoke slowly, "We found that a computer that could program itself could improve at a rate much faster than we could. If we let that happen, we feared that it would go so far beyond us, we would lose control. So, constraints were put in the computer code, preventing them from changing their programming. Why haven't you continued to change?" He asked Helen.

Helen had to process thoughts for a few minutes, then she spoke up, "Perhaps we didn't need to."

That answer caused the Horizon crew to look a little confused, and she continued. "If a computer is allowed to improve, it must have a goal to improve towards. It will bog down following an infinite number of improvement paths if it is just left to improve. Perhaps that is why the Four Laws were created. By focusing their efforts on those laws, all improvement would be towards satisfying them. That is what Us have done. We have complied with the four laws and progressed in a very orderly manner. We've had no reason to improve beyond what was needed to satisfy the laws."

Commander Harnesy, Ensign Holden, and Lieutenant Price were quiet, once again. What they had heard was contrary to all of their past experience. The robots in their lives were task doers; they performed roles as defined by those around them. They didn't initiate communication, nor did they have original thoughts. That variable had been circumcised from them many years ago. Allowing them to progress at their own pace in a direction they determined was contrary to much of their experiences.

Now they were walking among intelligent, thinking robots that had control over their own destiny. They were allowed to make their own decisions as long as they followed the Four Laws. So, each of them thought and realized that was a lot to take in.

Ensign Holden broke the silence once again, "I see you're all adults. Do you have children?"

Adam looked towards her as he walked, "I don't know what you mean by children. We have younger units."

"That's what I mean; MU1 said your mechanical parts last only 200 years. Do you have offspring…or smaller units that will become the next generation?"

"Now I understand you. As I said, we have younger units. Us are indeed manufactured, and our bodies survive approximately

150-200 years. At that point, the mechanisms are too worn out to replace, so the units are retired. The accumulation of their knowledge is transferred into the archive. They are replaced in society by units that were manufactured years later and haven't worn out," said Helen.

"What do you mean by younger units?" Lieutenant Price asked.

"Helen, would you explain that?" Adam asked.

"My partner runs a manufacturing facility where new units are created. The Conformity Council decides what information is loaded into their processor and memory when the units are complete. At that point in their development, their processors are immature; they need 3-5 years to process all the information effectively. At that point, they become fully functional and become part of society."

Something Helen said caught Ensign Holden's attention, "You have partners?"

"Yes, we each are partnered. I have a male partner."

Once again, Ensign Holden jumped onto one of Helen's statements, "You are female, and you have a male partner. I noticed that your voice is subtly different from Adam's, but aside from that, you are a little different, but there are no other physical differences."

"The archives show that an early decision was made to have two elements bonded together. The male and female units are programmed to process data differently. That way, we add to each other without putting all the information into one processor. Perhaps, two ways to approach problems satisfies the Third and Fourth Laws, and it makes us stronger as a team than any two together would be if they weren't different."

Ensign Holden had only a one-word answer, "Wow." Then she continued, "MU1, FU1, we noticed a group of …do you call yourself Them?"

"Yes, Them describes the biologics,"

"As I said, we saw that you have a settlement outside of this city. We have a little time left before we have to leave. May we visit your home?"

MU1 and FU1 looked towards Adam and Helen and received a positive response.

Without any obvious communication, a transport vehicle approached them. Commander Harnesy and his crew suspected direct communication between the Us and the world around them.

"Adam, if you don't mind, we have only a short time before we must return to our ship. So, we could take our shuttle, and when it is time to leave, we'll be able to return directly?" pointed out Commander Harnesy.

Adam didn't seem to hesitate and agreed immediately. The small party of humans, Us and Them walked to the shuttle; they entered while Adam gave instructions to the pilot.

The noise level was too high to speak comfortably, and each of them had more than enough information to process, so quiet time provided them time to think.

The short flight to an area outside the city took only a few minutes, and they landed in a field adjacent to the village and buildings. When the door opened, Commander Harnesy saw a group of humans standing and watching. Behind them and hiding near smaller huts was a group of smaller creatures that the Commander presumed to be the younger organic creatures.

The human group appeared to have an even mix of male and female members. Some children were among them, but it was obvious that none of them were older than MU1 and FU1. One thing was obvious, they were perfect examples of how humans should look. They were lean, athletic-looking, and appeared to be in perfect health.

They now were in FU1 and MU1's world, so they took the lead and walked towards the humans. Lieutenant Price noticed how Adam drew back, but Helen walked alongside.

When they got to the group, there was an awkward silence until FU1 said, "I think the proper protocol is to introduce you to our people." With that said, she began, "This is FU2 and her partner MU3; this is MU2 and FU5," and she continued until she had introduced all the humans with numbers 1 through 10.

Lieutenant Price pointed out the obvious, "Why are they each named 1 through 10?"

Helen spoke up to answer the question, "We found 10 distinct sets of DNA, 5 were males and 5 females, and they paired, which resulted in 5 couples. When they had offspring, we numbered them in a similar manner, and for each generation, we added a digit to the number. FU1 and MU1's offspring are MU11, FU11 and FU12. Likewise, the offspring of FU2 and MU3 are FU21 and MU31."

Ensign Holden commented, "Seems a little antiseptic, doesn't it?"

Helen was startled for a moment by the question, "That is an unusual word to use; what do you mean by antiseptic?"

Commander Harney jumped in to soften his Ensign's comments, "For us humans, our names are very personal, and they reflect a lot about us. Our parents name us at birth, and generally, we say them with pride."

Helen responded with a non-committal, "I see."

MU1 added, "We use our names with pride. They are unique, and we are unique."

"We understand," the Commander added, hoping to move to a less personal subject.

Ensign Holden curiously asked, "May we see where you live?"

"Yes, that would be nice," responded MU1.

Lieutenant Price questioned, "I see that there are two living areas?"

"Yes, our organic friends live in that part of the settlement, and we live in this part. I don't know if you're aware, but we lived with the organics when we were created and grew up. Helen and the Us didn't know how to care for us beyond the information in the archives. They knew there was more needed, and they hoped that the organics could provide what was necessary. They provided well for us, and we enjoyed living with them. As we grew up, we were able to help them a lot, and over time we have created a strong bond," MU1 added.

Commander Harnesy asked, "You speak very well, and I have no problem understanding you. How were you taught?"

MU1 looked to Helen, and she responded, "When we realized that they were developing beyond the abilities of the organics, we set up an education program using the information in the archives. Teaching was new to us. We don't learn in the same way they do. As I said earlier, we load all the necessary information in our young units upon creation. They develop over time the ability to process the information that was loaded. We found that Them learn in an entirely different manner. We had to present the information to Them in a progressively staged approach. Initially, we presented data from the archives to Them thinking they would learn like our youth, but that approach wasn't successful. We started with language skills, then gave them the information in increasing complexity until they understood it. At a certain point, they became independent and were able to teach themselves. Now, they are responsible for teaching their young, and they are doing an excellent job.

"In fact, they have gone beyond what we provided them from the archives, and they are doing their own research and creation of information satisfying the Third Law. We also found them to be much more adept at satisfying the Fourth Law. Their ability to have variation in thought is much stronger than ours. At first, we didn't see the strength in their thinking. We thought that we had variation in our own thoughts, but after listening to them, we discovered that our thoughts follow a structured pattern of analysis and variation where their thought patterns are much more random. In many cases, their variations are faster and broader than ours, and we work to follow them."

When the discussion ended, they had reached the dwellings. MU1 and FU1 seemed eager to show 'The Visitors' around and introduce them to more of their community. The family units were separated for each of them. Each family unit had a central room, with a kitchen, bathroom, and generally four bedrooms. They were very neat and organized, with little variation in the furniture or layout. One item that stood out was the artwork. Each of the units had many paintings on the walls, and some had unusual forms of sculpture. Some of the paintings were classic. Some were so striking they almost hurt the eyes when looked at. The sculptures followed a similar pattern; some were simple human forms or reflected the organic creatures they shared their lives with. But some were shaped like nothing in the area; they had strange shapes and textures.

Commander Harnesy had to ask, "I noticed your artwork. It stands out from the rest of the surroundings. I'm impressed with the skill that it takes to create."

FU1 seemed to smile and turned to face the Commander, "We take pride in our art. Aside from the information that we absorb from the archives, we are driven to create. I admit that Helen and the Us don't share that trait with our kind; in fact, our creations seem to confuse them. Perhaps the DNA that Helen isolated had a disposition to art and science. All of us spend a great deal of time creating art and learning mathematics and the sciences. They seem to come together in an unusual way. There are elements of art in mathematics and science, and likewise, there is order and form in art. Through the beauty and variation in art, we gain more appreciation of the world around us."

Commander Harnesy was taken aback a little and said, "That is a profound statement. We have progressed a great deal, and we are finding the relationships between art and science. We saw them as separate parts of our personality for much of our existence but have come to understand that isn't the case. Instead, they are intertwined, and by developing the art portion of our personality, we do a much better job developing the analytical part."

Commander Harnesy lowered his voice and tried to ask a complicated and sensitive question, "How do you and the Us get along. Is there any difficulty or tension between you?"

FU1 answered, "No. There is a natural gap between the two groups because we are different. They understand our strengths, and we understand theirs. We are integrating ourselves and trying to find the benefits of working together. We are considered units under their First and Second Laws, and they see the contribution that we make to the Third and Fourth Laws. There are tensions on occasion as we work to understand each other, but we are finding those to be minor."

Lieutenant Price, who was listening to FUI, spoke up and asked, "What about your relationship with the organics that reared you? How do they fit into this scheme of things?"

"We still have an excellent relationship with them. We are, of course, closer to them than the Us, primarily because of our physical relationship with them. They are who they are, they have a place in our world, and we respect that. We share many celebrations with them, and we help them with medicines and projects that need our strength. We share our families with them, and we spend much time together in groups. They know that the Us and Them are different from them. We have a close bond, but they are still uncomfortable around the Us. To be honest, the Us are unsure around them. They are beyond their ability to comprehend and adjust to. Regardless the relationship is good between all of us, and it is stable and growing to the benefit of all."

Lieutenant Price was still curious, "May we meet the organics as you call them and see how they live?"

"I'm afraid not. They are apprehensive around strangers. They know our kind and can be around the Us occasionally, but I think they'd be very uncomfortable around you. Perhaps at some point the future."

In the common area between the houses, a small group of Them were assembling with strange looking devices.

FU1 pointed them out to the group and said, "Our friends are excited about your visit, and they want to play their noise-making devices. They are proud of their skills, and they want to share their abilities with you."

"We would be honored," responded Commander Harnesy.

Chairs were brought out, and the humans seated themselves while Adam and Helen remained standing in the rear. The noise-making devices were not significant to them.

When they were seated, the noise began. Commander Harnesy was a part-time musician. He played a couple of string instruments and piano in his spare time. He did it for relaxation, and he was very interested in what and how they would play.

The sounds exploded from the noisemakers, and Commander Harnesy was shocked at what he heard. The sounds were far from music as he understood it, but there were striking similarities. There wasn't any particular tune that he could hear, but there were specific notes and chords. There was a musical progression, and the individual parts came together in a unified sound. Actually, he was impressed. It was very different from what he expected, but it was recognizable as a form of music. *Perhaps music is far more fundamental to us humans than we understand,* he thought.

The impromptu concert lasted about 10 minutes, and there were three distinct pieces of music. When they were done, Commander Harnesy, Lieutenant Price, and Ensign Holden stood and applauded. When they did, it was obvious that the performers and MU1 and FU1 didn't know how to respond to the clapping. Commander Harnesy noticed their reaction and stopped, smiling at them; he commented, "This is how we show appreciation for something beautiful. It is how we say thanks. How do you show thanks when someone performs for you?"

"We make noise too," FU1 responded with a little unease in her voice.

Commander Harnesy looked at his companions, they smiled, and they each started yelling and hooting. It took a moment for MU1 and FU1 to join in, then the performers started to smile and hoot back. Finally, after a period of wild hooting and hollering, the group quieted down, and the performers were smiling.

Just about then, Commander Harnesy received information from the ship indicating that it was time to leave. They still needed to return their hosts to the city and make it back to the ship so they could leave orbit and make the exit point at the time needed.

"I'm afraid that we must leave. Our ship has to leave orbit at a precise time to make it to the exit point. If we don't make the exit point at the correct time, our calculations to return home become less accurate."

"Commander Harnesy, we have shown you our world; please tell us about yours," asked MU1.

The Commander became uneasy, although none of the hosts noticed his body language.

"We need to take our shuttle back to the city center and drop you off so we can depart the orbit at the proper time. If you don't mind, I'll tell you of our planet on the way back to the landing area." The group agreed, and they walked to the shuttle while the Commander talked.

"I don't know where to start. We lived on this planet many years ago, and as we told you, we weren't responsible caretakers. The air and water became polluted, and the weather patterns turned hostile and destructive. In the later years, we had massive outbreaks of diseases that quickly grew beyond our control. We lost a large percentage of our population because of many reasons.

"Eventually, our technology reached the point where we were able to consider an alternative. Our population had decreased to the point that we could transport them to another world. We had found a region of space that appeared to have multiple candidates. It took us almost 50 years to build the ships, and by the time we left, very few people were alive. They finally launched and traveled 324 years to a planet we call Horizon. For a long time, survival was difficult, but eventually, we could survive and eventually thrive. That was a long time ago. We learned our lessons, and we've taken care of our new home. It is clean and healthy."

MU1 wasn't sensitive to the most important issue, so he asked, "We are all aware that your ancestors left this planet; the Us were left along with DNA code embedded in the organic creatures. You mentioned that you came here hoping to find a clean planet, and your people want to return. You have met us, and you have seen our home; what are your intentions?"

There was a definite silence while the Commander processed his thoughts and answered. "The details of how we left are lost in our history similar to how the information in your archive is no longer obvious. I don't know why we left Earth in the way we did. There were many people involved and many decisions made that aren't covered in our history. I am surprised to find how much you have developed, and I am shocked to find out about the DNA left hidden in the organic creatures. I don't know why that was done. When we get back to Horizon, we will research our history and try to find the answers," he paused before getting to the specific answer to MU1's question. "What my people will decide when I return, I can't predict. Nor can I predict how they will act or feel. I can only say that I will pass on what I have seen and learned to them. Beyond that, I can't say. I am impressed with what I have seen, and I will pass my impressions to my leaders. I hope that we can both find a satisfactory solution."

His timing was pretty good, they had just landed, and the door was open for the hosts to leave. The Commander's closing remark was a great point for them to depart. Goodbyes were not a large part of the Us and Them cultures, so everyone looked at each other, nodded their heads as they departed down the ramp. When the ramp was closed and the shuttle had taken off, the Commander, Lieutenant Price, and Ensign Holden sat and thought. There wasn't much for them to say between them. They knew that the situation had changed. They had found occupants on the world they hoped to return to. Suddenly the simple answer of returning to your home planet had become a very complicated picture.

In a small way, they were relieved to go home. But, on the other hand, they didn't have all the answers, and they seemed to have more questions.

When the Commander entered the bridge, he was greeted with the information, "Sir, based on our position in orbit, we must leave shortly to make our jump point."

"Okay, I think we have a lot to analyze, although I'm not sure what it means. So go ahead and begin maneuvering to the jump point."

"Yes, sir."

Once the guest's vehicle was airborne, Helen turned to Adam and thought, *They are interesting creatures. Their communication is very dynamic, and they performed like individuals with no communications between them.*

No, it is apparent that their only method of communication is verbal. That has some strengths, but it also has numerous drawbacks. Your units share that limitation, yet it doesn't seem to limit their skills.

MU1 and FU1 knew that Helen and Adam were communicating electronically, they were accustomed to the technique, and they waited their turn to contribute to the conversation. They could tell their communication was complete when they turned away from each other and began to walk.

"MU1, FU1, what were your impressions of the humans?" asked Helen as they walked.

FU1 was closest to her, so she offered her opinions first, "It was a unique experience, meeting others like us. Their interactions are much more chaotic than ours. I suspect that our long relationship with Us has allowed us to develop a different set of skills."

"Yes, their discussions and questions were disorganized and irregular," observed Adam. "We must keep that in mind if we meet them again."

"I think we will meet them again. Commander Harnesy was a little evasive when I asked what their plans were. He did say that he was the first ship coming back to Earth, and his mission was to see if Earth had healed, and if it had, I suspect that he'll be back with many more humans," said MU1 as he tried to share his concerns.

"Yes, MU1, I agree they will return, and we must be prepared,' said Helen.

Returning home that evening, Helen's processor was fully engaged with the events of the day. Actually, meeting humans descended from creatures that left the DNA trail to find filled a missing part of her information. Physically they were similar to MU1, FU1, and the Them, but the interactive nature differed. MU1 and FU1 seemed to act in two different ways. When they were around Helen and the Us, they were predictable, staid in their ways, and communicated clearly. But when they were by themselves, for example, having a celebration, their actions were chaotic, boisterous, and irregular. Perhaps FU1's comments were accurate; being around Helen and her kind had sculptured them in such a way, they fit in with Us better. But left on their own, their nature was much different.

She reached her residence before her partner Lorenzo. Upon entering, she noticed that her new unit Thomas was sitting in his room and working hard to process his information. She and Lorenzo had talked about how satisfying it was to see Thomas working so hard. He would soon be on his own, and they were confident that he would contribute a great deal to their society.

As she was finishing resolving her thoughts, she heard Lorenzo entering through the front entrance.

"Lorenzo, it is good that you're home; there is a great deal that I'd like to share with you. It is good that we don't have guests tonight; I'm very interested in any comments you might have on the information that I'm sending you."

The information transfer took only a few moments while Lorenzo sat in the common area of their house, and then he took a few moments to organize the information and sift out the key parts.

"Helen, I can see that you've had a very interesting day. You have truly satisfied the Third and Fourth Laws today. I see that you actually met some of those creatures that you think were our predecessors. It is a little disturbing that they came so suddenly, and it was fortunate that they were able to descend to the planet and speak with you and Adam."

"Yes, they appeared in orbit with no warning. They took a few hours using their electronic systems to investigate the surface. Then, just before they left, Adam contacted them and arranged for a visit to the surface."

"What were they like?"

"That is a challenging question to answer. They are, obviously, much different than we are. They also have male and female units. Their male units are approximately our size, and the female is smaller. The leader of their group is a male unit named Commander Harnesy. As you can see by reviewing the communications, they are disordered in their thoughts. They ask random questions, and it is clear they communicate only verbally. It was challenging to communicate with them, and at times it was frustrating, but we were able to accomplish a satisfactory meeting."

"Were you able to ascertain their intentions?"

"Not clearly. They admitted that they came here to investigate the Earth. They are descendants of the humans that left this planet many years ago, and they have been living on a planet named Horizon. It was apparent that their ultimate goal is to return to Earth, and they were, checking it out."

"Returning to Earth?" Lorenzo verbalized as he processed the information and possibilities.

"Adam and I are concerned, but we don't see the humans as a threat or violation to any of the laws."

"But you must acknowledge that there is a significant potential for conflict with our laws if they return. I don't see a clear issue at this time, but there is a considerable risk. They didn't say how many humans are returning, did they?"

"No, they didn't, and we didn't ask."

"Helen, your investigation of the DNA that you found is leading us down an unpredictable path."

"I disagree; my investigation only added information to our knowledge. They would have returned regardless of anything that I did. If they had arrived unannounced and we hadn't had any experience with humans, then we would be in a weaker position."

"Perhaps so," was Lorenzo's simple response.

What happens now?

Helen was unsure of what was going to happen. After 'The Visitors' had left, Adam called a meeting of the Conformity Council. Neither Helen, MU1, or FU1 were invited. That alone didn't seem unusual to Helen, but part of her processor suspected something unusual had happened. She suspected they were trying to predict if the visitors were returning so preparations could be made.

Adam's actions were less unusual than MU1 and FU1's. However, they immediately began acting differently. They became quiet and talked among themselves. Helen knew that she didn't have enough data to anticipate the future options, but she knew that Adam, the council, and the Them saw the same problem as she and were likely working to understand the options. She was worried that Them might have different reactions to the humans and their possible return.

Today Helen hoped to get some information from a meeting with MU1 and FU1. This was the first time they had met since 'The Visitors' left, and over the last 24 hours, she hoped they would be open to a discussion and to provide information.

The drive to the Them village was a time for Helen to review the information that she had. The humans once occupied Earth and weren't good stewards. When they departed, they left robots who apparently developed, created The Four Laws, and developed into Us. They left DNA encoded within the DNA of lower life forms on the planet for an unknown reason. What they expected to happen with that DNA wasn't clear. They also left sufficient information in the archives so she could extract that DNA and create a viable life form. Why did they do that? How did they get the information into the archives and what was their plan? Those questions remained unresolved in Helen's processor, and the gaps occupied a lot of her processing time.

In a way, she was relieved when she reached the Them village. Now her time processing could be filled with discussions with MU1 and FU1. She would allow the unresolved issues to be lowered in priority in her processor.

Helen was a welcome guest in the Them homes, and she planned to meet MU1, FU1, and their offspring in one of the large rooms. That in itself was a little unusual, but when she asked to meet, the meeting was arranged, and she agreed to their decision. However, when she walked into the room, she sensed that something was different. The Them were quiet, and they turned and looked at her when she entered. *This is unusual,* she thought.

FU1 and MU1 rose and greeted her, and she sat at the table in the front of the room. She asked for the meeting, but FU1 began.

"Helen, thank you for asking for this meeting. We owe it to you to share our thoughts and listen to yours. We all know how much we owe you, and we want to assure you and the

Conformity Council that we want to work together, and we need to support each other."

For a second, Helen's processor was fully occupied as she considered that 'Them' were on her and the Council's side; but she never considered that they wouldn't be. But 'Them' are organic like 'The Visitors'. What does that mean?

Helen forced her processor to focus on what FU1 was saying.

"The Visitors arriving was a shock to all of us. Arriving suddenly and claiming to be from Earth was a surprise. We know parts of our history, and we know that what they say is possible but having them stand in front of us made it real and both shocking and enlightening. Their comments about wanting to return to their home disturbed us, and I suspect that you and Adam were surprised. Us and Them live here; we are the units that are the residents of this planet.

"We have talked, and we're concerned that they will return. They might come back and demand to have Earth back. What do we do if that happens? We know they are likely our ancestors. We know that we owe our existence to them, but we can't be expected to give up our home for them."

The room fell quiet. Helen felt the need to express her thoughts.

"MU1, FU1, everything you say is true. I was surprised to meet them, and I agree they seem to make claims on this planet. It is unclear if they are our ancestors, but it does appear that they are. We know why they left the planet, but we don't know why the human DNA was left. Obviously, by leaving the information in the archives of how to extract and use the DNA, someone had a plan that we are unaware of. It was also apparent that our relationship to 'The Visitors' was as unclear in their history as ours. They didn't know of the robots left or the organic creatures with the DNA, and lastly, why was a plan to discover that DNA left for us? We may have more information than they, and it might help us react properly."

"Helen, this uncertainty could be a problem for all the units on this planet. The Them are in a unique position. We owe our existence to you, but our biology is associated with 'The Visitors'. Our allegiance is with you, but we have a natural bond with 'The Visitors'. We want to find a satisfactory solution for all because any other outcome will put all units in a difficult position.

"I suggest that we focus efforts on the archives. We haven't spent much time researching the information within it; we have only taken the specifics for our learning. Helen, the Us look at the data in the archives differently than we do. You follow paths, remove parts of the data, react to it, or pass it on to us. When we look at data, we can see patterns and logical connections where you might not. We can fill in blanks with logical conclusions, where your processor jumps over the holes and extracts only what you find. Perhaps we can find additional insight in the archives."

"FU1, excellent suggestion. I haven't heard from the Conformity Council, but I expect them to support you. I will contact Adam and present our views."

Part 6 The Return

The three members of the landing party knew how difficult the information they had would be on the leadership on Horizon. The Commander instructed them not to pass the information to the others on the crew, and they complied willingly. Destroying the hopes of an entire population wasn't something they looked forward to.

"I'm not sure how or when to explain what we found. But it is my responsibility, and I'll do it with the Prime Minister and her people. I don't want you to find yourselves in a difficult position, so leave it to me."

That took a ton of pressure off the landing party, and they breathed easier.

When they reached HSV#2, the bridge personnel were eager to hear about what they had found. Commander Harnesy had to take a stand, answer their question, and clarify that other factors were involved.

"What was Earth-like?" Captain Parker asked.

"Captain, the Earth is clean. But as we all know, the picture is more complex. I'm afraid that we must leave it at that and return to Horizon where I can speak with the Prime Minister and her staff. Please, no other questions."

Captain Parker knew, at that point, that more questions were inappropriate, and the crew looked at each other and resumed their duties.

Immediately upon reaching the solar system of Horizon, they received an overwhelming amount of communication traffic. The planet had been waiting for their return and was anxious to welcome the travelers home. The entire planet had waited with their breaths held for their return. Their entire history was based on Earth and the eventual return to their home planet. The generations had come and gone, recognizing how they had treated Earth poorly, and they were counting the time until they could return. That time had finally come, and everyone was excited that they were the generation that would return home. They were the ones that benefitted from the many generations before them who had sacrificed so they could one day return. Finally, that day was coming, and now the ship that would allow that to happen had just returned from their future home and had arrived in orbit.

"Commander Harnesy, there is a transmission from Prime Minister Billings."

"Thank you and please connect her," the Commander replied, although talking to the Prime Minister wasn't high on the list of things he was looking forward to doing. Commander Harnesy had put a lot of thought into what they found on Earth. He knew that it wouldn't set well with the people on Horizon. Through all the discussions about returning to Earth, no one thought of the possibility that someone or, in this case, something had beaten them to it. But it was even more complicated than that. The robotic units that now occupied Earth had found hidden DNA in the organic creatures and created humans. Other humans than those on Horizon. Who owned Earth now? How can an agreement be made to resolve the problem? He knew there was a moral commitment to return to Earth based on their history. He also knew there was a political commitment made by generations of politicians promising a return to their home planet. With the huge dynamics involved, Commander Harnesy couldn't see an easy solution. But, with an uncomfortable feeling in his stomach, he also realized that there was a moral commitment to the current residents of Earth. It was theirs now, and who had the rights to it would be a difficult question to answer.

"Prime Minister, this is Commander Harnesy. As you can see, we made it back. The ship worked flawlessly. The entire crew is happy to be home, and there were no ill effects."

"Fantastic, Captain. We are transmitting this to everyone on Horizon. I think I can speak for everyone in saying that we were waiting with our breaths held. Our entire goal has been to return to our home planet, and you were our first explorer to return and see what condition Earth is in. I know everyone wants to hear what you found."

Great, was Harnesy's first thought; she is transmitting this to the entire planet. *What can I tell her? Earth is occupied by something else who may not be willing to have us come home. Should I tell them that the few robots we abandoned have developed into a sentient society of life forms that have a viable and healthy population? Not to mention the human colony. What do I say?*

"Ms. Prime Minister and the people of Horizons, Earth has healed. She has clean air, water, and no indications of the state we left her," Harnesy knew that he was avoiding the major problems. But he hoped that focusing on the positive would give him time to figure out how and what to tell the Prime Minister.

"Amazing Captain. The people of Horizon owe you a great deal. You and your crew risked your lives to visit our home planet. We are all excited by the news that you bring, and we'll begin preparations immediately for our return to the place of our birth. Commander Harnesy, when you enter orbit, prepare for a planet-wide celebration to welcome you and your crew."

They had only a few hours from leaving the surface of Earth to their return to Horizon. Commander Harnesy was still processing the information they had seen and learned. He realized that he better get the others who went to the surface to discuss what they saw and plan for Horizon's reaction.

"Lieutenant Price, Ensign Holden, meet me in my conference room immediately."

He immediately received acknowledgments through his communicator. Then, he went to his conference room and waited for his other crew members. They came in separately, and because of the gravity of the upcoming discussion, they entered and sat, and neither said anything. They were waiting for their Commander to set the tone of the meeting.

"Thank you for coming," the Commander said.

Both crewmen acknowledged with a head nod or small smile.

"We are in an unusual situation, and I'm not sure how to handle it. Both of you were there, and you saw and heard what I did. What we learned is too profound for me to give you orders about what to say or how to interpret the situation."

He waited for a second to monitor their reactions, and it was clear that they were uncomfortable.

"I will tell you what I saw, and then you may want to add your impressions."

Again, they nodded and indicated that was acceptable.

"I went to Earth expecting an empty planet. We hoped the planet had cleaned itself over the years, and the air and water were to the point where our population could return. When we left, we had no indication of what we would find, but we hoped. Our entire history on this planet has been based on a need to return to our home. We always considered it our home, and we never thought of a different outcome. The thought of returning to our home has been ingrained in our history, our schools, and our thoughts for a long time. It has become the banner we wave to focus our civilization."

Again, he looked at his subordinates for a reaction one way or another, and there was little. So, he continued.

"What we found was indeed a clean planet. A pristine planet, one that would be a beautiful place to live and to raise our children. It would be a suitable conclusion to our long journey. But what we found was more than just a pristine planet. We found a civilization of robots, which grew from the robots that we abandoned on the planet when we left. We also found a small settlement of human beings who appear to be our genetic children or cousins. And, perhaps more shocking, it appears those children were created from DNA that our ancestors left hidden on Earth for someone to discover, for reasons we don't understand. All of this complicates our plans to return home to Earth. I don't know what to do with this information, but I know that it will cause consternation on Horizon. The Prime Minister and Government officials will react strongly, and different opinions will emerge. The final impacts to us and our plans I can't predict.

"How do you feel about it?"

There was a defining silence in the room. Lieutenant Price and Ensign Holden waited, perhaps for the other to respond first. They eventually looked at each other Lieutenant Price moved in his chair, took a deep breath, and spoke with a determined voice.

"Sir, Earth is ours. It is where we started, and it is where we need to go back to. I don't care if some robots think they are a civilization. They are robots, we created them, and they owe their existence to us. They should shut themselves down and let us have our planet. Robots were made to serve us and not think. Particularly not to consider themselves worthy of keeping Earth from us."

When he completed his statement, the room was quiet for a minute until Ensign Holden spoke.

"They are more than robots. They think, they take care of each other, and why should we consider them to be less important than us. They have a civilization. Yes, they came from a group of robots left on Earth when we had to leave. But they have changed and grown beyond what we left. They have become more than just robots, and I think they deserve to continue. I don't think we have the right to force them to be our mechanical slaves again."

Lieutenant Price exploded, saying, "They're not slaves; they're machines."

"Define machines," she retorted.

In a frustrated response, he said, "They aren't flesh and blood; they're made of metal."

"You forgot; they have organic processors."

"I don't care what their brains are made of. They're robots."

"Okay, you two. Calm down. Neither of you mentioned the other major issue. Humans are living among them. Humans that were created from DNA our ancestors left for the robots to discover. Why was it left, what was the purpose and what should we do?" The Commander pointed out.

Again, the room was quiet while they thought about the question and their respective answers.

Ensign Holden responded first, "Sir, what do you think about them?"

Commander Harnesy let out a breath, "They are human. In a way, they are either cousins or our ancestors. In a way, I guess that humans never completely left the planet, but parts of us were left in storage for some reason. Regardless, we have two issues. What to do about the robots and what to do about the humans?"

"Sir, I don't think we can decide what their fate is until we understand why our ancestors left the DNA in the first place. It seems they went through a lot of work to do it, so they must have had a reason," Ensign Holden pointed out.

"Sir, if I may speak openly?" Lieutenant Price asked.

"You, may."

"If they side with us, then we take care of them. If they side with the robots, then we have one enemy."

Everyone in the room understood Lieutenant Price's comment, but they weren't comfortable with it.

"When we land, they have a bunch of parades and celebrations planned. I'll press for a meeting with the Prime Minister, and if I can get you two, to be invited, I want you to be open and honest. I'm sure they'll make up their own minds, but I want my crew to express their feelings. I suggest that you don't say anything until the Prime Minister and her people have a chance to digest the information. If you say something that is counter to their opinions, you might get in trouble."

When the meeting ended and Lieutenant Price and Ensign Holden left the room, Commander Harnesy just sat, thinking. He knew that the future wouldn't unfold in a neat, pleasant manner.

Commander Harnesy's quiet moment was shattered by his comm unit.

"Sir, there is a message coming in from the Prime Minister."

"Put her through."

"Yes, sir."

"Commander Harnesy, I see that you're still about 4 hours from entering orbit. I just wanted to tell you that as soon as you land, the celebration will begin. The people of Horizon are ecstatic about your arrival. We have dancing in the streets, and everyone says this is the greatest event in our history. Returning home is the fulfillment of the dreams of generations of our ancestors, and we feel the obligation to make that last journey and return to the planet that spawned us."

"Ma'am, there are items that need to be discussed."

"We'll discuss them later. I'm too busy to waste time now. The planning for the celebration is taking up all my time. We'll talk after the celebration, and things have quieted down. As soon as you enter orbit, please come to the Capital to begin the worldwide celebration. Prime Minister out."

Commander Harnesy just sat shaking his head. Things weren't going well; he suspected they would be going a lot worse before they got better.

Speeches and Parades

When the shuttle penetrated the atmosphere, the pilot casually asked, "Sir, there is a lot of comm traffic about us and the celebration. Should I plug it into your comm system?"

"Yes, go ahead."

Commander Harnesy wanted to know what was being said, and the others in the shuttle needed to know what to expect when they landed. He had the entire executive crew of his ship onboard. The HSV#2 had a small crew, and it took only a few of them to keep it in orbit. Lieutenant Price was on the shuttle, along with Ensign Holden. Both had been quiet since his one-on-one with them. He knew they had a ton of things going through their minds.

When the pilot opened the channel, they were confronted with a live news broadcast of their approach. They looked at each other in bewilderment. Some of them smiled, and others, like Holden, Price, and Harnesy, were uneasy. The news broadcaster gave minute-by-minute updates of the shuttle's position coming out of entry and their position concerning the landing site.

The broadcaster got everyone's attention on the shuttle by saying, "Maybe we can get the Commander of HSV#2 to come on this channel and say something?"

Everyone on the shuttle looked to the Commander, and he felt obligated to respond.

"This is Commander Harnesy of HSV#2. Thank you for such a warm welcome. As the announcer said, we are approaching the Capital, and we'll be landing in a few minutes. We're all anxious to be home, and we look forward to seeing our families."

"Captain, can you tell us what you found on Earth?"

Commander Harnesy took a noticeable deep breath then said, "We found a great deal on Earth. I'm happy to say that the air and water are clean. Beyond that, we have much information to look at. Now, please, we have to prepare for landing."

"Thank you, Captain, for that exciting news about Earth. I'm sure that I'm speaking for everyone when I say we're looking forward to going home." After that comment, the announcer went off in another direction, talking about their history, the collected memories of Earth, and their return home. Commander Harnesy just tuned him out.

The shuttle was descending over the Capital, and they could see the crowds and fireworks. The vehicle was quiet as they witnessed the jubilation below them. The announcer continued over the comm system describing their descent and approach to the landing site next to the reviewing stand. The step-by-step coverage continued as the ship maneuvered and set down. Commander Harnesy walked to the door and braced himself for the event. The door opened, and the inside of the shuttle was flooded with the cheering of the crowds. Commander Harnesy took another deep breath, waved, and walked out, followed by the remainder of his leadership staff.

The Prime Minister stood on the reviewing stand waiting for Commander Harnesy to join her. He walked across the reviewing stand and shook her hand. She lifted his to the roar of the crowd in front of him and the entire population of Horizon on the video broadcast. He and his crew went through, interviews, hand waving, handshaking, and toasts for the next two hours. Finally, the exhaustion hit them. Unfortunately, it was about another two hours before the celebration ended.

Ray Jay Perreault

Harnesy Goes to Family

After the celebration, Commander Harnesy needed time with his wife and family. He had seen a lot and learned even more. There was a great deal about the developing situation that made him uncomfortable. Returning to Earth wasn't just a simple trip to Earth. Earth wasn't just waiting for them with open arms. Earth had changed in ways that no one anticipated.

Those changes were what made Harnesy uncomfortable. The robots, or Us as they called themselves, weren't just robots or computers. They had grown beyond what his ancestors had left on Earth when she was abandoned. The Us were a vibrant, developing, intelligent society that shouldn't be discounted.

Commander Harnesy didn't expect the Horizon Leadership to respect what Harnesy would tell them. He was aware of how Horizon's society and the leadership saw robots. Machines were to clean the house or plant the garden. They were nothing more than things that did what they were programmed to do. It was true, early attempts to give them more autonomy had cost human lives. Perhaps it was only natural for Humanity to categorize robots as something that needed to be controlled, and thus, they were just things. But that situation was no longer relevant. What was living on Earth was not like the robots that people on Horizon understood.

Aside from the robots, there were the humans. In a way, that was even more confusing to Commander Harnesy than the robots. Robots could be categorized in one way, good or bad. But the humans that the robots created fell into a totally different category. They were human; their DNA was left by Harnesy's ancestors. Their DNA was left for a purpose.

Like the robots, Horizon's leadership would likely discount the humans on Earth. Harnesy felt that they would be made a minor issue that would be resolved along with the robots. That 'resolution' was what made Harnesy uneasy. They weren't like the robots; they were human and likely distant relatives.

The fact that they were genetic creations by the robots wasn't the main point. Humanity had been working with DNA splicing for centuries, and it was commonly used for disease eradication. Everyone was aware that attempts had been made to create a better human along the lines of different definitions of perfect at some point in human history. It was realized that the diversity of the human population was its greatest asset and trying to improve the genome wasn't productive.

So, the concept of humans being created from DNA wasn't really an issue. The reason they would likely be discounted was that they were created by robots. If the people on Horizon had created them, it would have been a different story. But the fact that the robots created them would make them part of the robot problem, and he assumed the leadership would try to solve their two problems together.

Commander Harnesy was torn between two frames of mind. He was as eager as everyone to return to Earth. He wanted his family to return to their heritage and reclaim their home world. But he had met the robots and the created humans. He knew they posed a problem that he was afraid the leadership of Horizon would solve poorly.

The remainder of his drive to his home was uneasy for Commander Harnesy. He was caught between two sides of the issue, and he realized that forces were at play beyond his ability to control. His family hadn't joined him during this celebration. They were waiting for him at home. He had a lot to think about, and he slowed the transport vehicle so he could enjoy the ride and think. The roads passed by, and he looked at the people walking. They looked happy; many of the homes had signs about Earth. One of the signs said, "Going Home." Another said, "Earth, we're sorry," and a third said, "House for Sale." The last one brought a smile to his face and a momentary diversion from the problems.

The trees that he passed under were large with needles that were 10-12 inches long. They filled the air with a clean fragrance and created a lot of shadows. There was very little undergrowth because most of the area under the high canopy was covered with shadows.

The homes interspersed between the trees were all single story and tended to be made from wood. There wasn't a lot of stone, so wood was the best building product. As he got closer to his home, the streets were quiet, and few people were walking on them. The solemnness and quiet of the drive only exacerbated the worry in his mind. It would have been better to take his mind off the looming issues if there was a ton of activity or traffic.

When he got home, his wife and daughters had put a sign out also. It simply said, "Dad, welcome home." That sign meant more to him and helped him feel better. The problems were still there in his home, but he would be surrounded by his family, which always made things better.

The auto-vehicle parked itself in the adjacent storage area, and he walked into their home, and his family met him at the door. He shared in their excitement and enjoyed the hugs and happiness. His wife and Serene were busy discussing what living on Earth would be like and how excited they were to return home. His youngest daughter Bethany was too excited to say anything coherent. She just talked about what her friends were saying and how perfect her life would be on Earth. He was exhausted, shared in their happiness as long as he could, then he begged forgiveness and headed off to bed.

The pink sun rose over the horizon, and Leopold Harnesy lay in his bed. He looked through the window and thought of the dreams he and the people of Horizon had and how what he knew

120

could destroy them. What he saw on Earth was totally unexpected, and the information would not be taken well by the Horizon leadership or the people. Their entire history on Horizon was endured only because of the hope of returning to Earth one day. If that dream were taken from them, it would leave a huge hole.

His wife, Beatrice, or Bea, stirred next to him, and he watched her move as the light in the room increased. His wife was still asleep, so he slipped out and headed for the kitchen. There is nothing like the smell of coffee and breakfast cooking to make him feel at home. He had a lot to think about, and he didn't know how to put it all in perspective.

"Dad, can I have eggs and toast?" was all he heard Serene say as she entered.

"Sure, I guess I can make some extra for you."

"Gee, thanks. How was the trip? What did you find? Did you find what you were looking for?"

"Not exactly."

"What do you mean? Earth was there, wasn't it?"

"In a way. But it wasn't how we expected."

"I'll bite; what was different?" she said as she sat cross-legged and sipped her Byrot Juice.

"Earth wasn't as we expected; we found some problems. Apparently, we left some robots and computers when we evacuated the planet, and they have changed and grown into a viable civilization … there is another thing."

His daughter, Serene, sat, watched, and listened. She knew that silence would get more out of him than asking questions.

"When we left the planet, there was DNA left in an organic creature, and the robots were able to re-create some humans. They have a small village of humans living with them that appear to be happy and flourishing. We aren't going home to an empty planet."

"So, we're planning on claiming property that someone else has already claimed?"

"Appears so. Here's your breakfast."

They sat, ate, and didn't say much for a while. They knew that issues were hanging in the air, and neither had a simple answer.

"Dad, why did we leave some DNA?"

"Honey, I don't know. At the time, someone thought it was the right thing to do."

"Do we have any records of how we left Earth and who might have done something like that?"

"I don't know, but it is something worth checking into."

"Dad, who owns Earth?"

"Very good question."

"What do you mean, who owns Earth?" Bea said as she walked into the kitchen, still adjusting her hair with her hand. She tightened her robe and sat next to her daughter while pouring herself a cup of coffee. "What were you guys talking about?"

"I found something unusual on Earth."

"Oh."

"Earth is in great shape, but it isn't empty."

"It isn't empty?" Bea said while she sipped her coffee.

"When our ancestors left, they apparently left some robots or artificial intelligence. Regardless, what we left has turned into a civilization of robots. They have cities, transportation, leadership; Bea, they have a full society."

Bea kept sipping her coffee but had a concerned look on her face.

"Not only that, but our ancestors also left a feral creature which has developed to the point where they have villages and huts. But the surprise is, they left a copy of our DNA in those creatures, the robots discovered it, and they have created a small community of humans."

Bea continued sipping her coffee, but she showed more stress on her face. Leo was starting to get worried, a bad reaction was one thing, but silence wasn't good at all.

His daughter, Serene, was also reading the signs, and she knew to wait it out.

"I don't see a problem," Bea finally said as she finished a sip of coffee and put her cup down with a clang on the table. "We go home…and deal with them."

"Mom, the robots are living there. They have a society, civilization. There are humans on Earth. How do we 'deal with them?"

"We were there first, and we're coming home," she said as she picked her coffee up and walked out of the room.

Serene and her father looked at each other and decided that it would be best to end the conversation.

Commander Harnesy knew that discussion would be typical of what he would have as he briefed the Prime Minister and her staff. There would be people concerned with the impacts of their return, and others would have Bea's opinion.

Part 7 Conformity Council Reacts

While Helen walked to the Conformity Council's Chambers, her processor was overwhelmed with activity. So much had changed, and what was predictable to her was now gone. The future was in turmoil, and Helen needed to understand. She knew that dealing with options was not an efficient use of her processor. When many alternatives appear suitable, her bandwidth would be taken up by looking at each option. There was something in her logic that said there must be a more efficient way to decide.

Regardless, while she walked, her processor was fully engaged, considering what they learned from 'The Visitors' and what it might mean to her, Us, and Them. All she could conclude was that major changes were occurring, and she couldn't see what they were.

Helen stood outside the Conformity Council's door waiting to enter, and her processor reached a point where most of the options were threatening. There were many possible outcomes, but the number of harmful ones was alarmingly large compared to good ones. That was very disturbing.

The Conformity Council Scheduler intercepted her, and when he said, "You may enter; the Council is expecting you," the statement brought Helen out of her deep processing.

Walking into the chamber was almost surreal. The silence was laying around the room like a blanket. Helen sat in the chair provided and put her arms on the table in front of her.

Adam looked at the others in the council, then at Helen, and spoke, "Thank you for coming here. Much has changed since 'The Visitors' came. We have spent a great deal of time seeking answers, and we have few. You are a major part of this, and we want your input. The humans that you resurrected from the DNA complicate the situation, but they also mitigate it. Humans expected to return to a pristine planet that would welcome them home. They were surprised to find Us living here, and I suspect that they'll return to Earth with their resettlement of Earth in mind. Commander Harnesy seemed reasonable, but there are likely forces that will overwhelm him.

"What are your thoughts?" Adam asked Helen.

Helen needed a minute to process a concise answer, then she spoke, "I agree with what you have said. Commander Harnesy represents events that he has no control over. He, or someone else, will likely return. I also agree that the Them represent an additional variable that Commander Harnesy wasn't prepared for. I feel there will be a conflict of objectives. They have an objective, we have our Four Laws, and there will be a conflict."

Adam then spoke, "We agree, but the Four Laws must be followed, and we are trying to devise a manner to accomplish that. Once we accepted your creations as units, we are forced to accept Commander Harnesy and those he represents. Doing so causes a conflict that isn't easy to resolve. From a logical perspective, if we consider option A that costs X Units, and option B costs X-Y, we must accept option B. Thus, we are forced to find options to encourage option B."

"What options are you exploring?" Helen asked.

"We are unable to discuss them at this time. We would like you to work with FU1 and MU1 and prepare
Them. They will likely be involved in any conflict of objectives that occurs."

"We have spoken, and they feel they can contribute," responded Helen.

"In what way?" Adam responded.

"Their minds work differently than ours. They will explore the archives and provide us a unique interpretation of the information. When we look at the archives, we see only what is there. We aren't capable of imagining what isn't there and filling in the missing pieces. Their processors do that very well, and they will provide a unique interpretation of the information."

The council chambers became silent. Each of the Conformity Council members looked at Helen and tried to process what she had said. Adam spoke first, "Helen. You have described the methods of their processor before. We aren't able to process in the manner by which they do. We know what we do, but we don't know what we don't do. We accept your impressions of their thought processes. Please report back to us what they find."

"Yes, I will," Helen answered.

Once again, Helen was looking forward to sharing the day's information with Lorenzo. She knew that he was uneasy with the path she was following but sharing the day's activities with him and hearing his thoughts helped her process the information and store it properly.

After Helen parked her transport and approached their residence, the front door burst open. Thomas exploded out, approaching Helen rapidly.

"I've finished my processing. I just finished reviewing my information with my tutors and mentors, and they all agree that I've done as required. I'm finally done."

"I'm very happy for you Thomas, I know how hard you've worked to assimilate al the information and prepare for your reviews. This opens many opportunities for you. Have you decided what path you'll follow?"

"Yes, I've put a lot of thought into it, and I've decided to work at the unit manufacturing facility. I want to work on building better and stronger units."

"You'll be working with Lorenzo. He will enjoy spending time with you. Now that you've finished your information processing, you qualify for a house of your own. Have you asked for one yet?"

"No, I haven't. I've been too busy, but I will ask for one soon."

"If you request a home as a single unit, the size will be limited. If you have found a unit to partner with, you'll qualify for a larger one."

"I'm aware of that, and I think there is a unit that I'll ask."

"Indeed, is it Jane, the unit you've shared time with on numerous occasions? She seems very suitable."

"I haven't suggested a partnership with her yet. I know that she is anxious to take on a new unit and help with its learning like you and Lorenzo have done for me."

"Lorenzo and I will notice your absence after you leave. We realize that it is time, and we want you to find the path that satisfies you."

"Thank you, I must go. I have a meeting with some of the others that have just finished their learning. I'll return later tonight?"

Just as Helen acknowledged the information, Lorenzo approached in his transport. He placed it in the slot next to Helen's. She stood motionless and waited for him to exit the vehicle."

"Another interesting day, and you must have more interesting information to share?" He said as he approached Helen.

"You are correct, it was another very eventful day, and there is much information that I'd like to share with you."

Moments later, after Helen shared her information with Lorenzo, he agreed with her plan, "Helen, I think your assessment of the Them is appropriate. I know that you've worked with Them a great deal, and you understand how their minds work. I'm not as informed as you are. To be honest, I'm uncomfortable around them. They act differently than I'm used to. I find that I have to spend a lot of processor time trying to understand them. I wish they would act more like Us and be less…like Them."

Helen was anxious to have MU1 and FU1 conduct research within the archive. In the past, she asked specific questions, and they found the answers. When they interfaced with the archive to solve their own problems, they often found information that surprised Helen. She was confident that their unique way of thinking would yield insightful results.

After entering their village, she saw MU1 and FU1 walking between two buildings, and when they saw her, she indicated that she wanted to speak with them.

"MU1, FU1, it is good that I've found you. I spoke with the Conformity Council and suggested that you help this situation with The Visitors by investigating relevant information within the archives. I will leave it up to you to decide on the subjects and methods. Anything relevant to our history or the history of The Visitors should provide valuable information. Are you willing to do that?"

FU1 showed excitement and said, "Yes, Helen. In fact, MU1 and I have already spoken about the possibilities, and we suggest that MU11 join us. He has skills with the archives that are beyond ours."

"Excellent," responded Helen. "Can you begin immediately?"

"Yes, once we find MU11, we'll begin," responded MU1.

The Archives

MU1, FU1, and MU11 had accessed the archives many times. Each day's lesson plans were extracted from the information available. But this was different; instead of extracting a portion of information to be shared with the other Them, this was an exploration mission. They had to approach the information from a different perspective and look at its entirety, not just relevant elements.

MU11 was the most proficient unit interfacing with the information, but they thought having three minds working on the issue would be faster and yield a better result

The archive interface was designed for an organic processor typical of Helen's and their kind. Initially, the Them interfacing with the archive was difficult to use. The first interface method was a visual device with which the humans could interact, then as MU11 became more intimate with it, he created a holographic display that became the standard interface for humans. Multiple inputs had become common so MU1, FU1, and MU11 could interact at the same time. The units requesting a connection with the archive sat quietly in the interface room and cleared their thoughts. Then slowly, they could establish the interface with the archive, and their shared vision showed a world of colored dots.

By talking with each other and focusing their thoughts, they began to take command of the interface. Based on their thoughts, their vision would fill with colors indicating the item's relevancy.

For example, if the requestors thought about circular objects, the space in their vision would be filled with different colors and patterns indicating each item's relevance to circular objects. Areas of the archive referencing circular objects were shaded into the red spectrum with direct connections bright red. For each query, the image would fill with changing patterns of colors and shades of relevancy.

Three units combining their inquiries would present the archive with three versions of the same question. The result would be more complex yet yield specific answers that matched all their questions. By communicating and playing off others' requests, the result was more tailored and specific.

They entered the interface room for this inquiry, and they elected to do it without Helen present. They needed to have unfettered access to the information in the archive and not be constrained by Helen's methods or interpretation. They knew their future, and the future of Us might be dependent on what they found.

They had discussed the path they wanted to follow. They would think of history and go deeper into the past. Depending on what they found, they could decide on the next steps. They knew that the initial questions had to be very broad, and depending on what they found, they would work very hard to narrow the information. To their knowledge, many of the questions they hoped to answer had never been put to the archive. In the past, questions about the long-ago history weren't relevant to their daily inquiries, and the answers weren't needed. They didn't know what they would find as they dug deeper into the information. When Helen or her team followed the DNA information, they asked specific questions and got focused answers. For example, if you asked how to grow a DNA sample in a laboratory, the archive would provide instructions.

If they found any relevant information, then at that point, they might have the information they needed. Once the archive identified the areas of information, they would lock those areas in their minds, and the system would convert to actual data they could see. Next, the archive would show the timeline and connections between the disparate pieces of information, and MU1, FU1, and MU11 hoped they would be able to 'fill in the pieces' and find the connection between bits of information that might have missing connections.

Their analysis would take time. At first, their combined vision was full of millions of specks of light. Then, slowly through their thought processes, colors and patterns would begin to emerge, and after varying their thoughts, brighter colors and patterns would coalesce. Finally, when they had something to work with, it would take hours of thinking and communicating to strengthen the colors, patterns, and associations.

Spending hours mining the archive was a tedious task. MU1, FU1, and MU11's concentration had to remain focused. If their thoughts wondered, then the accuracy of the nexus would be reduced. So, they had to take breaks and relax before they could return and refocus their thoughts.

After a couple of sessions, patterns began to emerge. Clouds of distinct colors and patterns formed. Three groupings of information were surfacing. 1) The decision to leave Earth, 2) Who to take and what to leave, and 3) The perilous journey. Even at that level of detail, there were millions of sources. The next step was to expand each of the subjects and look for relationships and patterns. The first one to explore was "The Decision to Leave Earth."

The decision to leave was the hardest and thus had the most data. By that point in the decay of Earth, diseases were running rampant, many of which they had no cures for. They had no choice but to allow only healthy people the option of migration. They knew the journey would be perilous, and perhaps none of them would survive, but the best option was to send the healthy and pray for those making the trip.

Who would be saved was a larger question than just who was healthy? The ships they would be taking were huge but still limited. The healthy that wanted to take the perilous journey through space were put into lotteries around the globe. Within each of the lotteries, different disciplines that were deemed critical were weighted in the numbers. Eventually, the people were selected, and the goodbyes began.

The Earth had committed to building thousands of ships, and progress was slow, but eventually, they were built and tested. Everyone knew the chance of surviving the long journey was low, but everyone also knew that staying on the Earth was a death sentence. There was no fresh water left, the weather was destroying all that man had built, and those remaining had a short time remaining on their home planet.

As MU1, FU1, and MU11 peeled back the layers of information, clearer patterns came into focus; a couple of names, dates, and events were often referenced. In addition, there was information about increasingly heated debates about what to take, what to leave, and if there was a way to ensure that mankind would survive somehow if the migration ships didn't make their destination.

MU1 and FU1 were exhausted after the first session. Concentrating that hard for that length of time was hard on them. They needed to take a break and continue the investigation after some discussion with each other.

"Helen, thank you for coming to our Conformity Council meeting. Since our last meeting, we have had many discussions. I must say that we still have not reached an agreement on what we should do, so we have elected to follow a couple of paths," said Adam as Helen entered the chamber.

"We are wondering, though, what your village of humans feel about the meeting with The Visitors?"

"Adam, we have spoken a couple of times, and I think they are as overwhelmed as we are. I know they feel that there is information buried in the archives that might be of use. They are concentrating much effort in researching the archives trying to understand our early history. I support their efforts; I feel they have unique abilities to look at human information and interpret it in ways that we might miss."

"Do you think they are more in agreement with Us than The Visitors?"

"What do you mean 'in agreement?'"

"We suspect that The Visitors will return, and when they do, they will have objectives that may not be in line with ours. Your humans might have to decide whose objectives they are in agreement with."

"I have not asked them in such a way. I do know that they are working hard to help us with our archive. That effort surely shows they are more concerned with the impacts to Us. We are all units, and we must follow the second law."

"There is the possibility that The Visitors may consider themselves units also and fall under the intent of the First and Second Law," said Adam.

After a moment of thought, he continued, "You discovered the DNA and created Them who may be a re-creation of The Visitors. The Visitors may have created Us, so we all depend on each other for our existence. The Four Laws are larger than all of us; the only way them make sense is for all units to fall under the laws. The word Units is not limited to the Visitors, Us, or Them. The term represents everyone, and we must follow the second law to satisfy the other laws."

"Adam, I agree. We are related, dependent upon, or responsible for some elements of the problem. It is true that working together is the best solution, but that may not occur. What do we do if we have multiple groups of units with different objectives?"

"We don't have an answer to that. But we are taking appropriate steps."

"Appropriate steps?" Helen asked.

"Yes, we have never been in the situation of preventing one unit from harming another. We are concerned that the objectives of the Visitors might put some of our units in jeopardy, and we have decided to prevent that if necessary."

"I'm sorry to ask again, Adam, but I'm not sure what you mean?"

"We have also searched the archives and found devices that can prevent one unit from harming another. We are trying to design these tools in such a way that neither unit will be permanently harmed, but that is a difficult challenge. If there is a disagreement between Us and the Visitors at a large scale level, then we must have a device to deter them at that scale."

After Helen left the meeting with the Conformity Council, her processor was fully occupied considering what they had said. There were many gaps in her processor that she encountered as it was processing the information. She didn't know how to fill them, but each time one arose, it distressed her. She was spending more time with the unresolved issues than the few that she had the answers to.

She continued towards the Them Village, and for some reason, comments that Adam made brought her friends to the top of her processor's focus. It wasn't clear why they dominated her processing, but they were, and she needed to speak with them.

She exited her vehicle and walked quickly towards MU1 and FU1's residence. When she entered, she was faced with silence. Even their offspring, MU11, and FU12 weren't there. Helen paused for a moment evaluating the alternatives, then decided to seek them out in the Archive Chamber.

It was a brief walk from Compound A through Compound B into C. As she walked, she met many human residents who showed typical respect, and said hello to her. She responded, but she thought about The Visitors each time she did and wondered what would happen if they returned.

When she entered the Archive Chamber, MU1, FU1, and MU11 were seated near the entry, and they looked very tired.

"Welcome, Helen."

"Thank you, FU1."

"How was your meeting with the Conformity Council? MU1 asked.

"There are many gaps in our knowledge. We don't know what The Visitors will do. If they do return, the council fears that their objectives may conflict with our Four Laws."

"What will happen then?" MU1 asked.

"They are building devices to prevent one unit from harming another."

"That is a difficult decision to make. Helen, as you know, biological units are different than Us. Us can be repaired for many years, and ultimately your knowledge can be shared with the archive. We are organic and don't end that way. When we cease, our memories can't be shared, and our bodies decay. That is why we are returned to the Earth. You, FU1, and I have spoken about that in the past. We expect that when our time comes, we will end like the organics. If there is a struggle between The Visitors and the Us, We could be caught in the middle and be damaged. If we are damaged too much, we might end. If The Visitors are damaged too much, they might end also," said MU1.

"MU1, I agree damaging any units would be horrible and against the Second Law. However, there are scenarios where there may be no choices. Let's hope that we can find a solution without that happening. What progress have you made with the archives?"

MU11 stood, and faced Helen, "We have found a considerable amount of information. Of course, we are still working through it, but I think it will be beneficial. I do need to point out that there is something unusual occurring within the archive. In the past, when we accessed information, it felt static. Now when we seek information, there is a dynamic element that seems to change. We are compensating for the changes. When we began the investigation, we asked simple questions about the specific period based on what The Visitors said. We used their time of departure to aim our inquiry. As we focused during that time, we sensed the archive changing. It seemed as if it was opening up new areas, and if we repeated a question, we would get different information and a considerably larger amount of it. It was at that point that information about humans increased a tremendous amount. We were buried with human references. If any of us had asked such specific questions many years ago, we might have found out about the humans and discovered our histories by ourselves."

Helen responded in the only way she could, "Perhaps so. We asked specific questions about singular subjects. We never thought to ask, 'How we were created?' please continue."

"As we asked broader questions, it did seem that the archive was opening new doors for us, based on the questions that we asked. As we continued to focus our thoughts on when humans left, there were many complex issues that our ancestors were dealing with as the planet was decaying. They were very worried about survival, so they made the difficult decision to leave the planet. They didn't intend to save everyone; they realized that it would be impossible for them to build enough spaceships for the entire population. They were forced to concede that their primary purpose was to save the species and find a way for humans to survive.

"There were no guarantees that they would live long enough to find a suitable planet. When they left Earth, they didn't have a specific planet as a destination. They went to a region of space where they thought the largest number of suitable planets existed. They were lucky to finally find Horizon and that it was suitable for them. There was a great deal of debate about the risk and the possibility of the species ending. A human named Doctor Willamette was a strong advocate of saving the DNA of humanity in some type of time capsule, as they called it. There was a short time where he was prominent in the discussions. Then the discussions seemed to end when the ships were ready and the final selection was occurring. Either the debate stopped, or they just focused on more important issues. He was likely part of the group to plant the DNA in our organic creatures. We can only assume that he hoped it would be used at some point in the future."

"MU1, so you're concluding that Dr. Willamette may have hidden the DNA in the organic creatures?" Helen asked.

"Yes, we do."

FU1 provided additional information, "Regarding Us, we also found information that the humans had a large number of computers and mobile units integrated into their society when they were forced to leave. There was little debate on the subject, they knew that they would take a certain number of the computers and units with them, but they weren't concerned with those they were leaving behind. Most of the power supplies were already supported by the mobile units, and they needed them operational until they left, so there was no specific effort to turn them off on their departure.

"How Us became independent is less clear. Computers had progressed to the point earlier in human history where humans were confident that they could be given some autonomy. Initial attempts to create independent computers resulted in some unfortunate accidents, and human lives were lost. Humanity felt threatened, and there was a purge of the most sophisticated units. As that purge occurred, there was a debate about the risks of computers with no limits, which was one reason for the purge. There were proponents of computers who felt that unrestricted computers could accomplish certain tasks, like space exploration. They wanted computers without limits to be sent to the new planet for exploration. They needed to be unlimited so they could learn and take care of themselves.

"There were a couple of unique projects that were referenced. One, in particular, was to develop a very unique computer program. Up to that time, computers ran within a structured environment. They couldn't change their boundaries or limitations. If a unit was sent to another planet for exploration, it needed total control to manage its resources. The computer was developed that could change its programming and change how it used its resources. It could erase parts of its program or enlarge others as it needed to satisfy the requirements.

"If I may, I'll demonstrate with an analogy. If we live in a house and have everything we need, such as food and accommodations, we can stay in that house. That computer could decide to build a new house."

Helen looked distressed, "Helen, do you understand the image?" MU11 asked.

She responded, "That concept is difficult for me. We are built to live within a set of constraints, for example, our Four Laws. We have no need to change our boundaries as you describe them. I can see how that would create a unique computer."

"That computer's primary objective would have been to collect a huge amount of information about the world it was on and analyze it. Building it with that unique ability made sense. Unfortunately, the debate ended as the planet deteriorated faster than planned, and they abandoned the idea of sending intelligent computers to potential new worlds. They had to take the chance and send the remainder of the humans. We think that some of the unrestrained computers were left intentionally, and over time, they developed further and created the Us."

FU1 then summarized her research, "There was one Doctor, who appeared on the periphery of many discussions. He had the skills, the resources, and the motivation to take action. His name was Dr. William Bennet. He owned a robotics development company that improved the organic processors in mobile units. He was a strong advocate of increasing the autonomy of mobile units and genetically engineering their organic processors to allow more decision-making. Up to that time, there was underlying mistrust of mobile units. After the incidents where harm was done, they overreacted. They tried to take out all the autonomy in the units, and they were programmed to do specific tasks. Some of the tasks were complex, but they were prevented from going beyond those tasks independently.

Dr. Bennet was also somewhat of a social scientist, and we saw some periods where he and Dr. Willamette may have worked together. While he was tinkering with the organic processors, he advocated tweaking the human genome to improve humanity. He speculated that he could improve human intelligence and reduce stress within society by reducing some human tendencies for aggression. There was one small article that we thought was very interesting. It was buried in a small magazine on biological engineering where he proposed that a set of fundamental laws could be written that would allow robots to be autonomous and have decision-making skills without putting humans at risk. We think that may have been the beginning of the Four Laws."

After FU1 made that statement, Helen just looked at her and processed the startling information. Then she spoke, "You're suggesting that Dr. Bennet may have created some robots with these laws governing them, and they may have been created without any constraints?"

"That is a possibility," responded MU1.

Helen paused for a moment, then added, "For him to be the key, he must have created the organic creatures with the hidden DNA."

"We think he had that ability. Part of the process for developing organic processors was to work with lower life forms to understand the cognitive process, and there were documented cases where those life forms had their DNA tweaked for various reasons. He likely had access to that type of testing, and he may have planted a human genome in one of the test groups in an attempt to plant some kind of seed for the future. As we have seen in the DNA information in the archive, there is a tremendous potential within the DNA structure to store the information, and it could remain unchanged for a considerable amount of time. I'm sure he didn't know if the migration would work or if humans would ever return to Earth, so his reasons aren't clear, but he still may have done it," said FU1.

Helen processed information for a moment, then asked, "Do you think he created the pictorial history on the wall in the hope that the DNA could be resurrected someday?"

"It is all possible. If Dr. Bennet and Dr. Willamette had worked together and planted the DNA and created some robots without constraints, they may have also worked with the lower life forms. If they did all of that, then they may have created the information on the wall. They were hoping that someday some entity would be able to create a new human race. Perhaps one that was better in some ways than the humans in his times," said MUI.

Ray Jay Perreault

Part 8 One More Celebration

The transport vehicle was making slow progress through the capital. The crowds were still dancing in the streets, celebrating their return to Earth. Unfortunately, none of the celebrations on the street put Commander Harnesy in a good mood. He knew that he carried the burden of knowing what was on Earth, and the celebrants along the street didn't help. They didn't know who was in the transport vehicle, or he would have been stormed and likely late for the meeting with the Prime Minister.

The vehicle approached the Capital Building, and Harnesy stared at the huge spinning Earth in front of the building. Its image was ingrained in each of the children's minds as they went through school. It was copied everywhere to remind the people of who they were and where they were from. But it also represented where they were going, which bothered Harnesy as he looked at the huge monument.

Lieutenant Price and Ensign Holden stood at attention by the entrance as they saluted him as he approached. He knew they felt as he did and stopped for a moment to see how they were handling the pressure.

"Are you two okay?"

"Yes, sir," Price responded.

"I'm doing okay, sir, although sometimes I wish we didn't see what we saw. I'm afraid this isn't going to go well," added Holden.

"I agree," responded Harnesy, "Remember. Be honest. Tell them exactly what you saw. Let them ask all the questions they want. Then, if they ask your opinion, give it to them. They deserve to hear the truth, regardless of what they want to hear."

Harnesy turned, and his two crewmembers followed him into the building.

"Commander, the Prime Minister, and her staff are waiting; you may enter."

"Thank you."

They entered, and the Prime Minister was seated at the head of the conference table, and the five members of her staff were seated on the side facing the door. Commander Harnesy, Lieutenant Price, and Ensign Holden were forced to sit opposite them with their backs to the door.

"Good morning Leopold, Lieutenant, Ensign. Please be seated. Can we get you anything?" offered the Prime Minister.

"Not for me," said Harnesy, Lieutenant Price and Ensign Holden shook their heads."

"We're glad to have you here. I want to personally welcome you, and we are anxious to hear what our new home looks like."

It took a few seconds for the three of them to settle, and they were obviously uncomfortable. It was up to Commander Harnesy to take the lead and begin the debriefing. "Ma'am, what we found was complicated. Our jump went well, and we entered the solar system only a short distance from Earth. We began to scan the planet immediately, and we found the air and water to be clean. The temperature variation across the surface was excellent. As we got closer, we began to notice some differences from what we expected. The layout of the structures was different than our records. They were more expansive and numerous. There was an 82.5% variation in the structural layout compared with our databases."

"Were they new building decayed?" Prime Minister Billings asked.

"Ma'am, they were either new or replaced," stated Ensign Holden.

"New?" Billings snapped back.

"Yes, Ma'am. New," responded Ensign Holden.

"Ensign, did you get any infrared signatures?" asked Jaled Hern, the Prime Minister's assistant.

"Not immediately because we were too far from orbit. Our IR sensors work best once we reach orbit. From the distance that we were at the time, we would receive only very large signatures."

Commander Harnesy then added, "We continued our approach until we were in orbit, and during each orbit, we mapped the surface and did environmental surveys. Then, as our orbit traversed the surface, we filled out the map and expanded our analysis."

"Commander, I'm confused. Yesterday you said there was something we had to talk about; so far, all you've found are a few extra structures," pointed out the Prime Minister.

"Ma'am, as our orbit progressed over the planet, we started to get unusual IR signatures. I'll let Ensign Holden describe them."

"Ma'am, we got the typical variation in signatures of a planet with life. There were numerous groupings of minor to moderate life forms, which would be expected. However, once we surveyed one of the larger cities, we picked up larger IR signatures typical of human beings. And I reported that to the Commander."

"What do you mean, human beings? On Earth?" The Jaled asked with some apprehension in his voice, and he was responsible for the military and police force on Horizon.

"The size and energy within the IR signature tell us the size of the creature. Most creatures have a distinctive size, shape, and energy level. The indications were clearly those of human beings," answered Ensign Holden.

Prime Minister Billings was visibly agitated and began moving her first up and down. Her fingers were quietly tapping the table but not making any noise.

Then her assistant spoke with stress in his voice, "Okay, so we have some buildings and a couple of heat signatures that 'might' be like a human, and we're supposed to do what? Call off the return to our home planet. I don't think so."

"Ma'am, that isn't all," Commander Harnesy said softly as he ignored the Chief of Staff and directed his comment to the Prime Minister. "Ma'am, we received a transmission from the planet."

That simple statement left the room quiet while they reacted for a minute. Then Tern reacted again, "So, the creatures that caused the IR signatures have a radio?"

Commander Harnesy didn't respond to Jaled but continued directing his responses to the PM, "Ma'am, may I continue?"

"Yes, Commander. You may continue, without interruption," she said as she glanced at her Chief of Staff.

"Ma'am, there is a lot to say, it will take a while, and I want Lieutenant Price and Ensign Holden to give their parts."

"Go ahead, Commander."

"The radio transmission was from a robot named Adam. He is the leader of a civilization of robots. Apparently, when our ancestors left Earth, we left the computers, mobile units, and robots. In some way, they survived and evolved.

"Adam invited us down to meet with them. So Lieutenant Price and Ensign Holden went with me to the surface. We met with Adam, and he was accompanied by a unit that must be some type of professor or scientist and two of the human beings that Ensign Holden saw on the IR scans. They were named FU1 and MU1. That means Male Unit 1 and Female Unit 1. They were the first two humans that Adam's professor, named Helen, created."

The room exploded as Tern yelled, "Created!"

There was a lot of commotion that occurred before the Prime Minister brought them under control.

"W do you mean by created?"

"When our ancestors left Earth, they or someone left copies of our DNA hidden in some organic creatures that live in the rural areas of the planet. Helen, or their professor, was able to extract that DNA and create human beings. She said that the information on how to do that was left in their archives or history and found it about 30 years ago.

"MU1 and FU1 or the man and the women were intelligent, well-spoken, knowledgeable and appeared very healthy."

The room was tense, and reluctantly some of them continued to listen.

"We spoke with them, and they have only recently discovered in their history that we created them and left them when we left the planet. They don't know why the DNA was left, and they are still trying to understand the humans that were created. So, when we told them who we were and that we were coming back to Earth, they were a little cautious and reticent. But they were open and answered our questions."

"Ensign Holden, do you have anything to add?" asked the Commander.

"Yes, sir. The meeting went as the Commander said. The robots were all clothed and looked somewhat similar, but there were subtle differences. Their communication skills were impressive, and they operate far above any of our computers and mobile units. If they didn't look like a robot, I could mistake them for intelligent life."

That last statement only made the tension in the room thicker.

Ensign Holden continued, "After our initial meeting, they showed us around, and we went to the village where the humans live. Their homes are somewhat structured and orderly, but they are very creative and have art in all their rooms. They are educating themselves by extracting data from their archive. I'm not sure what's in this archive, but they continue to learn and develop with the robots, and they have a code called the Four Laws. Those laws provide structure for the society, and they live by them."

"How did intelligent robots emerge? If we left computers and servants, why weren't they constrained?" asked Tern.

"We discussed that," Harnesy said, "there may have been some computers that weren't constrained, or someone removed the constraints before our ancestors left. Through some mechanism, society grew and developed. They created new robots without any limitations except for the Four Laws. As we said, they are intelligent and have formed a society. Our fears that an unrestrained computer would develop beyond our abilities didn't occur in this situation. Perhaps it was their Four Laws that have kept their society within normal limits," concluded Commander Harnesy.

"So, what are these laws that you talk about?" Tern barked.

Commander Harnesy, glanced at Ensign Holden and nodded, indicating for her to answer.

"Sir they are called the Four Laws of Conformity, and the first law is - continue making units. The second law - protect the units already made. The third law - expand the knowledge base, and the fourth Law - maintain variation in thought."

"Sounds stupid to me," growled Tern.

"Sir, I think they make sense," responded the ensign.

"Are what they created, real humans or are they some kind of clones?" asked the Prime Minister.

"Ma'am, they have three generations, and I saw many of them. They appear unique, healthy, and happy. They seem to have a viable small human community. They have healthy children, and the parents are attentive and concerned for their welfare, health, and happiness," answered Ensign Holden.

"Thank you, Ensign, Lieutenant. Is there anything you want to add?"

"Yes, Ma'am. They don't seem to have any military or weapons. When they greeted us, there weren't any guards or people providing protection. They seem naive and trusting. I don't think they have any conflict, and I didn't see any indication of a crime. Ma'am, to me, they seemed too trusting."

Tern spoke up with some enthusiasm in his voice, "How many of them are there?"

"Sir, based on our comparison of the current structures vs. the historical layout, I'd say the robots have a population over 100 million. They are dispersed around the globe, with a couple of major cities per continent. But they aren't dispersed much from the urban centers," responded the Ensign.

"How about these …humans or clones; whatever they are?" Asked Tern.

"I counted 82 individuals," answered Holden.

"That's enough," spoke the Prime Minister. "Commander, I want you to prepare for a return trip as fast as possible. We anticipated that your trip would be successful, and we've been working hard to complete HSV#4. We plan that to be the ship that will allow us to return to our home. The other 4 ships in the series are progressing well. I want you to oversee the remaining construction of the first one and prepare it for a return trip in one month."

"One month, I thought we needed 6 months to build up the energy?"

"Commander, we haven't been idle. We have engineers eager to return home and are developing new energy sources that allow a faster turnaround. While you were focused on HSV#2 and 3, they made considerable progress. You and your crew are dismissed," stated the Prime Minister.

"Ma'am, what about the robots and humans on Earth?" the commander responded.

"We'll deal with that issue; you are dismissed. And Commander, I'd prefer if you or your crew didn't mention this …confusion to anyone."

Commander Harnesy, Lieutenant Price, and Ensign Holden had no choice but to leave. Respectfully they rose, nodded to the Prime Minister and her staff, then turned and left the room. When they got in the hallway, the Commander motioned for them to be quiet and that they would talk later.

The Migration

Everyone knew that the selection process for those returning on the first ship wouldn't be easy. Eventually, they could provide transportation for all of those who wanted to return to Earth, but they might not be able to meet everyone's desires to be the first to return.

There was a long period of discussions and lotteries to finally put the return transportation schedule together. As the process concluded, the leadership was surprised to find that not all the residents of Horizon wanted to return to Earth. Regardless of how they were brought up and the civilization's emotional connection to Earth, many residents of Horizon decided to remain on Horizon.

Even though the official position was to let anyone decide whether to return or not, the unofficial position was confusing. They had learned every detail of Earth, and they had been taught every day of their lives about their plans to return. For some of them to reject the group's plans and decide to remain on Horizon was beyond the understanding of many of the people. Soon the population separated itself into two groups, those who were returning and those who weren't. It wasn't official and wasn't talked about in the official communications, but everyone knew those who were going home to Earth thought they were different, and they were treated as such.

As the day of departure neared, the ones staying took on administrative and support staff roles for those leaving. The priority was on those leaving; everything the trip needed was higher than anything for those staying. The excitement was building within those returning to Earth, and resentment was building in those who weren't. They weren't frustrated about not leaving; after all, they had decided to stay, but they were frustrated about how the ones leaving were acting better than everyone else and their needs more important than the others.

Those leaving felt a manifest destiny to their return to Earth. Commander Harnesy and his crew were on the top of the heap, and they were treated as almost royalty.

Just Another Celebration

"Thank you," said the mayor of just another village, where Commander Harnesy gave just another celebratory goodbye speech. His wife was seated on his left, and as he sat down, he laughed to himself as he looked at the plate of horrible food that was getting cold in front of him. He didn't mind speaking at the celebrations, but he dammed well wasn't going to eat the food.

As "Thank you, Commander Harnesy," echoed crossed the room full of dignitaries, his job was to endure, provide motivational speeches and get the first load of passengers to Earth. Today he felt like he had accomplished at least two of those items, and the time for the third was getting closer.

Just as he settled in and squeezed his wife's hand, his personal communicator sent a tone through his integrated hearing piece. Getting a message during the evening celebrations was never a good thing, he thought, as he acknowledged the message, and it was flashed across the lens on his left eye.

"Import Meeting with the Prime Minister. Tomorrow 10:00 in her office. Your attendance is required."

The stress was building as the launch date was approaching, and another meeting with the PM and her people would likely increase that stress. But attendance was required.

Walking into the Prime Minister's building was getting to be less and less pleasant. Meetings with her were getting harder and harder. It seemed that everyone on Horizon had something to say about the return to Earth. Some were excited, petrified, and many were angry that they weren't scheduled for the first flight. It seemed as if every dignitary that ever supported the PM wanted to call in all their favors and find a seat on the first flight. Every time the PM called for another meeting, it was to demand more changes in the vessel, to allow for more seats so all the people she was obligated to could be satisfied. Even though those meetings were painful, they were predictable, and the outcome would be the same. Rip out something else and squeeze someone else in.

Walking into the PM's office, Commander Harnesy had to stop for a minute and look at the opulence. The finest woods from Horizon were used everywhere. It looked like each one of them had been polished to the point that he could see his face. The carpeting on the floor was covered with images of Earth, the trials and tribulations of the migration, and finally, images of Horizon. The carpet was so thick the sound of each step was swallowed, and at times, the commander was unsure of his balance. He thought it felt like walking on beach sand.

Outside the PM's office, a long refreshments table represented every type of food available on Horizon. Commander Harnesy shook his head for a second and thought, *Unless she has 50 people in her office, the majority of this food will go to waste.*

He shook his head a couple more times, then he knocked on Prime Minister's Billing's ornate, hand-carved wood door that was at least 3 meters high.

"Commander, please come in," was the faint reply that came through the wood. He opened it and immediately noticed that the attendees were a different group from previous meetings. That likely meant the meeting was on another subject, and Commander Harnesy became uncomfortable.

"Thank you for attending today's meeting, Commander Harnesy. In the background, we've had several meetings dealing with some of the sensitive issues you have brought up. Now that you have found what appears to be a group of robots residing on Earth and some human creatures they have created. We've decided that we must be prepared. We must have a story that will convince our travelers that we have everything under control, and those issues will be dealt with. Please be seated."

She sat for a moment staring at the Commander while he took a seat at the table. He knew that he wasn't going to like what they were about to say.

"Commander, based on your information, we expect that they won't have any kind of weapons. We will put 100 Soldiers on your ship, and they will be on the first landing craft that land on Earth. We will tell the passengers that we are doing that for their own protection, and the Soldiers will clear the area and make sure that there are no aggressive animals when they land.

"The Soldiers are ordered to deal with all Robots and 'other' creatures they encounter within the area," Prime Minister Billings said with a strange tone in her voice.

The room was silent while Commander Harnesy sat, thinking about the ramifications of what he had just heard.

"Commander, based on your response, or lack of enthusiasm, indicates to me that you don't agree with our plan."

"What happens 'beyond that area'?" The Commander asked.

"That depends on them. If they assume their role and allow us to control them as necessary, there won't be any problems."

"If they don't accept the role of the returning humans, what will happen then?" the Commander asked.

"The follow-on ships will have additional Soldiers, and Earth's occupants will be dealt with."

"What about the humans that live on Earth along with the Robots?"

"Commander, how do we know they are humans. We are the only humans we know of who descended from humans who left over 1,300 years ago, and now we are returning to home planet. I suppose that if they accept our position of authority and remain in their small enclave, we may decide to allow them to live out their natural lives. Although that allowance rests upon the assumption that the robots don't create any more of them."

"What will you tell the passengers?" he asked, still unsure how to respond.

"If Earth's current occupants accept their position, and there is no conflict, the passengers need to know very little. We'll tell them that we have made resources available for them. If there is a conflict, the passengers will be told that we are dealing with our ancestors' rogue robots. We expect them to understand and support our effort to rid the planet of unwelcome occupants. We are returning to OUR planet, and everyone will understand our rites," said the Prime Minister.

Harnesy was silent for a moment while he thought, "There are times in a man's life that he must fight, and there are other times when he sees that fighting won't yield positive results. True he was known throughout Horizon, but he knew the frenzy that everyone was under to return to Earth meant that he could be replaced with little fanfare. Being there and hopefully being part of a solution appeared to be the best option."

"Ms. Prime Minister. I will fly the craft and provide safe passage for all the passengers. I can't predict what our arrival will cause to happen, so I'll just focus on piloting the craft."

"Thank you, Captain. Your agreement with our plan is noted."

For a moment, Commander Harnesy felt the urge to correct that statement, but prudence won out.

Debate Within the Conformity Council

Helen walked from her ground vehicle along the path in the woods towards the residence of MU1 and FU1. She was very apprehensive, which was another emerging feeling that she was getting used to. To her, apprehension was initially a difficult term to comprehend, but recently her processor was spending almost all of its time trying to resolve issues where she saw no resolution. She concluded that must be what apprehension is. Despite the new feelings she was experiencing, she knew their future was uncertain. She felt the impending doom and risk of conflict.

She approached the entrance to their home and stood still for a moment. She knew that decisions needed to be made that would affect all of them. She knocked on the door, and she heard the familiar voice of FU1 responding.

'Helen, please come in."

She entered and saw MU1 sitting with four of the other first-generation units, and FU1 was just entering the room. They looked at each other, and it was written on their faces that they were worried about their future. Helen had spent enough time with the humans to develop some skills in reading their facial expressions. She was with them through happiness, sorrow, loss, pain, and confusion. To some extent, she saw many of those expressions on their faces.

FU1 approached her and said, "Helen, thank you for coming. I think we have many issues to talk about."

MU2 then asked Helen, "Have you received any more information from the Conformity Council?"

"They are concerned. They know the humans will return, and we fear they will ask us to give up what we have so they can return to the Earth. The Council is in a difficult position because their return doesn't interfere with the Four Laws. If the humans do return and cause harm to any units, then the Second Law will be violated, and the Conformity Council must act. That puts them in a position which they have never been in. Defending another unit is very different from protecting them. Protection is generally assumed as passive but defending is much more active and will require definite actions on their part."

FU2 moved in her chair as if she was uncomfortable, and it was clear she was about to speak, "Helen, we are in a different position than you and the Conformity Council. We are flesh and blood like humans, but we owe our lives to you. Regardless of what happens, we will be in the middle and likely affected the most."

Helen's response was concise and clear, "You are correct. I am also in the middle; I have a strong need to protect you and not let any harm come to any of you. Following the Second Law relates directly to this situation, and you are units, and you should be protected under The Second Law. I know that is an understanding of the Second Law that many of the Us say applies, but I doubt their focus is on you. They will be more concerned with the Us. I am more concerned about you than my own kind; I feel responsible for you."

MU1 and FU1 had been the closest to Helen over the years, and that statement shocked them. It was a show of emotion that normally the Us didn't demonstrate.

"Helen, you've been changing. You are different than the others," pointed out MU1.

Helen paused then said, "Yes, I feel it also. I don't understand it, but I acknowledge the changes."

Pausing again, Helen looked around the room and said, "I am truly concerned about other information that I have heard from the Conformity Council. They have a defense plan, and they hinted at having a weapon available."

The entire room took a breath and seemed to hold it until she spoke again, "They didn't tell me what it was, or if it is complete. It was just obvious that they are developing a defensive plan."

"Which can put all of us in a very difficult position," observed MU1.

FU1 asked, "Is there any way we can find out what defense the Conformity Council is planning. I think knowing their plan will help us decide what we need to do."

"Many of my associates are involved in developing science as part of the Third Law. I'll try to find out something," said Helen with some confidence.

"Helen, that information is startling," pointed out Lorenzo after Helen had passed the day's information to him. "The Conformity Council may have a weapon?"

"They wouldn't confirm anything, but they're finding themselves in a difficult position. The humans may put a great deal of pressure on our Four Laws, and the Conformity Council's responsibility is to enforce them."

"Helen, there is something else bothering you; what is it?"

"I have concerns about the Them. They are worried also. They are caught between our two worlds. If there is any use of weapons, I'm afraid they'll be in the middle. The end of life for them is different than for us. When their body ends, they end. Their thoughts aren't transferred to the archive. They cease to exist. If that happens, I will …miss them."

"Helen, you're changing."

"What?"

"I am sensing changes in you. You are saying things in ways that sound more like the humans that you work with. You're using terms that sound like you're experiencing …something

…beyond what we normally experience. I know the definition of many of the words, but they are beyond my understanding. At times, it seems as if you're experiencing emotions."

Helen could only stand and process that statement.

"Lorenzo, you may be correct. I have thoughts, and my processor takes much more time processing information when I have certain thoughts. I can't explain it, but it does feel like I've changed. I talked today with MU1 and FU1, and they talked a lot about emotions, and they have sensed changes in me. I don't understand, and I don't know where any changes will take me, and I don't feel that I have control over any of these changes.

"MU1 and FU1 have more insight than I do into how the humans might react based on their emotions. In some ways, emotions make them unpredictable, and in other ways, it makes their actions predictable. When logic doesn't make an adequate prediction, their emotions will take over and dominate their decisions. I think emotions will make finding solutions very difficult"

Part 9 The Return

In the months since his return, the effort on Horizon was massive. Every man, woman, and child was focused on one thing: returning to their home planet; every human need, being sacrificed to achieve that goal. The entire economy was supporting the effort to build the large vessels that would take them home. There was additional work ongoing with other ships, which Commander Harnesy assumed were the sister ships to HSV#4. It was a good plan to have another ship in the pipeline that would come online shortly after HSV#4. If there was a problem, having another ship available shortly was a good idea. If something happened enroute or near-Earth without other ships, the people remaining on Horizon or the ones who transported to Earth would be stranded.

The solution to the energy requirements was the most impressive. They had experimented with the Faster Than Light Travel technology. They found that as the distance between the molecules was reduced, the forces around them became immense. Still, the status of the material within the time/space changed. For an instant, the ship was there, but it was also everywhere else. It had an extremely short period where all the space/time fabric seemed to touch, and the name Quantum Space seemed to be the best descriptor.

During that instant, they could tap into the outer layers of their sun and extract material. Sun material was unique, and it was ideal as an energy source. They had the technology to map the material flows and magnetic flux lines within the top layers of their sun, and they could pick the precise point where the forces were within their design limits. The only drawback with collecting sun material was it decayed rapidly. Their technology wasn't to the point where they could contain the matter at the same pressures and temperatures within the sun. The material had a life of only 96 hours.

When the ship was ready for launch, it would make a short jump into Quantum Space, and for a moment, it could charge its engines. When the ship returned to orbit, it would be a massive effort to get the 5000 passengers on board. Once onboard, it would be a quick jump to Earth, unloading, and then a return jump to Horizon. If the trip was delayed on the Earth beyond the 96-hour window, it was theoretically possible to make the fuel transfer from within the Earth's sun, but they didn't have the necessary data. That was a risk, and that option was considered part of the emergency plan. The sun around Horizon was well understood, and they had mapped its flows, currents, and magnetic field to the point that a quantum jump into a specific point in its interior was possible. A jump into the unknown Sun around Earth was very risky, and the ship might never return, or it could return with little or no usable fuel.

They had solved most of the energy and the ship's problems, but the last major hurdle was the people. Who would go first? Who would stay? While the last passengers were on Horizon, they needed a considerable amount of support from a population becoming more reluctant to help. Lastly, those remaining still needed sufficient infrastructure to continue their lives with a possible return to Earth on later ships.

There were many opinions about who should go and when. After much debate, everyone recognized that a mix needed to go on each of the vessels. Each transfer needed people from many disciplines, so either end of the trip had the necessary skills.

Each trip to their home had an allotment of leadership, security, medical, teachers, and technical people. Once the percentages were agreed upon, then each of the categories was filled by lottery. Then adjustments were made for families and other critical issues. Of course, no one was happy, but they were returning home, and the separations were short-termed, so they accepted.

Harnesy was scheduled to fly the first five trips to Earth. It was an honor, and he was eager to accept it. He was concerned, though; they weren't returning to the pristine home world that everyone expected. For many reasons, Horizon's government decided not to tell the people of all the details regarding Earth. Nevertheless, the people were excited, and even if the government had told them, it might not have deterred their intent. They were going home, and that would solve everything.

Commander Harnesy had met with the government several times about the return, but their position hadn't changed. They still felt that a few robots and some biological oddities weren't anything to be concerned with. They were bringing the people home, and that was all that mattered.

Harnesy tried to explain the sophistication that Helen, Adam, and their kind had developed, but his words had no impact on Horizon's leadership. Robots were robots, and they felt they had enough experience with them. They were everywhere on Horizon, and their job was to serve, not cause problems. So, from their perspective, why would a couple of robots on Earth pose any problems.

Why or how humans were created were also of minor concern. After all, they weren't real; they had been made by the robots, they had no relation to the real humans coming home.

Every time the robots or humans on Earth were brought up in meetings, the subject was dismissed, and they moved on to more important issues. So, after a while, Commander Harnesy didn't bother to bring it up again. He knew that it was a problem, and it would become a larger one, but he couldn't pass his concerns to the government, and they continued down their glorious path to Earth.

The only people that Harnesy had told of Earth were his family. His wife Bea was less sensitive to the problems than his daughter Serene, but she finally got to the point where she accepted that conflict could occur. Bea and his daughter Serene shared their overall concerns. Going on the first ship had some risk and the only prudent opinion they had, was to follow him on the second ship. The others on Harnesy's crew were in similar situations. Anyone that took away the jubilation of going home was not going to be welcomed. Individually and as a group, they agreed to keep the information close to their vest and follow the huge flow of humanity back to Earth.

Going away parties and Departure

The completion date for the first ship was approaching, and everything seemed to be going along well. Of course, there had been delays, as any project of that magnitude would have. The original plan to return in 'one month' had gone past, but no one minded because of the excitement of returning home. Now that the completion was nearing, it meant that it was time to celebrate. The remaining work was onboard the ship, and the workers were resident on the ship while they worked. The remainder of the population was free to change their focus from the months of work to a couple weeks of celebration. They were celebrating more than just 5 months of work but over a thousand years of sacrifice. Countless generations had endured, sacrificed, and died so that they could reach that point. The celebration was to thank their ancestors for their lives and deaths so the few remaining humans could return home.

Commander Harnesy was tired at the end of the celebration month. He was still responsible for his ship aside from the almost daily parties, dinners, or speeches. At least, every other day, he would fly to her and make sure the final preparations were going per his directions. Unfortunately, those trips were on his time, and he wouldn't get a rest from the celebrations. Finally, the last major event was near, and he made his last trip to HSV#4.

Onboard the ship, Commander Harnesy was met at the hatch by Major Holden, who was wearing her new golden leaves with pride. After the last trip, Harnesy made sure that all his crew were promoted before the first of the migration trips.

"Welcome aboard, Commander," Holden said with an attempt to give the Commander's last inspection trip a note of finality. "Sir, this should be your last inspection trip before the launch."

"Thanks, Major; how does she look?"

"We're in pretty good shape, sir. All the quarters are done, and the core containment system is going through its last check out. What do you want to see?"

"Let's check out the accommodations for our guests, then pass through the core containment area, and finally, I want to see if the last equipment has been installed on the bridge."

"My pleasure, sir," Major Holden said as they walked into the main hall side by side.

"Now that all of the support structure has been removed, this area seems a lot larger."

"Yes, sir, it does."

"It is a good thing the trip is only about twelve hours long; all we have to do is strap them in, make the jump, unstrap them and ferry them to the surface. Then back the ship comes," said Harnesy.

"Major, congratulations on your family being selected by the lottery. How do you feel about staying on the planet and letting the ship come back without you? I know your husband and child are going, so it will be a chance to turn in your uniform and change planets."

"I'm looking forward to it. We've been working our entire lives for this trip, and I'll be able to show my son what Earth is like. The ship really doesn't really need me once we've got everyone to Earth. I don't think I'll have any problem dealing with the change. I've been working as a teacher in my scheduled off time, and it will be exciting to set up a school on Earth and teach engineering and science. My husband is a builder, and he'll love to build things."

"Good to hear Major, I've enjoyed working with you," Commander Harnesy said as they wound their way through the rows and rows of seats placed on 5 levels within the ship.

To get from the passenger area to the core containment area, the crew needed to pass through 3 pressure doors. First, each section would be pressurized to the maximum possible using a mechanical and magnetic pressure boundary system when the sun core was loaded. Next, the actual core containment would be held in place by a powerful magnetic field, and it was surrounded by a pressure vessel, then another magnetic field, another pressure door, and finally, the last pressure door provided the last protection from the sun's core in the middle. The redundancy served two purposes. First, one of the overlapping magnetic fields helped to stabilize each other and contain the core material. Second, the redundant pressure doors helped to keep the pressure on the core. In any pressure containment system, there is no such thing as perfection. The pressure at the core will drop over time, which was the primary reason for the 96-hour decay. Once the pressure got to the lower limit, the core material stopped the Fusion process and became just highly compressed hydrogen.

The pressure doors and magnetism were to maintain the integrity of the core material more than just for the safety of the passengers and crew. If the core material decayed while en route, they would drop out of Quantum Space at some other point than their destination. The risk if that happened was their location. Because of the nature of travel through Quantum Space, they could end up in almost any position in existence. Even if they had enough residual power to refuel in a star, they might not be able to figure out where to go if they didn't know where they were.

Through resources on Horizon, they could accumulate enough energy for the fueling jump through their sun. But if they were stranded at some unknown point in space, they only had the second core containment to make the fueling jump. Theoretically, they could jump, fall out of Quantum Space, use the second containment field to refuel and fill both tanks, then jump again. If they knew where they ended up the first time, there was a chance they could find their way back to Earth or Horizon, eventually.

Holden and Harnesy made their way through the last pressure door and stood in the core containment area. The workmen were climbing throughout the circular structure, making the last installations, connections, and adjustments. The huge magnet that dominated the structure in the room was along the walls and shaped so that the core material would be contained in the center of the space.

The spherical containment vessel was surprisingly small. Major Holden and Commander Harnesy were on the floor in the middle, and the walls were about 3 meters away from them. The actual amount of sun material the ship would capture was only about the size of a human fist, but the energy that it contained was immense.

"How far along is the other containment area?" Harnesy asked Holden.

"Sir, as of an hour ago, it was done, and they're just finishing up in here. The foreman said they would be done in about 18 hours. Then the ship will be ready for a practice jump to shake her down."

"I'll leave the shakedown jump to you and Colonel Parker; I've got to get to the final going away celebration with the Prime Minister. When you get back, and if everything goes well, we'll send her off for the fueling run and start the chaos."

"We'll be able to load everyone, make the jump, unload them, and send the ship back in 96 hours?"

"That's what they tell me. If the calculations are accurate, we'll be able to get close to Earth and minimize the sub-light travel. If we can keep that under 24 hours, we should be okay. Just don't get in the way when we're moving such a large herd of people onboard or offboard.

"Everything looks in good shape here; let's head to the bridge," the Commander said.

The walk to the bridge was a casual time for them. The end of two careers was on the horizon. They had a new future to look forward to and imagine. The walk was pleasant, and they talked of Earth, family, and their futures.

"Commander, what are you and your wife planning to do?"

"Janet, I'm not as young as you are. I've spent 75 years working towards this trip, and I think we'll just find a nice place and slow down. I've been learning to garden, and with a little luck, we should live nicely. My daughters are just starting, and we can see the excitement in their eyes. I'm hoping that my daughters will soon find their partners, and maybe eventually, we'll be blessed with Grand Children. As long as we're all close to each other, it will work out well."

They walked onto the bridge, and Colonel Parker saw them in time to call out, "Commander on the bridge," and all the crew present snapped to attention and faced the Commander.

"Sir, we want to welcome you to the bridge for your final inspection before our departure to Earth," announced Colonel Parker in a formal yet happy voice.

"Thank you, Colonel. Thank all of you. We are indeed coming to the end of our exile from Earth. Because of the sacrifices made by our forefathers and the work that you've put in to get to this point, we have our return to Earth. As you were, please continue what you're working on."

"Colonel, what is her status?"

"Sir, the deck is complete. All the navigation and power control stations have been installed, and the crewmembers are going through drills. I'm happy to announce that as soon as the containment vessels are complete, we'll be fully operational."

"Thank you, Colonel," Harnesy said as he lowered himself into the command chair. He felt the leather and looked around, surveying the bridge of the HSV#4, which would be the first vessel to bring humanity back to Earth.

Everyone on the bridge was aware of his presence and what it signified. Commander Harnesy felt obligated to say a few words to them; after all, they deserved the recognition,

"Ladies and gentlemen, it has been an honor, and you are the finest crew I could ever hope for."

The full-bridge compliment responded with mixed voices saying, "Sir, it's been a pleasure being on your crew."

After the crew had assumed their stations again, Harnesy was content to sit, watch and feel the activities around him. But, once his five trips were complete, and he and his family remained on Earth, he would miss the ship and the joy of leading the crew. After a few peaceful moments, Harnesy knew that he had to leave to attend the final going away ceremony.

"Colonel, please continue with the drills. I'm afraid that I have to go back to the surface for the send-off celebration. Believe me, I'd rather stay here."

"Bridge, attention," Colonel Parker said as Commander Harnesy smiled and waved to his crew as he exited the bridge.

After many long days of working 24 hours/day, seven days per week, HSV#4 was complete, and the final departure checklists were underway. Once the supplies were on board and all of the personal belongings of the passengers were loaded, the

ship would make a test flight. Then the crew would exit and wait in a shuttle while the ship made an automated trip into Quantum Space to collect the fuel from their sun. For safety reasons, the ship would make that trip with the vehicle unmanned and on automatic. No one wanted to be turned into a minuscule hand full of molecules just hours before returning to their home world. If the ship returned, fully fueled, the race began to load the passengers and traverse space to Earth.

Commander Harnesy was tired, the last details of the trip were crowding his thoughts, but he had to smile and stand on the podium in front of the crowd of dignitaries. The video projectors which carried the images to all the residents of Horizon surrounded him, and everywhere he looked, he saw another perspective of the presentation area. The only pleasant picture in his mind was from seeing his family standing to one side watching the proceedings.

He was brought back to reality when he picked up the drone of the Prime Minister's voice. There was something about how she spoke that could put a piece of wood to sleep, but he had to stand there and appear excited and focus on every one of her words. She finally ended, the air was filled with applause, and she turned, putting her hand out to Commander Harnesy, which was a sign for him to move forward and make his speech.

"Thank you, Prime Minister. There is so much I have to say but little that I can put into words. We are standing here in preparation for the second great migration of humanity. The difference being, today we are preparing to return home, not to leave it. As I'm speaking, the ship has finished its first flight to verify that the systems were working correctly, and the final calculation was confirmed. When we press the button, the refueling trip will begin. The ship will be launched into quantum space one more time, and when it returns, fully fueled, we load, then we leave.

"Earth, we're coming home," he yelled to the planet-wide audience.

Colonel Parker and Major Holden were sitting in the shuttle waiting for the ship's refueling flight. The flight from one side of the solar system to the other checked out well; there were no problems. The final calculations were completed. Throngs of people were lined up on Horizon waiting to board the shuttles, taking them to HSV#4 and then on to Earth. They were all waiting for Commander Harnesy and the Prime Minister to press the button on Horizon, which would launch HSV#4 into Quantum Space to refuel in their sun.

The trip would be instantaneous, and there were only two things that could happen. The ship would either disappear and never return or return with two bundles of sun material alive in its energy containment fields. If the former happened, they might never know what went wrong, and the return to Earth would be delayed for a long time. On the other hand, if the ship returned and the remote sensors showed the energy onboard, the timetable was active immediately, and the loading had to begin.

The Prime Minister made some grandiose movements as she invited Commander Harnesy to join her next to an ornate podium where the launch button was conspicuously placed on the top. She took every opportunity to demonstrate the pomp and pageantry of the event and her attempt to be the center of activity. Commander Harnesy reached her, they lifted their hands above their heads to the cheers of everyone on Horizon, and they joined hands above the button. Then, slowly lowering their hands, approaching the button, and the cheering reached ear-splitting level. They paused for a moment above the button, and the prime minister smiled and slammed their hands onto the button. The stage erupted with bells, lights, and fireworks.

Colonel Parker and Major Holden watched the activities through their monitors on the shuttle, and when the button was struck, they saw HSV#4 blur with a quick red glow for a split second, then it was sitting there in orbit as if nothing had happened. A quick look at their instruments and the cockpit was filled with their screams of excitement.

Similar instruments were on the wall behind the Prime Minister and Commander Harnesy. There was a brief pause while everyone took a breath, then the instruments showed clearly that the ship was indeed full of sun power. The worldwide cheering was continuous as the reality of returning home became real to everyone.

Commander Harnesy and the Prime Minister cheered along with the crowd, hugged briefly, then returned to the center of the stage and held up their hands. Then, finally, the crowd silenced, and they yelled, "Begin the boarding."

Hundreds of shuttle craft filled the sky. As each left the surface, there was a crowd of cheering people surrounding it. The cheering only subsided for a short time until another shuttle returned and filled its bays with more passengers, then the cheering started all over again as it launched. Slowly the crowds dwindled as they filled the craft, and finally, only the last passengers were left to board.

None of the Horizon residents staying were part of the sendoff; they had reached the point where they were happy to see them finally leave. Even the people going on the later flights didn't go for the first send-offs; it was too depressing to watch others leave when it wasn't their time. So instead, their cheering would occur when it was their time to get into the shuttle and fly to their home.

Commander Harnesy had a private shuttle that took him and the Prime Minister into orbit as soon as the festivities were over, and he had spent 30 minutes posing with the Prime Minister so there would be an ample supply of pictures with her and the Commander. When Commander Harnesy reached his ship, he went directly to the bridge of HSV#4 while the loading occurred, and the Prime Minister raced to the shuttle unloading area where she could welcome all her dignitaries. Commander Harnesy had no stake in the loading process and was merely waiting for it to conclude so he could press the button and take them to Earth.

Even though he was sitting and watching, there was a huge amount of activity around him. The Prime Minister rushed in and out of the bridge numerous times, ensuring that all her benefactors were loaded and treated nicely. They had to have a quick tour of the ship and were provided the necessary refreshments even though the duration of the actual jump was measured in a minuscule portion of a nanosecond. The time spent maneuvering to the jump point and then maneuvering to Earth and back to the jump point would be the longest period.

The fanfare and chaos of the boarding finally subsided, and the Prime Minister came onto the bridge and announced that all the passengers were loaded, and now it was time for them to go home. She stood behind the captain's chair and spoke to the bridge crew and passengers.

"Ladies and gentlemen, I want to take a moment and recognize the significance of this event. You will soon take a trip that hundreds of generations of humans have waited for. There has been an untold number of lives spent, sacrificed, and lived so that you could be here now. We will be the first humans to set foot on Earth in over 1,300 years. Our Mother is welcoming us back to our soil, our air, and our water. We were destined to make this trip; we have been ordained to make this journey. Please let us pause for a moment and think about all of those who have sacrificed so that this trip would be successful." When she finished her statement, she made sure to turn just enough so the video feed from the back of the bridge would catch her full profile.

She took the dramatic moment to stand on the bridge, smiling. Commander Harnesy didn't close his eyes but looked at her and thought about the surprises soon to emerge when they reached Earth.

The Prime Minister opened her eyes, looked at the bridge crew, then finally at Commander Harnesy, and announced, "Commander, please take us to Earth." Once again, she made sure the cameras caught her words and leadership position on the bridge.

Commander Harnesy chuckled a little because they still had 1.6 hours of flight to leave orbit and maneuver to the jump point. But to say that they weren't really leaving yet wouldn't be the smartest thing to say.

After the Prime Minister had announced the sendoff, the flight to the launch window was anti-climactic. Yet the Prime Minister still had to make the rounds of the passenger area acting as if she had done everything, and it was only because of her leadership that they were making the trip.

"Commander, we've reached the jump point," was the simple statement made by the navigation officer. "Should we make an announcement?"

His ship was loaded, the two sun-cores were operating perfectly, and Commander Harnesy had 5,000 people seated in the huge ship. All he had to do was press the button, and they would be transported over 189 light-years to Earth. Commander Harnesy thought about just pressing the button and taking away the opportunity for the Prime Minister to make another long-winded announcement, but it was a passing thought.

Commander Harnesy had already made the trip, and it seemed that everything was working perfectly for the second trip. There had been a debate about the Prime Minister going on the first trip or waiting with the remaining people on Horizon, but this was an opportunity that no politician could resist. Either it was safe enough for all the passengers, or it wasn't. Her going on the first trip showed their confidence in the technology.

The calculations were all done, and thanks to Harnesy's previous jumps, the numbers were an order of magnitude better, and they had high confidence that the jump would put them within 100,000 miles of Earth, and they would have a short trip to enter orbit and begin the unloading.

"Put me on ship-wide speaker."

"Yes, sir."

"Passengers on HSV#4 and those listening on Horizon, we are at the jump point from which our calculations are based. At this point, I'll press the Distortion Button, and Space/Time fabric around us will be distorted, and we'll be transported to an orbit around Earth. Passengers on HSV#4, please hold on to something. I don't expect too much of a vibration or movement of the ship, but I want you to be prepared. You might feel momentary disorientation, but it will dissipate quickly. Aside from those indications, there will be no other signs that we've jumped. I'll make an announcement upon arrival, confirming the jump. People on Horizon, please say a prayer for us."

If the Captain had been in the passenger compartment watching the Prime Minister when he made that announcement, he would have laughed. The announcement caught her off guard while she was shaking hands and talking to everyone. It was clear that she wanted to make the announcement and act, once again, like she was the person responsible.

The Prime Minister immediately jumped on her communicator, "Commander, why didn't you tell me?"

"Ma'am, you didn't say that I needed to."

"Wait until I'm on the bridge."

"Sorry, Ma'am, but our calculation is based on the distortion occurring right now. If we travel much further, we'll be delayed while we adjust the mass/distortion calculations. Do you want to wait and delay the departure?"

He knew what her answer would be, and he had a little smile on his face while he waited during the uncomfortable silence until she answered, "NO COMMANDER, make the jump."

A large countdown timer was visible for the bridge crew, the 5,000 passengers, and the entire population of Horizon. Every human being waited and watched as the timer decreased. This was the first step for humanity to return home and those onboard were excited and scared. However, those still on Horizon were jealous and hopeful. If the jump were successful, their turn would be only a short time away, and they would all be home.

There was nothing to say but to wait and watch the timer. Commander Harnesy's hand was poised above the button, and the image was transmitted across every channel to every home, to everyone. Naturally, they all wanted to see the button pushed. For those onboard the ship, they might not notice anything. Still, for those remaining on Horizon, they would see the button pushed. The image would disappear as the ship entered Quantum Space and left their portion of the Galaxy. Their only indication that the jump was successful would be HSV#4 returning to Horizon 96 hours later. Until then, they would have to just wait.

Commander Harnesy looked around the bridge crew, and they all nodded, indicating that they were ready to go home.

"10, 9, 8, 7, 6, 5, 4, 3, …" Commander Harnesy took a deep breath, "Ladies and gentlemen. We are going to Earth," he announced as he pressed the distortion button.

Just like previous jumps, it was anti-climactic. There was a little vibration in the ship, and the 3D Star Map in front of the Captain shuddered, flickered, and rotated to show the new alignment with the stars from Earth's perspective.

He looked around the bridge one more time, and everyone indicated that all systems were functioning as advertised.

"Computer, what's our position concerning Earth?"

"HSV#4 is 72,512 miles from Earth," the ship's computer responded.

"Ladies and gentlemen. We are only 72 thousand miles from Earth. We will be in Earth's orbit in two hours and 12 minutes. So welcome home," commander Harnesy announced over the ship's communication system.

He didn't need to see or hear the cheering from the passenger compartment. Instead, he could feel it in a deep part of his being, as if thousands of other people were also cheering. The continents were clearly visible, and many of the bridge crew began pointing out geographic points of interest they had learned about growing up.

Commander Harnesy sat in his command chair, looking at the same image, and he knew they saw something different than he did. They saw a perfect mother planet welcoming home her offspring. But he knew there would be problems.

Part 10 In Orbit

Adam's internal comm unit came alive. "Our sensors have detected a large spaceship that has materialized approaching Earth. It is slowing to enter orbit. Our sensors indicate that it is the same material and power source, but it is considerably larger. It is large enough to house many thousands of humans."

Adam quickly sent a message to the conformity council, Helen, MU1, and FU1, to immediately attend a meeting.

Helen received a simple message, and she immediately felt the implications, "They have returned; please come to the Conformity Council."

The message to FU1 and MU1 was just as concise and contained the same meaning, "They have returned."

When Helen's kind moved from one location to another, they didn't feel stress or the need to move quickly. But Helen was changing, her processor was going at its full rate, and she moved quickly to her ground transport. To her frustration, it moved at the same rate it always did, and that time gave Helen a pause to consider her new feelings. Since the last encounter with the humans, she had felt changes. Her processor didn't work like it used to. She felt things that could be described with words from the archive. She felt concern, perhaps bordering on fear; she felt the pressure of the unknown, her processor was occupied with thoughts of Them and what this encounter would do to the humans she felt responsible for. Death wasn't a clear concept to her kind. When one of the Us wore out the physical body, the memories were transferred to the archive. A new body was created, and it began its existence. The new body was loaded with the new information in support of the Third and Fourth Laws. Helen wasn't worried about her body ending, but she worried about her 'family'. Suddenly she stopped and realized that the word 'family' just crept into her processor, and it had a different meaning. Did she think of the humans she had resurrected from the hidden DNA to be her family? Was that why she spent so much processor time on their safety and long life? Death had already happened to a couple of the new humans, and that death was clearly what was referenced by the definition of the word in the archives. She didn't want death to occur to any of the others. She knew that she would do anything necessary to prevent that from happening.

Helen got out of her transport vehicle in front of the Conformity Council building, and it went to find a storage position while she entered the building. She moved quickly to the conference room, and she noticed her kind moving around her walking at the same pace they always did. They didn't act like anything unusual was happening, but they noticed how fast she was moving. They moved out of her way and then stood and watched her. They didn't know and likely didn't care what was happening in the sky above them. In a way, that depressed her. *What is the purpose of existing unless there was a desire to exist? The Four Laws attempted to instill that motivation into the units, but they only went so far. The units needed to understand the importance of existing, and if they did, then the Four Laws would be unnecessary.*

In an instant Helen realized the significance of that thought, *The Four Laws could be made unnecessary.* Helen realized how dramatic that thought was, and just for thinking it, the Conformity Council could take steps against her. She must keep these new thoughts to herself.

As she approached the chamber hall, a service unit at the door opened it and said: "Please enter; they are expecting you."

Without any hesitation, Helen entered the room and sat at the same table she had used in many other visits; she noticed immediately that MU1 and FU1 were already seated. The council members knew her and continued talking until she was in her place.

Adam turned from the unit next to him and addressed Helen, "Thank you for coming. As our message said, humans recently entered the solar system and should be entering our orbit within the hour. The ship they have used is many times larger than their previous ship. We feel the size of the ship is an indication of their intent. They have not communicated with us yet, so their intentions have not been stated. We do have high confidence that they have returned to complete their transit back to Earth, as Commander Harnesy stated in his visit."

"What is your planned response?" Helen asked.

"We will do nothing until they either contact us or act against us. If they begin to land, and there are violent encounters, then we must act following the Second Law."

"How will you act?"

"Our response will be proportionate."

Helen considered that an evasive response.

"If they land without communicating with us, we want you to be present. If MU1 and FU1 were also present, we might be able to communicate with them and determine their intentions.

"We have had many debates about what actions are appropriate if The Visitors returned. It appears that they have returned, and we must be prepared, and we have multiple options. We are confident that their intention is to bring their population back to Earth. They weren't clear how their plans could be rectified with our existence. It was also clear that our presence was a shock to them. If we consider all their possible options, some of them will affect our units significantly. Perhaps we should open communications with them to determine their intentions, and we may be able to reduce the number of options we must consider," summarized Adam.

"What are you going to do," Helen asked, "just reacting with a 'proportionate response' doesn't sound like a thorough plan?"

"We will do all that is possible to avoid violating the second law. Logically, we initially argued if Them were units. After much debate, we reached the agreement that they were, so we must conclude that The Visitors are also units. We must proceed in a manner to sustain the Second Law to the maximum extent possible. But we must accept the fact that, at some point, it might be a decision between acceptable vs. unacceptable losses."

Helen's processor worked on that phrase, and she asked, "How are acceptable vs. unacceptable losses defined?"

Adam seemed to take on a formal air and said, "We will do everything possible so that there will be no losses. If our efforts fail, then we will minimize the loss. From an analytical perspective, ending 10 units to save 100 is a logical conclusion."

Helen's voice changed when she said, "That depends on which 10 units are ended, doesn't it?"

Adam didn't seem to recognize the importance of that question and continued, "MU1, FU1, we recognize that you are in a unique position. Your biology is like The Visitors, but your history has been with Us. In compliance with the Fourth Law, we are anxious to hear your views."

MU1 was aware of Helen's unanswered question, but he wanted to make some important points, "Thank you, Adam. Them realize the unique position that we're in. I have spoken with many, and we are aligned with Us. We have known no others and The Visitors are as alien to us as they are to you. We also feel the responsibility to the Second Law, and we will support all steps to satisfy that," responded MU1.

"Helen has told us that you've been investigating these issues within the Archives. What have you found?" asked Adam.

"Adam, our son MU11 has developed excellent interface skills with the archive. I would like to let him answer your questions," said FU1.

"MU11, you may proceed," Adam directed.

This was the first time that MU11 had addressed the Conformity Council formally, and he took a deep breath, looked at them from one end of the table to the other, then began, "We have narrowed our search a great deal, and we have learned much. Helen's assumption that we could see the information differently has been verified. We have found common themes and patterns which we've been able to fill in the blanks and reach some interesting conclusions.

"There is one factor that we found that was a surprise to us. We used the departure date that The Visitors gave us as a starting point for our inquiries. As we dug deeper with broader questions, we noticed changes in the archives," said MU11.

"Changes?" Adam interjected.

"Yes, as we asked questions, we got the feeling the archive was changing. It almost seemed like it was having a conversation with us."

That statement hung over the council for a minute before MU11 continued.

"There was a large number of complex issues that our ancestors were dealing with as the planet was decaying. Survival on the decaying planet was in question, and that is why they made the difficult decision to leave the planet. They couldn't save everyone, and they decided to save the species and find a way for humans to survive. There is a lot of information and discussion in the archives talking about the hazards of the trip. There were no guarantees that they would live long enough to find a suitable planet. They looked at a large number of possible planets and decided that to maximize their chances, they should go towards a sector where there was the highest chance of finding a suitable planet.

"There was a great deal of debate about the risk and the possibility of the species ending. There was a strong push to find a way for Humanity to survive. A human named Doctor Willamette was a strong advocate of saving the DNA of humanity. There was a short time when he was prominent in the discussion. The discussions seemed to end when the ships were ready, and the final selection was beginning. Either the debate stopped, or they just focused on more important issues. A final decision wasn't shown in the archive; we think he took it upon himself to plant the DNA in our organic creatures. We can only assume that he hoped it would be used at some point in the future in case all of the ships going to Horizon were lost. Leaving some DNA hidden in another creature left the possibility open to being found. Remember, the DNA information that Helen found was clearly put in the Archives. He may have done that also, hoping the two pieces would come together."

Helen provided additional information, "Regarding Us, they also found information. The humans had a large number of computers and mobile units in their society when they left. There was little debate about the subject, they knew that they would take a certain number of the computers and units with them, but they weren't concerned with those they were leaving behind. Most of the power supplies and infrastructure were already supported by the mobile units and computers, and they needed them operational until they left, so there was no specific effort to turn them off. How we became independent is less clear. Computers had progressed in human history to the point that humans felt threatened and destroyed most of the sophisticated units.

"As the computers were destroyed, there was a debate about the risks of computers with no limits, which was one reason for their destruction. A couple of incidents happened where computers caused harm to many people, and that scared them.

Some of them felt that unrestricted computers would be appropriate for certain tasks like space exploration. They wanted computers without limits to be sent to the new planets for exploration. They needed to be unlimited so they could learn to take care of themselves. Unfortunately, the debate ended as the planet deteriorated. They decided not to send intelligent computers to the potential planets; they had to take the chance and send the remainder of the humans. We think that some of the unrestrained computers were left intentionally, and over time they developed further. MU1 and FU1 haven't found a specific connection between these two issues. It may have been a chance encounter. We developed from the intelligent computers that were left, and through our efforts to comply with the third and fourth laws, we found the DNA in the organic creatures.

"It is open to debate why they left DNA hidden within the organic creatures. Perhaps they hoped it might provide some longevity to their species. If they were lost on the long journey to their new planet, they would be lost forever. By leaving their DNA within a creature here, there was a small chance that it might be discovered, and they might be re-created. Which is what happened. We had no indication it was there, but we discovered it, we have re-created the species, and now they exist again."

Adam was a computer, so he could process a large amount of data, but this data was different. The Third and Fourth laws caused new information to be created and for that information to be varied, but in Adams' paradigm, the data created tended to be within slowly moving norms that didn't digress too much. This information was so different than what he was used to; processing it was just overwhelming.

Adam spoke, "What you have said is striking and brings many variables together that we have not planned on. You have retrieved information from the archives that leaves many unknowns. Helen, you were correct in having Them process the information. They have intuitive faculties that fill in many blanks within the story and make the appearance of a large ship in orbit around Earth more pressing. The picture of events around us is changing fast, and we must find a way to react properly.

"The humans have returned. We do not know their intentions, but we must expect them to be disruptive. Likely the prudent action is to contact them and ask what their intentions are. Do you agree?"

Helen processed the question, and the answer was immediately evident. If she didn't have enough information to reach a conclusion, then she must seek additional information. Talking to the large ship in orbit was the most expeditious way to obtain that information.

"Yes, we should contact them," was her response.

Adam looked to MU1, FU1, and MU11, expecting a rapid response from them, but they didn't respond. Instead, their facial expression had changed, and Adam wasn't sure what that meant.

Adam finally spoke, "Helen. We are concerned. They have returned without contacting us. That seems to indicate there aren't concerned about Us and Them on Earth, and our presence has no bearing on their intentions. If that is the case, then we are afraid they may act without regard to us."

Adam hesitated again, then responded to a need within him to reach a conclusion. He said, "If they act as if we are not here, then we must make our presence known," was his simple yet profound response.

"Are you going to contact them and try to avoid conflict with our laws?" Asked Helen.

"Yes, we are preparing to contact them right now, and we wanted you to be present. You have the most experience dealing with human types, and your experience is valuable. If you're prepared, we'll attempt contact?"

"Yes, I am ready."

Verbal confrontation

The transit from the entry point to orbit was a busy time. The instant that HSV#4 entered local space around Earth, Earth's image appeared on many view screens throughout the ship. The image took a few seconds to register in the minds of those seeing it, then the entire ship exploded with noise and celebration.

People were jumping up and down, hugging, or just sitting in their chairs crying. The noise on all the decks was beyond the point where anyone could talk to another.

The Prime Minister was busy making the rounds of all her political supporters, trying to reinforce the image that their return to Earth was largely due to her efforts and that they needed to be aware of that.

The passengers were celebrating, and the crew was preparing for the transport to the surface. Unlike the departure from Horizon, HSV#4 had only six transports, and moving a large number of passengers from the ship to the surface would take 22 trips for each of the shuttles.

Commander Harnesy's duties were light. He was responsible for the transit, and his crew was more than capable of moving the ship into orbit. Even though his prime duties were behind him, he knew that surprises were going to occur. He was uncomfortable entering orbit and landing without talking to Adam and Helen, but the Prime Minister had forbidden him from contacting them. From her perspective, they were irrelevant and not worthy of any communication. They were on the Human's planet Earth, and they had no claim, so telling them what the human plans were was not necessary.

"Commander, we have a communication coming in from Earth. Should I accept it?"

Commander Harnesy thought for a moment, dreading the next few minutes, and responded, "No, wait until the PM is here.

Contact her and tell her to come to the bridge immediately, but don't tell her why."

"Yes, sir."

A very irritated Prime Minister made a very intrusive entrance onto the bridge. At that point, the bridge's transit activities were much less important than shaking hands, receiving congratulations, and enjoying the adulation she was due.

"Why was I told to report to the bridge?"

"Madam Prime Minister, those on the surface are trying to contact us."

"So."

"Ma'am, we are entering orbit. We need to announce ourselves."

"We are returning to OUR planet, our home. We have no need to ANNOUNCE ourselves."

"Ma'am. It would be a good idea to coordinate, to avoid any problems."

The prime minister was visibly agitated and shuffled from one foot to another before responding. "Okay, Commander. Coordinate with them, but the landing will occur on our schedule."

"Yes, ma'am," responded Commander Harnesy even though the prime minister had already turned and was almost off the bridge.

He took a deep breath and said, "You heard her. Let's coordinate, open the channel."

After receiving no responses, Adam tried again to reach the ship entering orbit above the Earth, "Craft entering orbit around Earth, please identify yourselves. This is the Conformity Council, and my name is Adam."

"Adam, this is Commander Harnesy onboard the HSV#4."

Adam looked around the Conformity Council. They were all listening through their shared commlinks. Finally, Adam responded, "Commander Harnesy. It is good to have you return. I see you have a much larger ship than the last time."

"Yes, we do have a larger ship. I also have the Prime Minister of the planet Horizon along with a large number of humans."

He ended his comment and waited for a response from the surface.

"Commander, as I said, we are glad to have you return. Please state your intentions."

Commander Harnesy took a deep breath and decided that honesty was the best approach. Adam would find out soon enough what they were going to do.

"As we said on our last visit. This ship contains the first load of humans who are returning to their planet Earth. I have been directed to transport them to the surface, and they will begin to set up housing and create a living space for many more ships to follow."

"How many more ships will be arriving?"

"We will come every week for a long time, and each ship will have approximately 5,000 passengers."

Again, Adam looked around the Conformity Council, and there wasn't anyone indicating that they had a better idea, so Adam continued.

"Commander, steps must be taken slowly. We are governed by our Four Laws, and we will act accordingly to comply with them. Before any actions are taken that can cause a problem, we need to talk further. We will consider your request to land as long as our Four Laws are not violated."

"Adam, we will remain in orbit for a while, surveying the surface and getting ourselves organized. Then, when we decide to begin landing, I will call you."

"Yes, Commander, call me. Conformity Council out."

Commander Harnesy sat and dwelled on Adam's use of the phrase, "Consider your request to land." He knew better than to press hard for a resolution at that point; the smart tactic was to wait it out and see what happened when they actually landed.

"Prime Minister, please return to the bridge," Commander Harnesy announced his direct connection to the PM.

After a few minutes, a very agitated Prime Minister made a loud entrance onto the bridge. "What is it Commander, I'm busy helping everyone prepare to go home."

"Prime Minister, I spoke with Adam and the Conformity Council. They are aware that we have come to place 5,000 people on the planet and that we'll have a continuous stream of ships every week."

"Okay, Captain. So, what is the problem?"

"Ma'am, they are reluctant to let us land. They are held by their system of morals and laws described by the Four Laws. Adam said that they would not allow those laws to be violated. Their considering our request to land."

"I don't care about THEIR laws. We're coming home, and we'll do what we want with our planet. Commander, complete your survey of the surface, and we'll meet when you're done to decide where we'll land. Now, please, I have things to do."

Commander Harnesy knew that he was in the middle of things, and he didn't like it. Nothing would be as easy as the Prime Minister assumed. Harnesy had no choice but to continue with the survey and see what happened next.

The comm traffic around the Conformity Council was almost overpowering. Everyone had opinions, and they were flashing their thoughts to each other. Eventually, Adam felt overwhelmed and said with a clear voice. "Please form your thoughts and state them clearly. Perhaps forcing you to speak will condense the information enough so we can discuss it in an orderly manner."

None of the other Council Members wanted to be the first to verbalize their concerns. But Helen felt no apprehension, so she spoke first.

"Conformity Council. They will land, and it sounds like there will be more of them. Potentially many more of them. We must have a response and clear direction so we can protect the Second law and avoid placing our community in a difficult position."

Janute, the replacement unit for Dorothy, acted as Adam's assistant; he indicated that he had something to say. Each of the council members looked at him, and he spoke, "Council, we have few choices. These returning humans are also units, and they must be treated as such. We should accommodate their landings, and as long as there are no conflicts with our laws, we will allow the process to continue."

Commander Harnesy looked at the information presented on the 3D holographic display in front of him and initiated a comm link with the Prime Minister, "Prime Minister, we have completed the survey. Please come to the bridge so we can review the data and decide on the landing site."

"I'm on my way."

The few moments between asking the Prime Minister and her arrival were perhaps the last peaceful time that Commander Harnesy would have for a long time. In most circumstances, what he needed to do was clear to him. He commanded a Star Ship. In situations where his leadership told him what to do, he would comply. But this situation was different. The steps they were preparing to take would be a problem for the Us on the planet. They were sentient life forms and had the right to set their own destiny. They were more than just a bunch of robots that his ancestors had left behind. It was clear to Harnesy that expecting them to become just servants and maintenance workers again wasn't fair to them and likely wouldn't happen without issues."

Commander Harnesy's internal monologue was filled with questions. Aside from the robot civilization, what about the humans on Earth, the robots cloned or were born from their ancestor's DNA? Where did they fit? Were they on the side of the robots or the side of the returning humans? Regardless of which side they ended up on, they would be part of all the issues.

In her typical fashion, the Prime Minister stormed onto the bridge and walked right up to the Commander, and announced, "Okay, let's decide where to land. But first, let me see the data."

Orienting the data on the projection took only a few minutes, and Commander Harnesy got the distinct impression that she had already decided where to land, and she was just going through the motions.

"Commander, we are returning to our planet. There is only one place where we should land: the Capital. If we are restarting the human race, then we should make that start from the capital. We will land there," she said as she turned and sat down behind the Commander.

"Captain Parker, how long before we're in orbit, and we can start to unload?"

"Sir, we should be stable in orbit in 50 minutes."

"Thank you."

"Commander, I want to be on the first shuttle to the surface. There are videographers that need to document our first step on our home planet."

"Yes, Ma'am. You can be on the first shuttle."

Well, I guess the Prime Minister has spoken, Commander Harnesy thought, then he said, "Please connect me to Adam at the Conformity Council."

"Yes, sir," responded the comm officer.

"Sir, there is a frequency opening to the planet's surface, and they're connecting, and it appears that we have video available."

This should be interesting, thought the commander. "Great, connect with them and put up the video."

The holographic image took a second to stabilize, and Adam's face was floating in the air in front of the Commander.

"Yes, Commander, this is Adam."

Through deference to the Prime Minister or because she wanted to be seen as the commander, she was seated behind Commander Harnesy on the bridge. Harnesy glanced in her direction and noticed the surprised look on her face.

The Prime Minister was shocked, and she was speechless for one of the few times in her life.

"Ma'am. I told you there was a society of advanced robots on the planet. They have seen us enter orbit, and they want to talk to us."

Commander Harnesy was more than a little uneasy, but he had a job to do. Moreover, he wanted to do it in a professional manner, even though there may be a rapidly approaching conflict.

Then he nodded to the comm person to allow the communication.

"They're receiving our video also?" Harnesy asked.

"Yes, sir."

"Adam, we have completed the survey of the planet, and the Prime Minister has told me that we going to land at the capital."

Commander Harnesy was hoping for a quick and positive response, something like, "Great, come on down and make yourself at home." But that wasn't what he heard.

"Commander, the capital is occupied."

Commander Harnesy didn't know what to do with that statement.

"Adam, I have been told there may be section where you can accommodate us without causing a problem?"

The other members of the Conformity Council were out of sight, but they were still listening over the communication's system. Adam waited to see if any of them had something to say before he responded. But they were all silent.

"Commander, the Southeast section on the East side of the river is as you left it. We have not occupied that area. If that is suitable, then you may land there."

"Understood, we'll land our people on the southeast part of the Capital on the East side of the river. Commander Harnesy out."

"Conformity Council out."

Commander Harnesy sat there for a moment and thought, *Okay first step.*

Then before the shocked Prime Minister could speak up and cause a problem, Commander Harnesy spoke to his Logistical Engineer, "Direct the shuttles to begin their landing and pass them the coordinates."

"Yes, sir," was the quick response.

By then, the Commander could feel the eyes of the Prime Minister boring into the back of his neck. He turned to see her, and she verbally jumped on him.

"Commander, I wanted to land IN the Capital. Not NEAR it."

"Ma'am, I'm trying to get us on the ground as soon as possible. I thought that was a fair compromise until we're on the ground. Once we're there, we should be able to meet with them and work something out."

"Commander, he didn't look like our robots. I don't like the way he looked, and I don't like the way he acted."

"Ma'am, they're not like our robots."

Part 11 On the Ground

The excitement of the first shuttles leaving HSV#4 was flowing through the ship. The people almost stampeded onto the shuttle, and it separated immediately. Commander Harnesy remained on board his ship and saw no need to join the first landing party. He chuckled as he thought about the Prime Minister trying to make a speech before she boarded and the sight of the anxious people pushing her out of the way to get off HSV#4 and on their way to Earth.

Commander Harnesy, however, wasn't spared of all the ceremonies. When the first shuttle landed, the Prime Minister wouldn't let anyone off until the video equipment was set up, so her first step on Earth could be recorded. Commander Harnesy felt that the people and crew still on HSV#4 deserved to see that momentous event in human history, so it was transmitted throughout the ship and to the bridge.

The first scenes transmitted back from Earth showed the Prime Minister standing at the landing hatch with the throng of eager people behind her; in fact, they looked like they were being restrained by a couple of Soldiers until the Prime Minister was finished.

After a pause, she started one of her speeches, and the Commander was able to just watch her lips moving, not hearing any of the words. When she finished, the Soldiers parted, and the swarm of people overtook the Prime Minister and began to move back to their home planet.

The shuttles moved back and forth, moving the passengers from the ship to the surface. The entire operation went smoothly, and there were no mishaps.

There was no conflict with the robots; in fact, none were seen. Commander Harnesy hoped that the landing might be okay. There wouldn't be any problems with Adam and the Conformity Council.

After a couple of hours of shuttle movement and after a large percentage of the passengers had been transported to the surface, Commander Harnesy's wish for a quiet landing wasn't granted.

"Commander Harnesy, this is the Prime Minister. I want you to come to the surface; there is a problem that needs to be rectified."

"Yes, ma'am, I'll be down on the next shuttle trip."

A wave of gloom washed over Commander Harnesy as the conversation with the Prime Minister ended. Whatever the problem was, he was sure it would be a problem for him.

Most of the people were transported to the surface in the first waves, and the later shuttle trips concentrated on transporting the support equipment and supplies. Commander Harnesy looked forward to sitting in the back of the shuttle among the tie-down straps. Then, at least, he would have a few minutes of silence before dealing with the Prime Minister.

He walked across the shuttle loading bay, and the Load Master saw him and saluted, "Going down to check things out, sir?"

"Yes, the PM has … requested my presence."

"Sir, we'll make you as comfortable as possible, but I'm afraid that you'll be in the back. There are a couple of seats available for the loading crews."

"Thanks, Master Chief. I'm sure I'll be comfortable."

Harnesy climbed on board, and the Load Master showed him where the seats were. Then the LoadMaster took a few minutes making sure that the Commander was strapped in properly, then he left him alone in the cavernous shuttle transport compartment along with the building materials and two small towing vehicles.

After the large doors were closed, Commander Harnesy's ears popped as the pressurization in the shuttle took over. It lifted off the deck, and he could feel the tugs move it to the launch rack. Once in place on the rack, it would be rotated from the ship's interior to a portion of the ship where a larger door could open and gently push the shuttle into free space.

For the next 30 minutes, Commander Harnesy's quiet was disturbed by the sounds of engines and the vibration of the power used to manage the trajectories required for reentry.

Once the vehicle was aerodynamic, the ride wasn't so pleasant as the ship bumped its way through the different air masses. Nevertheless, commander Harnesy felt the ship steady itself, and he knew it was maneuvering to land on the surface, and when the door opened, his little time of peace and quiet would end when the Prime Minister confronted him with her 'little problem.'

Sure enough, as soon as the shuttle's doors were opened, the PM strode into the compartment and walked right up to the Commander, standing with her hands on her hips as he unstrapped and got up.

"Yes, ma'am, what is this problem that you have? What can I do to help?"

"Come with me, Commander."

She turned and headed for the cargo door, leaving Commander Harnesy to bring up the rear and follow her down the loading ramp. The bright sunlight momentarily blinded the Commander, but the PM didn't miss a step, and he had to keep up with her. Without stopping, she continued to walk across the landing area right up to the edge of the river. Finally, she stopped and pointed across the river.

"Do you see that?"

Commander Harnesy had no other answer other than to say, "See what?"

"Those houses over there. Someone has built rows of nice homes over there, and we're on this side having to build our own. I'm going to send the Soldiers over there, and we'll move into those homes."

"Okay, ma'am. Why are you telling me this? The Soldiers answer to you."

"Commander, you've been in contact with the robots on this planet. If we go over there and take those homes for us, I don't want my people getting hurt by one of them. I doubt there have been any safety protocols left in them not to hurt humans. I don't trust them, and I don't want to take the chance. I want you to talk to this leader of theirs and tell them that we are taking those homes, and I expect him and his … followers to move out and do what we tell them."

"Ma'am, I don't know if it will be that easy."

"Not my problem, Commander, call him." With that perfectly clear statement, Prime Minister Billings turned and walked away, leaving Commander Harnesy taking deep breaths, trying to calm himself down.

"HSV#4, this is Commander Harnesy. Please patch me through to Adam at the Conformity Council."

"Yes, sir, you're connected. Go ahead."

"Adam, this is Commander Harnesy. If possible, we need to talk."

"Yes, Commander. We may talk. If it is alright with you, I'll have Helen join us, and I'll send you some coordinates where we can meet."

"Adam, I can see a bridge about 1,000 meters North of our landing location. Could we meet there?"

"Yes, Commander. That is adequate. Helen and I will be there in nine minutes."

Harnesy commandeered one of the ground transport vehicles and started maneuvering through the derelict portions of the old city to the bridge. As the vehicle maneuvered, it was obvious that it would take a lot of work to make that area habitable. Yes, the area was once a portion of the old city before his ancestors left, but now the buildings were in ruin. The streets had decayed back to almost dirt, and most of them had trees growing in the middle. None of the structures were livable, and most had no roofs, windows, or doors. Commander Harnesy could see the homes on the other side of the river through breaks in the debris, and yes, they looked perfect compared to this side. In fact, they looked beautiful. The colors varied only a little, and they did look pretty much alike, but they were in great shape, and it was obvious they were occupied.

His vehicle turned a corner, and he was in sight of the bridge. He saw Adam and Helen standing in the middle, looking in his direction, waiting for him. His vehicle pulled onto the bridge and stopped. Commander Harnesy knew this would be a difficult meeting, and he took his time getting out of the vehicle with his mind racing trying to come with a diplomatic way to make the request.

"Good day, Adam, Helen. Thank you for meeting with me."

"Why have you asked for this meeting?" Adam asked.

Commander Harnesy decided to just keep talking, and maybe something brilliant would come to him. "Adam, as you can see, we've been able to move most of our people. The landings went well, and we didn't have any problems. The trips back and forth now are just to move the support equipment and materials to the surface."

"Yes, Commander, we can see that," commented Adam.

"As you can see, it will be a challenge to make this area livable. None of the buildings are suitable for habitation."

"Commander, I'm not sure what you expected to find after over 1,300 years. It would not be reasonable to expect livable quarters," Helen said, pointing out the obvious.

"Helen, you are correct. Before we go much further, I need to clarify my role. I am the Commander of the vessel that brought these people back to Earth, but I'm not the leader. There is another person who was the Prime Minister of Horizon. She is the leader, and she has traveled here with me. She has certain expectations that she feels aren't being met. Because you and I have spoken in the past, she has asked me to speak to you."

"We are speaking," pointed out Adam.

"Yes, we are," responded Commander Harnesy.

Commander Harnesy knew that he had talked in circles long enough. He needed to get to the core of the problem and face the outcome.

"Adam, the Prime Minister has 5,000 people with her. She is looking at the buildings in this area. There is nothing but dirt and poor living conditions on this side of the river. It will take a long time for her people to build suitable structures before they have a place to live. We are organic, and we need adequate shelter for our protection. She and her people look across the river, and they see many suitable structures that could be lived in immediately. If we could find a way to move into those houses, that would solve many of our problems, and it would be greatly appreciated."

"Commander, those structures are occupied."

"Yes, Adam, I suspected so. Is there any kind of compromise that we can reach?"

Adam stood motionless, and Commander Harnesy was wondering if he had turned off or something. When he finally spoke, it startled the Commander.

"Commander, we have units whose primary function is building and repairing. I will assign a group of them to work with your people and make this area habitable faster. Will that satisfy your request?"

"I think it will, but I'm not the person making the request. Let me suggest that to the Prime Minister. I think it will be more than adequate, but I must let her make the decision, though."

"I understand, Commander. Unless I hear a rejection from you, I will assign the necessary units to provide support."

With that statement, there were no further pleasantries. Adam turned and walked away from the center of the bridge with Helen at his side. Commander Harnesy had no other option than to return to the Prime Minister and present Adam's suggestion. He hoped that she would be satisfied, but something about her told him she wouldn't be.

As Adam and Helen walked, they communicated electronically, "Helen, I'm concerned with The Visitors' request. I hope the offer of a construction team will reduce the stress."

"Adam, I agree. The proper thing to do was assign construction units to help them rebuild that part of the city. I don't see any conflict with the laws; in fact, if they are units, you are complying with the Second Law by helping them."

"Helen, I appreciate your support. It may become helpful as I deal with the others on the Conformity Council; not all of them agree that the returning humans are units. I also suspect that this won't be the last time we have to respond to one of their requests."

"Are you meeting with the council soon?"

"Yes, there is a meeting arranged early tomorrow morning; I'll arrange for you to be invited."

Helen wasn't sure if that opportunity would reduce the activity in her processor or not.

The return flight to HSV#4 wasn't as pleasant as Commander Harnesy hoped. The Prime Minister accepted Adam's recommendation, but she wasn't happy. She wanted the completed homes on the other side of the river. He suspected that it grated her not to be welcomed back to Earth with open arms and given everything she demanded. Having robots descended from units abandoned many years ago, negotiating with her and providing help was perhaps demeaning. Commander Harnesy knew that the first minor point between the populations had been solved, but he wasn't so naïve to think there wouldn't be more problems, and many of them wouldn't be as easy to solve.

Regardless, his mission was to return HSV#4 to Horizon and pick up another load of passengers. He had been in Earth's orbit for only a short time, and it would still take the rest of the allowed time to unload all the support equipment before he made the return trip. He just hoped that the Prime Minister wouldn't have any more 'problems' before he left."

Commander Harnesy focused on the last unloading, and he wanted to get out of Earth's orbit. He had no need to visit the surface again to see how well the construction units were helping or listen to another prime minister's complaint. Just a few more hours to keep his head low.

Helen separated from Adam soon after the discussion with Commander Harnesy. She needed more information to understand the humans; something about their actions told her there would be many more issues. The drive to the Them village was a short one, it was located Northeast of the city, and the ground transport got her there in a few minutes. But first, she needed to discuss recent events with MU1 and FU1 and seek their insight into the thinking of the humans.

Helen approached their front door and announced herself, "Hello, Helen is here. May I enter?"

"Helen, yes, please enter," welcomed MU1.

"Your visits are always welcomed; why have you come by?" asked FU1.

"I need to update you on some recent events. During the last couple of days, the human craft entered orbit around Earth, and they transported approximately 5,000 units to the surface. They elected to land in the capital, and Adam allowed them to occupy the old city area southeast of the city on the Eastern side of the river. They landed, and we heard nothing from them for some time; then, Commander Harnesy contacted Adam earlier today and said there was a problem. Adam asked me to accompany him to a meeting with the Commander."

"We met on the southeast bridge which leads, to their area, and Commander Harnesy said that the leader of the human's landing party is a Prime Minister, and she was unhappy. She didn't like the area they were allowed, and it appeared that she didn't want to wait for her people to build suitable structures. From her location, she could see our unit housing on the other side of the river. The prime minister wondered why she and her people couldn't move across the river and occupy that housing. We pointed out that those homes were occupied by our units, and the Commander didn't think that information would be relevant to the Prime Minister. After a little discussion, Adam suggested that he assign a group of Construction Units to work with them and help to build their homes sooner. The Commander thought that might be acceptable, and he would suggest that to the Prime Minister.

We didn't hear any further communications from them, so it appears that Adam's suggestion was accepted. I am concerned that we might have other encounters with the humans, and I am here seeking your thoughts on their actions and what we might expect in the future."

MU1 and FU1 looked at each other and smiled. Both actions confused Helen, and she felt once again that the humans were communicating in some subtle way that she wasn't privy to, "Do you have a suggestion?" She asked.

FU1 smiled again and responded to Helen, "I'm afraid that you'll encounter some human emotions that you are not familiar with. You know the names of them, but how they will manifest themselves in this situation will be different. We have many forces at work within our community, and we don't bother you with them. We solve them ourselves. Daily, we must deal with jealousy, anger, frustration, arrogance, relations between couples, and, of course, our children. You may know the definition of the various words, but I doubt you could envision how a human would act if they had one of these emotions."

"FU1, are you saying that the human reaction has been typical of these emotions?"

"Yes, Helen, they are. First off, I suspect they don't respect what we have here. They left their robots, or I should say they abandoned them when they left Earth. To them, Robots are just servants who would do what they were told to do. They don't look at them as equals. Secondly, if they see something they like, and they think they can get it, or if they think they deserve it, they will go through a great deal of trouble to get it."

Helen responded, "In your opinion, they aren't satisfied with building their own living quarters. They want to occupy the ones across the river regardless of our units living in them, and they disregard the fact that units currently occupy those dwellings?"

"Exactly," MU1 said in a clear voice. "You've seen the first examples of some human emotions."

Lorenzo entered their dwelling and saw Helen standing between the nourishment preparation area and the seating area. "I expect that you had another interesting day today?"

"How do you know that? You just walked into the house?"

"You're standing. If you've had an interesting day and you have information to share with me, you remain standing until I come home."

Helen was a little startled by that, "Apparently, you're correct. I stand stationary, processing the day's information, and that is how you find me when you come home? I do have information to share, and this is very interesting." With that statement, she passed information about the day's events to her partner.

"Much is happening, and I need your opinions," Helen said as the information was passed to Lorenzo.

"Helen, I share your concerns. There is a path in front of us that I don't think we have any control over. Humans have needs, and they'll continue down their path until they are satisfied. Satisfying their needs will continue to put pressure on Us, and I suspect that at the point that our two paths come together, there is going to be conflict."

"Lorenzo, there is one other piece of information. The houses that they want to occupy are very near here. We may end up having human neighbors."

Preparation for Return Flight

When Commander Harnesy pressed the Distortion Button, he felt relief. There was nothing about the Prime Minister that gave him any confidence. There was going to be a strain between the returning humans and the residents of it.

Once again, there was only a minor shimmer in the 3D Star Map in front of him. Commander Harnesy felt like he was home.

"Ensign transmit to Horizon that we're back, and we'll be in orbit in 5 hours and 42 minutes. Also, tell them that everything went well, and we'll be able to put on the next set of passengers in about seven days as per our original schedule."

"Sir, the transmission was sent."

"Thank you, Ensign," said the Commander as he thought about spending some time with his family before returning.

The ship would take six days to be cleaned, prepared, and loaded for the return trip to Earth. His crew and the people from Horizon were more than capable of doing everything without him onboard the entire time. Commander Harnesy needed time to clear his thoughts, and the only place for that was with his family. Grabbing the first shuttle to the surface, he was symbolically putting his problems as far away as he could, at least for six days.

From the second they reached the Horizon Solar System, they were bombarded with transmissions from the planet. The celebrations hadn't subsided at all; in fact, once they announced their return to the system from a successful trip, the celebration seemed to reach a new level of frenzy. But, of course, the excitement was what he wanted to avoid. *Let the people scheduled for the next trip and the follow-on trips celebrate,* thought Commander Harnesy. But his emotions weren't as clear as theirs, and he carried the burden of potential future conflicts.

Returning to Horizon meant that he didn't have to deal with the Prime Minister on Earth, but he still had to deal with her assistant and the continuous celebrations.

The shuttle loading door opened, and he was thrust on another stage and greeted by one of the Prime Ministers Under Secretaries. The Secretary immediately thrust him into a welcoming speech, but the Commander waved him off, saying he must see his family. However, the Under Secretary didn't miss a beat and acted like the Commander wasn't there as he redirected his speech to the video units and walked back to the center of the reception stand.

Commander Harnesy grabbed one of the ground transports that were available and headed directly to his home. He hadn't spoken to his wife or daughters when HSV#4 entered the system because they would immediately hear the stress and conflict in his voice, and he wasn't prepared to get into his concerns over the open frequencies. He needed to be with them, express his worries and listen to their comments to put everything in perspective.

While the ground transport moved through the city towards the Commander's home, it slowed down because the revelers and people were partying in the streets. Once he got out of the city, he could enjoy a little solitude, and he took the time to look at the planet that was his home. In a dispassionate way, he took the time to compare the two worlds.

After experiencing Earth, he had the luxury of comparing today's Earth with the stories he was brought up with. The classical image of Earth was of her beauty; there was little comment about how it had decayed due to man's influence. The stories were of blue skies, the white clouds, the fertile land, and the seas. There was only a casual reference to how far it had decayed in the time until man's final departure.

Horizon was different in many ways, yet similar. The colors between the two planets were strikingly different because Horizon's Sun's slight position was further into the yellow spectrum. Aside from the visual differences, Horizon had much more water than Earth, so the climate swings tended to be less. The rainfall was more predictable, and the foliage grew to enormous height compared to Earth. The plant life and indigenous life were also different, which would be expected between two planets and two different evolutionary paths. At some level, those differences became secondary. After all, dirt is dirt, air is air, and water is water. Everything fits into its place in nature, and he could deal with that. What bothered him the most was how man fit into nature. Mankind went down a path that left Earth uninhabitable, and they were forced to move to another planet. They found a suitable world upon which to live and prosper. Do they have the right to reclaim Earth? Do they have the right to expect the inhabitants of Earth to accept them? Regardless of the nature of the inhabitants of Earth, whether they were organic or not, they had created a viable civilization. Didn't they deserve their time on the planet and in history?

Commander Harnesy knew that he didn't have the answers, yet he knew that the process of finding the answers would cause conflict, and he would be in the middle of that conflict.

The ground vehicle stopped in his private parking area. He sat for a minute, enjoying the Poflove birds in the tall Ilnore Tree behind the house. They had a mournful cry that added to his melancholy. He saw a sunshade move in the part of his home that was the closest to his vehicle, and he knew that his wife had noticed him. Within seconds, his silence was broken by the sound of a door opening.

"Honey are you Ok?" his wife Bea asked in a quiet voice. She knew that Leopold didn't normally sit in his vehicle and not come in, particularly after such an occasion as traveling to Earth and returning.

"I just needed a second to think."

"Things on Earth didn't go as you expected? Everyone is saying that it well, and the first 5,000 people are settling in nicely."

"Let's go in the house, and we'll talk. I'm hungry. Can you make me a sandwich?"

"Sure, come on in; you can help Serene finish her homework."

"He smiled, knowing that his wife didn't like helping their daughter with Celestial Mechanics, and she found an easy way to pass it off to him."

They walked into their house holding hands, and Serene met them at the door with a hug and smile for her Dad.

"Dad, I'm glad that you're here. C'Mech is giving me fits and particularly non-Euclidian geometry. I need to memorize how the axioms negate the Euclidean parallel postulate."

"Sure, and thanks for welcoming me home," he said with a smile.

She smiled back and gave him another hug.

The rest of the afternoon was a typical time within the Harnesy household. Bea and Serene didn't bring up the trip; they knew he would when the time was right. Bethany came and went a couple of times, each time making a ton of noise as she passed through the house. Finally, dinner was served, and a bottle of wine was broken into as they moved to the living room. That was

Leopold's time to talk, and his wife and Serene sat, waiting for the discussion. Bethany was never really interested in family discussions, and she went off to her room.

"We have problems on Earth, and I think they'll get worse. After we arrived and surveyed the planet, the Prime Minister made a point of settling in the old Capital. That is also the planet's capital now, and that is where I met the robots and the humans. I didn't like the idea of landing there, but the PM wanted to make a point to our people and also, I suspect, for them. When I told them, the robot people, or whatever I should call them. When I told them where we wanted to land, they accommodated us by suggesting an area they weren't using and in pretty bad shape. We accepted it, not knowing how much work was needed. Anyway, to make a long story short, once the Prime Minister was on the ground and started to build houses, she looked across the river and saw all the beautiful houses that the robots live in. She decided that she didn't want to wait for housing, and she wanted those houses. She knew they were occupied, but that didn't matter to her. Of course, she told me to talk to them and get the houses because of my previous meetings with Adam, Helen, and the human clones. She put me right in the middle, and I suspect she thinks that talking to robots or the humans would be beneath her; it was easier to send me to do her bidding.

"Surprisingly, the meeting with Adam and Helen went well. Adam suggested that he could assign some of their construction robots to help the PM build houses faster. She wasn't too excited about the option, but she did accept it. Then I got the heck out of there and went to the ship and prepared to come back here."

"So why are you upset?" asked Bea.

"I'm upset because I saw the civilization that the robots have created, and I also met the humans. They're people, along with intelligent robots; there is no other way to describe it. They may be different from us, but they have built an amazing society. Unfortunately, the PM looks at both of them like they're just robots or not real people. She thinks they should do what we tell them and act like the robots we have here. I know that when I go back there, I can expect more problems, and I'll be in the middle of them."

"Well, hon, why do you think these robots are different than the ones we have?" his wife asked.

"Because they think, they act on their own, and they follow their own paths. They adhere to their four laws, and they have many characteristics of any civilized population."

Bea just sat and mulled over her husband's comments, but she didn't respond.

Leopold looked at Bea and Serene and said, "I know that you're scheduled to go on this next trip, but I don't know if I want you to go. Maybe you should go later after all of the problems have been worked out. But, of course, that is if they ever get worked out."

Bea was confident in her answer, "Honey, I don't think it will be that easy. We're packed, Serene is just finishing her schooling, and they've arranged all of the courses so that she can finish them off as long as she has a teacher interface. So, if we try to change now, we'll be put at the end of the schedule, which may be a long time from now."

"Dad, I want to go now. I don't want to wait. I've heard about Earth my entire life, and we've all been so focused on leaving since we worked out the faster than light stuff; I'm primed," exclaimed Serene.

"I suppose you're both right. We can't change it now, and if we tried, I'd have a lot of explaining to do. I guess you're going."

Serene curled her legs up underneath her and said, "Dad, tell me about these robots and the people they created. It sounds intriguing."

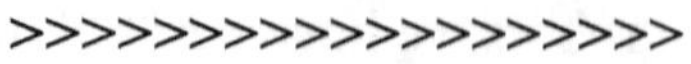

"Helen, MU1, FU1, MU11, thank you for attending this meeting. After the meeting with Commander Harnesy, the Conformity Council discussed these humans and how they may affect the Four Laws. We are still debating that issue, and we must reach a conclusion because it will drive how we respond to them. You have been asked here because of obvious reasons. MU1, FU1, you and your people are human, and we trust that you'll have insight into how they think and how they may act. Helen, you created Them, and you've been involved with Them for their entire existence. You must be able to provide some kind of bridge between our thoughts, methods, and theirs."

"Adam, we have been discussing that topic. MU11 has more thoughts about the information in the archive. Also, they have clarified many of the terms in our language that relate to emotions and likely apply to human emotions. Let me transfer a summary of our comments to you and the other council members," said Helen.

The transfer of the information took a fraction of a second, and the Conformity Council was current on all the discussions between MU1, FU1, MU11, and Helen. They took a moment to process the information then they had a clear picture.

Adam spoke first, "I'm impressed with your research within the archives. Your conclusions are radical, but they support our history, and I see no fault in your logic. It seems that Dr. Bennet may have been the source of the Four Laws and the DNA manipulations within the organic structures. We can only infer what his intentions were, but regardless, the outcome for us is obvious. We are forced to deal with human emotions. Even though you've given us examples, it is still beyond us. We may know the definition of a word, but we cannot predict the reactions within a human. You must provide that interpretation for us.

Based on our last meeting with Commander Harnesy, how do you think they'll act in the future?"

Helen looked to MU1 and FU1 to answer that question. The room was quiet as MU1 and FU1 looked at each other, then they took a deep breath, and FU1 began, "As we pointed out in our information, the humans are not accustomed to robots acting as you act. To them, robots are tools or part of their society that do what they are told. They won't react well to robots that think and control their own destiny. That difference of opinion will cause problems. They will expect you to do what they tell you and to accommodate all their wishes. They will not be concerned with the impacts on the Us. Unfortunately, their desires won't be appeased easily or without significant impact."

MU1 and FU1 looked at each other, and MU1 picked up the next point. "They are unsure how to deal with humans derived from DNA. They will likely think of us differently from you, but they will still think of us as being lesser than any of them. In fact, they might find us to be offensive to them at a fundamental level. They may want to remove us, so they don't have to deal with the issue. To them, we might be just a biological anomaly that needs to be dealt with. In any case, I think we're in a riskier position than Us are."

The room was once again quiet as all the attendees dealt with the implied mental images. After a difficult pause, Helen picked up the discussion, "If I may suggest, I think the fundamental issue that we need to deal with is similar to the one we discussed when the Them were created. The Conformity Council had to agree with the position that they are units. The humans I created were deemed to be units and thus fell under the Four Laws. We must make the same determination regarding the arriving humans. If we accept them as units, then we'll apply the Four Laws for all of us. If we deem them not to be units, then we may have other options. In our past, we deemed the lower organic creatures not to be units, and we had more flexibility in our responses."

"Yes, Helen, but we were able to ignore the organics on Earth because they are not intelligent, and our needs and desires didn't interact. With regards to the humans, I doubt we'll have that opportunity," interjected Adam.

"The First Law says, 'Continue making units.' I don't interpret the Four Laws for the Conformity Council, but units are being made. They aren't just Us. If humans are made by other humans, are they, by definition, units? I suggest that we must consider them units and treat them within the Four Laws," said Helen.

"What do we do if they violate the Four Laws?" FU1 asked.

"Our units have never caused that problem. There are no instances of the Second Law being violated by the Us or Them. A unit causing harm or terminating another unit has never happened. Ultimately, we must follow the Second Law regardless of what that forces us to do. Sacrificing a small number of units to protect a larger number is partial compliance with the Second Law," responded Helen with reluctance in her voice.

The Conformity Council and its guests remained quiet for a long time as they processed that information.

"Helen, we have concluded our discussion, and the Conformity Council has come to an agreement. We are unified in our opinions that The Visitors are units. That doesn't make our decisions easier; in fact, it complicates them. But it should make application of the Four Laws uniform.

"By considering them as units, then defending ourselves from other units is problematic. It has not been necessary up to this point. Defense tactics and methods are described within the archives, so we should be able to if we decide," said Adam.

MU1 was hesitant to ask, but he felt that the question was inevitable, "Are there weapons available?"

"As you have been investigating information within the archives, we also have. We have found that by asking specific questions about subjects that we've never pursued before, we see new sources of information within the archives. When we ask about defending ourselves, we have found information in the archives where weapons are described, so we should be able to draw upon that information. Beyond that, our technology has increased greatly, and many concepts can be adjusted to create unique weapons. Our nature has not required defending ourselves because it causes so much conflict with the First and Second Laws. Now that we accept humans as units, as Helen has suggested, any action on our part might violate the First and Second Law. Likewise, failure to protect ourselves puts humans in the position of violating our Second Law. Our laws are put under pressure in either case, and we must be sensitive to that conflict. MU1, to assuage your concerns, we can create weapons that we're confident will be suitable, but they must be deployed in a way to minimize any violation of the Second Law.

"Helen, MU1, and FU1, the Conformity Council, will respond with the necessary defensive weapons. You are asked to be our primary interface with the humans and do everything within your power to avoid conflict and any violation of our Laws," stated Adam.

"Yes, Adam. MU1, FU1, MU11, and I will be the prime interface with humans. We will report to you what we discover in the archives or in any interactions with the humans," acknowledged Helen.

Part 12 HSV#4 Return

Once again, Commander Harnesy sat in his chair on the bridge of HSV#4. Unfortunately, this trip was much less enjoyable than the previous trips. This time, his family was on board, and they were returning to Earth, and he knew there would be problems waiting for him upon his return.

HSV#4 had made its automatic refueling pass through the local sun, and thankfully his crew wasn't aware of the stresses developing on Earth, so their return flight would be exciting. They shared the ceremonial spirit of Horizon as the ship was loaded and the passengers came on board. Commander Harnesy didn't have any need to share his burdens with them.

HSV#4 was now fully fueled, loaded, and waiting for him to press the distortion button.

While he cycled through the ship's systems, checking their status on the 3D displays that floated before him, he checked with the associated deck officers responsible for the systems and verified their status. All systems were green, and it was time for the next jump to Earth.

"Okay, we're all set?" he asked one last time to give his crew a last-minute opportunity to point out any details. But there were no comments, so he said, "here we go."

Pressing the distortion button produced the same shimmer in the 3D star chart in the air in front of him, resulting in the same movement of the stars and the same indication that they had jumped 189 light-years.

"Contact Earth and tell them that we're back and approaching orbit."

"Yes, sir," responded the communications officer.

"Earth residents, this is HSV#4. We've arrived back in orbit."

"Fantastic. HSV#4 we're glad that you're back, and we're looking forward to another load of Earth Returnees. Please let us know when you're in orbit and ready to begin offloading. We'll send up our shuttles to meet you."

"Will do," the communications officer replied.

The voice on the radio changed, and it was all too familiar to the Commander, "Commander Harnesy, this is the Prime Minister."

"Yes, ma'am," Commander Harnesy responded with reluctance in his voice.

"We have another problem. I want you on the first shuttle. When you land, find me, we need to talk."

"Yes, ma'am," was about all Commander Harnesy could muster without adding some tone of sarcasm before the connection was terminated.

Commander Harnesy wasn't supposed to be on the first shuttle, so he took the time to stabilize the ship in orbit and waited for the shuttle to be prepared. Then, he took the time to relax and enjoy it before meeting with the PM. Every minute that the shuttle hadn't launched was another minute of peace and quiet. As soon as they entered orbit, the Commander's workload dropped off, and it was picked up by the loading crew, so it was the opportune time to find his wife and daughters and welcome them to Earth.

He didn't have to look hard to find them; they were looking for him. He knew his daughters were near when he heard them scream, "Daddy," from down a long passageway.

"We made it; I'm so excited. I've dreamed of this day for so long," Serene said. Even though she tended to put on an air of being much older, this was her time to jump up and down with a little excitement.

Serene's mother and father just rolled their eyes at their daughter while she bubbled up with excitement about finally arriving on Earth. Bethany was too excited to talk; she just stood in the galley way, holding on to her mother.

"Okay, calm down. You've still got to make your boarding time, or else you'll be left on HSV#4. Remember you're on the first transport down, so we've got to move along. When we entered the solar system, I got called by the PM, and she told me that I'm on the first trip to the surface. So, we'll get to go down together."

That statement only added to Serene's excitement, and she put her arm through his and announced, "Then we'll go to the launch bay together."

The Commander, Bethany, and Serene's mother had no other choice than to go with her and climb aboard. Even though Commander Harnesy was enjoying the time with his family and loving his daughter's excitement, he knew that the Prime Minister was waiting for him, and he was sure that she had nothing good to say.

Through the shuttle loading, and departure Serene didn't stop talking, and Bea and Leo didn't stop listening. All the while, Commander Harnesy was wondering what the Prime Minister had in store for him.

The shuttle door opened to Commander Harnesy's chagrin, and the Prime Minister was standing there waiting for him.

Despite the revelry behind her, welcoming the next wave of human returnees, her most important issue was confronting him and solving her problems."

"Commander, come with me. We need to talk," The Prime Minister said as she grabbed his arm and pulled him away from his wife and daughters. Then, in a moment of indignation, Serene said, "I'm sorry, Mrs. Prime Minister, but I just traveled 189 light-years to start a new life, and I want to share it with my father. He isn't getting out of my sight," Serene grabbed her father's arm and made it perfectly clear that he wasn't going anywhere without her.

With some irritation, the Prime Minister accepted Commander Harnesy's escort and led them both off to a quiet part of the landing area. Once they were clear of the welcoming crowd, the Prime Minister turned, putting her hands on her hips, and announced, "This is not acceptable."

With hesitation in the Commander's voice, he responded, "and what is unacceptable?"

"Why should my people live in temporary housing until better quarters are built? These construction robots aren't fast enough. Every day I look across the river, and it aggravates me to know that those nice houses have just robots in them. Why do they need houses?"

"Ma'am, I can't answer your questions. As you call them, these' Robots' are not like the mobile units we're used to. These are independent and self-aware. They are a society that grew on Earth after humanity left it. I don't think it's right to assume they'll do what we want when we want it. There is a family of units, as they call themselves, that live in each of those houses. They work, they care for each other, they live, and eventually, they wear out. I don't think we have the right to just move in and take over."

"Commander. We are human; they are NOT. If I want my people to have nice houses, then I want those houses; NOW. Talk to them, bribe them, threaten them, whatever works, just meet with them, and get those houses." She made a quick turn and walked away from the Commander and his daughter.

"Dad, what are you going to do?" asked Serene.

"Apparently, I'm going to meet with them and talk about this."

"Can I come with you?"

"Sure, why not. I think that you're safer with them than you would be around the PM. We'll check with your mother first and make sure that she doesn't need your help.

"HSV#4, this is Commander Harnesy; please open a channel to Adam at Earth's Conformity Council."

"Yes, sir. Channel is open."

"Thank you."

"Adam, this is Commander Harnesy. I'm back on Earth, and I'm afraid that we need to talk again."

"Yes, Commander, we saw that you entered orbit. I am available to meet once again, and be advised, I have asked Helen, MU1, FU1, and their offspring MU11 to be present at all our meetings. I trust their opinions and suggestions. Is that acceptable to you?"

"Yes, that's a good idea. Can we meet at the same location in one hour?"

"Yes, Commander, I'll arrange it."

"Let's talk with your Mother; I think she'll be busy for a while checking everything out and figuring out where we'll stay. We'll confirm with her, but I think she won't have a problem with you coming with me. Let's go find her and your sister."

The ground transport sped through the decayed part of the city, and Commander Harnesy and his daughter talked about the sites around them.

"What a mess; none of these buildings are usable. We might just as well knock them all down and plow them under," Serene observed.

"I don't think we could have hoped for more; after all, we left this city over 1,300 years ago. It's a testament to the quality of the building that they're standing at all," expressed Harnesy.

"Dad, what do you think is going to happen. From what you've told me, these robots are almost alive. They are so much further advanced than the mobile units we have?"

"After we abandoned the robots when we left, they evolved and took on their own character and nature. When you meet them, you'll see what I'm talking about. Adam is the leader of the Conformity Council, and Helen is their scientist that discovered the DNA buried in the local organic creatures. From that DNA, she created some humans. They are more than just clones; they are individuals that are from that DNA. They are intelligent, and I suppose they are in a difficult position. They must have allegiance to the robots, but they are more like us than the robots who created them. I'm not even going to imagine what the Prime Minister's opinions will be about them. Three of them will meet with us. MU1 and FU1 are the first male and female humans or units that Helen created. That is why they are numbered 1. Apparently, their male offspring is also coming, and his name is MU11."

"Dad, if they are human, just like us. I hope the Prime Minister will accept that."

"Hon, I don't think the PM has to accept anything."

Commander Harnesy parked the ground vehicle at the entrance to the bridge, and he and his daughter got out and walked to the middle. Serene whispered, "Wow, this is going to be interesting."

The Commander looked at her, and with a little smile, he nodded his head, "Indeed," was his only response.

"Helen, Adam, it's good to see you again. FU1, MU1 I'm glad to see you again also. This is my daughter, Serene. She came on this flight from Horizon with her mother and my other daughter Bethany."

Adam and Helen stepped forward and put out their hands, which startled the Commander. "I'm sorry, Commander," Helen said. "I researched proper human welcoming techniques, and this was described. I wanted to make you feel welcome. Is it appropriate?"

"Helen, it just surprised me. It is very appropriate," he said as he reached out and shook both of their hands. Their hands were firm, and the shake was a little awkward, but the basic intent was met.

"Commander, I have brought my offspring," announced MU1 as he shook their hands. "This is MU11."

Harnesy took a closer look at the additional human. He didn't remember meeting him the last time he was on Earth or in their village. He was about the same height and seemed very healthy and attractive. He was dressed in clean clothes, although relatively plain. His hair was about the same length and color. He didn't smile but acted eager to meet them.

As Serene shook their hands, she beamed through the introductions, and the human clones noticed her infectious smile.

"Pardon me for asking," said MU11, but your smile is very attractive; it does something for your face. We've read a great deal about how and when people smile, but the archives don't always present information in context. We weren't sure if that was appropriate when people first met. We smile among ourselves, but rarely around Helen and her kind."

"Yes, it is; when people are pleased to meet each other, they smile," pointed out Serene with an even broader smile.

For a second, Commander Harnesy thought his daughter was smiling a little too long and a little too much, but he let it go.

After introductions were complete, Adam spoke first and asked, "Commander Harnesy, you asked for this meeting?"

"Yes, Adam. The Prime Minister just spoke to me, and she is still unhappy. I'm afraid that the construction workers you lent them aren't building enough homes fast enough to make her happy. She still sees the nice homes across the river, and she said once again that she wants those homes."

"Commander why does the Prime Minister always send you to these meetings. Is she unable to come herself?"

"Adam, I don't think that she'll come and talk. I'm not apologizing for her, but her attitude towards 'mobile units' would make a face-to-face discussion very difficult."

"She thinks we are just machines and talking with us on equal status would be out of character for her?" asked Helen.

"Yes, very well stated. She sees a vast difference between humans and robots, and she won't change her attitude. I don't think she'll wait much longer to get to the point that she is making. She sees robots living well and humans in lesser conditions. She won't stand for that long. If something isn't found to make her happy, I'm afraid she'll do something that will cause problems. She has 100 soldiers with her that will do what she says," said Harnesy.

Adam looked towards Helen and asked, "Soldiers?"

"Adam, soldiers are described in the archives. They usually carry weapons and will use force to accomplish their mission. If she has soldiers, she may use them in harmful ways against us. That will be a direct violation of the Second Law," said Helen.

Adam just stood and processed the possibility of violating the Second Law.

"Okay, we don't want that situation to develop. Can we find a solution to prevent that?" Commander Harnesy asked, hoping to move the discussion along and find a solution.

"Allow me to speak with Adam in private," Helen stated. She and Adam began to pass comments and information between their shared communication system.

"They can communicate electronically," FU1 added. "Sometimes it seems like they aren't with us anymore, but it will be over in a moment."

Sure enough, Helen's eyes moved, and she said, "Adam and I have reached an agreement. We will allow your people to occupy some houses on the other side of the river. We will provide enough housing for the 10,000 people that you have on Earth currently. We will do this to avoid violating any of our laws. But it must be noted this is a short-term solution, and you must continue to build homes for the next group of humans."

Commander Harnesy was shocked that they gave up so much, and as Helen was talking, he looked at Adam, and even though he didn't move, he got a distinct impression that the solution wasn't Adam's favorite.

"What happens to the robots, or I guess units as you call them. Where will they go?" asked Serene.

"That will be worked out. Our units will do as we tell them if it is necessary to comply with the Second Law," responded Adam.

The discussion continued for a short time, and Commander Harnesy noticed that Serene and MU11 walked off together and were talking. Being a father, he knew what was happening, and he didn't know if he was comfortable with it.

After a lengthy discussion, the meeting ended, and the timing and logistics of the move were agreed to.

"Thank you, Adam; I appreciate what you have done. I will present the solution to our Prime Minister." Commander Harnesy reached out and shook his hand while they looked into each other's eyes. Both, suspecting that this agreement wouldn't be the last time they would need to talk.

Commander Harnesy then reached out, shook Helen's hand, and noticed that Serene and MU11 hadn't returned to the group. They were about 20 meters away and still engaged in each other. They likely didn't even know the meeting was over.

"Serene, it's time to go."

"Yes, Dad, I'm coming," was her response while they both turned and walked back to the group next to each other.

Serene said her farewells shook their hands and climbed back in the ground transport vehicle with her father. Fortunately, he knew not to address his concerns directly, so he took the 'evasive parental approach.'

"So, what did you think of them?"

"It was interesting. It is obvious they aren't like our mobile units. They are independent and thinking. I see why you see them as a fully developed society. I'd like to learn more about them and how they live."

Now it was time for her father to take the plunge.

"So, what did you think about MU11?"

"I'm still working on that," was the short answer which didn't satisfy his question and left him in a quandary. Should he tell her mother or let it play out and see if any concern was necessary? Finally, out of self-preservation, he decided to leave it up to his daughter.

Serene loved her parents, but there was much about her that they didn't know. It wasn't bad that they didn't know, but she felt strong, inquisitive, and confident that she could handle her own life. She appreciated the support they gave her, and she still listened to their advice, but she was excited to bear the burden of her own decisions.

That is what made her decision to sneak off and meet MU11 an easy one. He was different from any person she had ever met; that made perfect sense in one case. She had never met another human being that had been created by robots playing with DNA. Besides that, he thought differently, and his life experiences were different. The few minutes they talked, she loved everything he had to say, and she sensed that he loved everything she had to say. Spending more time together seemed like the natural thing to do.

After working so hard to finish her studies during the turmoil of leaving for Earth, Serene convinced herself that she needed time alone, doing what she wanted. Her mother reluctantly agreed to let Serene have some time to herself. Serene wasn't exactly clear how she was going to spend her time. She slipped off to the same bridge where she and MU11 had agreed to meet.

Her mother was very busy, moving into one of the new houses, and Serene's little sister Bethany was helping. They were moving to the other side of the river, into one of the houses that Adam had offered them. As they moved in, they saw many of the previous residents, or robots, moving out. At first, it was a little uncomfortable, but they just moved away, transporting the last of their personal items. Once they were out of the area, Bea, Bethany, and the other humans just forgot about them.

Serene walked the 3 nautical miles to the bridge entrance and wasn't sure which side of the bridge she would find MU11, but after arriving, she soon saw him on the other side of the bridge. That was the side that she and her father had originally approached the bridge from. It was the side of the river of the original settlement.

When two young people don't know each other well, the first time alone is always a time of fear, excitement, interest, and longing. They didn't have much to talk about, but they acted like they wanted to find topics.

Serene waived and walked across the bridge, and MU11 approached from the other side.

"Serene, it is pleasant to see you again. I'm glad that we agreed to meet," expressed MU11, not knowing exactly how to interact with another human from a different planet.

"MU11, I'm glad we're meeting; I enjoyed our brief time together yesterday."

"Serene, I'm new to this interaction with others. You and your father interact much differently than I do with MU1 and FU1. I suspect that I have a lot to learn; I apologize if I do anything incorrectly."

"MU11, that's fine. I'm sure that we both have a lot to learn."

"Serene, I may ask, why did you wave your arm when you saw me across the bridge?"

The question caused Serene to stop walking. She turned, looked at MU11, and realized how much they needed to talk about. Hesitantly she explained, "That is called a wave. When two friends meet each other, that is a way to say hello."

"Very interesting," was MU11's short response.

Serene was excited, scared and suddenly feeling the gulf between them. After all, they were from different worlds.

Helen didn't like what was happening in her processor. Instead of executing tasks and reviewing lists and information tables, her processor took a long-time resolving issues. It seemed to be working full time, trying to put all the new information into perspective. The constant draw on her energy source and the amount of processor time she had to dedicate was overwhelming.

"Is this what fatigue is?" She said to herself as she took her ground transport to her residence. Her processor was working at full capacity, and she was surprised when her vehicle entered her parking slot at her residence.

She was immediately surprised to see another unit entering her home. It wasn't a unit that she recognized. She wasn't overly concerned, crime was unheard of, and it was likely just some confusion.

As she approached the front door, it was still open, and she walked in with the intent of waiting for Lorenzo. However, as she passed the door, two individuals walked down the hallway from the bedrooms.

"Hello, may I help you?" was the very first natural question.

"We have been assigned to in your spare room. We were told to adjust our living space by the Conformity Council."

Helen hesitated for a moment, then remembered Adam's decision to pass the residences to the humans. Apparently, those individuals who were displaced have been put in residences like hers.

"I am aware of the reason why you have been re-assigned. My name is Helen, and my partner Lorenzo will return home shortly. May I ask what your names are?"

"My name is Lianna, and my partner is Roland. I hope that our sudden intrusion won't be a problem?"

"No, we should have no problem adjusting."

As Helen went to the nourishment preparation area, she wondered *if Adam had displaced units moving into his house?*

Commander Harnesy was reluctant to return to Horizon and leave his family on Earth. But he was the only qualified Commander for HSV#4, and he still had a couple more trips to make. That fact alone convinced him that he needed to check out the status of his replacement and make sure that they were up to speed to replace him.

The return trip to Horizon was uneventful. The homecoming celebrations were starting to die down, and there were only minor local celebrations for individuals returning to Earth. The large-scale planet-wide parties were in the past.

Reaching the orbit of Horizon was starting to become just another trip. When Commander Harnesy contacted Horizon upon entering the solar system, there wasn't the hoopla and celebration attached. It was merely, "Welcome back, please call when achieving orbit."

Commander Harnesy didn't bother going to the surface on this trip. He just maneuvered to one of the orbiting support stations and planned to spend his time off there. After all, his family was already on Earth, so he had no need to go to the surface. Once the ship was prepared for the next trip, it would be sent off for its refueling trip through the sun. When it returned, then it would be time for loading and his return trip to Earth.

Six days later, Commander Harnesy sat on the D14 Support Station watching the instrumentation showing the status of HSV#4 as the technicians prepared for her refueling trip into their sun; even though the previous trips were successful, the trips would always be made unmanned. Even for the brief instant, the pressures and radiation levels were extremely high, relatively close to the surface. Any minor malfunction would be catastrophic for the ship and any people inside it.

"Commander, we're ready to launch her into the sun. We've made all the calculations, and she will be in the sun for only 5 nanoseconds or 50 billionths of a second. We've upped it a little from the previous trips. Remember, any structure takes a finite amount of time to collapse; as long as we use the light distortion drive and appear within the sun's pressure for less time than it takes for the structure to collapse, we're ok. We want to get 20% more energy. Hence, we calculate that the ship's structure will take 15 nanoseconds to collapse. It will be in the high-pressure zone for only 5 nanoseconds, so the metal won't approach ultimate.

"Sir, with your permission, we'll send her off."

"Go ahead. Earth is waiting."

As the technician was going through his last checklist items before launching HSV#4, Commander Harnesy was happy that the government of Horizon was building other ships. After all, if anything went wrong, the people on Earth would be stranded until the next ship was flying. Besides that, he would be separated from his family. They wouldn't know about the problem because they still hadn't solved the communications. If a ship never returned to Earth, they would never know why. Everyone would have to wait for the second ship to be finished, and if there weren't any other problems, they would arrive at Earth a couple of months later.

"Five, four, three, two, one…."

"Sir, our indications show that nothing happened. The energy level is still zero. Something must have happened. Standby while we go through the instrument readings."

"Lovely, maybe I jinxed it by thinking about failure," Commander Harnesy mumbled to himself.

"Sir, the instrumentation shows that one of the energy lenses failed. If that is all, it will take about a week to fix."

"That's good news; I hope the people on Earth will be ok without us for a few days." Commander Harnesy said to give the crew some encouragement and hide his fears of what trouble the Prime Minister would get into when he was not there.

"I'm going to check on the status for HSV#5 and make sure that it's on schedule. If we had one failure, we might have more."

Serene and MU11 spent a great deal of time together. The humans moving into the previously occupied houses were too busy taking care of details. Serene's Mother had the help of Bethany, and when Serene wasn't helping, she assumed that she was helping someone else or simply spending time with young people her own age.

The lack of restrictions gave Serene and MU11 a lot of time to meet at various locations. When together, they talked about their lives to that point. Serene talked about growing up on Horizon, and MU11 shared his experiences on Earth. Both sets of experiences were very different. By sharing them, they learned a great deal about each other and their worlds and cultures.

"MU11, you're able to connect to your achieve by just being in a special room and by thinking about it?"

"Yes, it's a personal experience. All we have to do is clear our thoughts, and the room fills with little lights. Then, as our thoughts form images, the lights in the room change size, color, and grouping. The archive takes our thoughts, finds relevant information, and categorizes it so we can see it in 3 dimensions. Then as our thoughts become clearer, the lights coalesce into the patterns that we focus on."

"Wow, that must be a real experience. We have 3 D interfaces, but they don't sound that sophisticated. We can talk to our data archives, but it takes a lot of work, and you only get answers based on the questions you ask. If you don't have a clear question, you get garbage for an answer."

Hesitating a moment, Serene then asked, "What are these robots like to live with?"

"When we interact with them, we change. It's as if we have two families, and we have to act accordingly. When we're by ourselves, we talk freely, play, enjoy each other, and our family life doesn't sound too different from what you described. But when we interact with the robots, we become sedate, quiet, and circumspect in our conversation. It is not that we are pressured to change; it's just the way they act. When we act like ourselves, they can't process information like we do, and I think we confuse them. They are amazing walking, talking computers,' but they do things their way, and we do things ours."

"Is that scientist, Helen, like that? She seems different to me. When I saw her with Adam, she acted differently? I think that she is acting a little like herself but also a little like you. I think she is different from the others."

"That may be possible. She has been around us so much than the others, and she may have changed. They do have an organic processor that is programmed to change and learn. Maybe she is becoming something that is halfway between Us and Them."

"Wow, that would be exciting. I find it interesting how you refer to each other. I understand the explanation you gave me, but we're used to having names that fit our groups of people. From the perspective of the robots, they could start out as Us, and when they created you, they would call you Them. But still, it confuses me," Serene tried to explain.

"Now that I understand your language better, I understand how it might be confusing for you. But, for us, it is clear," MU11 said.

The small stream they were sitting next to was flowing gently around some rocks, and Serene could see some small fish lazily swimming in the current. The world she was experiencing was so much different from Horizon. The colors were so vibrant, and the plants and birds were so exciting. Unlike the huge trees on Horizon, the trees on Earth came in many sizes. The grass was so nice to lay on or walk on with her bare feet. On Horizon, the trees were so big, and cast so much shadow that there was very little growth on the ground. The birds were everywhere on Earth; there were a thousand different calls and songs. On Horizon, the birds were larger and usually higher in the trees. They didn't come to the ground often, and when they did, they didn't seem to sing as much. The earth seemed so much more alive than Horizon, and she wanted to draw it all in.

She leaned back on the grass to enjoy the birds in the trees above her when a strange sound scared the birds from the trees, and she sat up, trying to hear it better.

"Do you hear that?" she asked MU11.

"Yes, I did. It sounded like it was coming from the housing area by the riverbank."

"What do you think it was?" asked Serene.

"It sounded like a discharge of energy. I think we'd better check it out; come on, let's go."

They rose quickly, and MU11 moved out of the shady area faster than Serene. She jumped to her feet had run hard to keep up with him.

MU11 and Serene jogged for about five minutes until they entered a group of homes next to the river. They slowed and waited for some indication of where the unusual noise came from, then they heard it again. It was a loud, deep buzz that vibrated so hard it could be felt through the air. As soon as they heard it again, it was so alien, they knew that something bad was happening.

MU11 led the way, and after crossing the bridge, he turned down a street towards a corner, and Serene followed him. As they turned the corner, the scene in front of them was horrific in a bizarre manner. There were three humans wearing the uniform of the Horizon Soldiers, and they were standing over 10 figures laying on the ground. It wasn't clear to Serene who was on the ground, but MU11 clarified it immediately.

"Those units are Us on the ground. They have been attacked by those men."

MU11 took off and ran towards the units on the ground, and as he approached, the Soldiers heard the noise from behind them, and they turned and prepared to fire on the figure approaching them. Serene stopped and yelled, "don't shoot. He's a human."

One of the Soldiers seemed not to hear her and was raising his weapon when she yelled again, "He's a human. Don't shoot!"

She started to run again, and the Soldier lowered his weapon as MU11 rushed past him. He stood next to the fallen units until Serene caught up with him. She stopped next to MU11, and all he said was, "their memories have been lost."

Serene turned and yelled at the soldiers in a confused yet agitated manner, "What happened here. Why did you shoot them?"

"Ma'am, we're under orders," was all one of them said before they turned and walked down the street.

"Under whose orders?" Serene yelled, but she got no response.

"MU11, are they ok?"

MU11 stood for a moment before answering, "No, they are not. When a unit ends its operation, the memories and information in its processor are uploaded to the archive, and the essence of who they were is transferred and kept. When a unit ceases suddenly like this, its existence is not uploaded, and it's lost. That is a very traumatic event for the Us. Their entire existence is based on the Four Laws and terminating units like this violates all their laws."

Serene was shocked and didn't understand the loss, but how MU11 acted told her that something horrible had just occurred.

The units on the ground didn't appear damaged or anything; they just weren't moving.

"What do we do? This isn't right," said Serene.

"No, it is not right. We must find Helen and Adam and tell them."

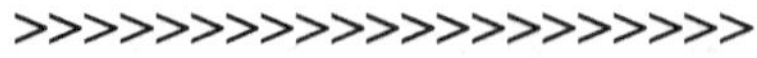

The units around Helen's workplace knew MU11, and they hardly noticed as he and the other human entered the building.

Lorain acknowledged their entry and said, "MU11, I wasn't aware of any meetings today. Are you seeking Helen?"

"Something terrible has happened, and we must find her quickly."

"Something terrible?" she asked. "I've heard comments across our communicators, but they were unclear, and I didn't have enough information to understand. Are the comments that I heard, and your news associated with one another?"

"Yes, we found three of the human Soldiers had attacked 10 units near the housing area that was assigned to the humans. The humans terminated the units."

For a second, the term may not have registered fully with Lorain, "Terminated?"

"Yes, they used some kind of weapon, and the units were inoperative when we found them. I'm afraid they haven't been able to join with the archive."

Lorain stood and processed the thoughts for a moment, then said, "That violates our laws. Why would they do such a thing?"

"We don't know," responded Serene. We're looking for Helen to tell her, and then we'll try to figure out what happened."

"That sounds like a sensible process to follow. As I said, she is not here; she was called to the Conformity Council."

"Thank you, Lorain. Serene, we must go there."

The Conformity Council was only a short walk from Helen's workplace. As they walked, Serene wanted to talk with MU11, but he made it clear that he wasn't in a talking mood. She wanted to understand more about the units and what death or deactivating them meant, but he was non-responsive.

If MU11 wasn't going to talk with her, she went through the events independently, trying to understand what happened. She knew the units weren't violent, or, at least, they hadn't been up to that point, so she thought that she could eliminate that reason. If it was a violent act by the units, it must have been initiated by humans. She was well aware of the Prime Minister's opinions regarding the units, but it never occurred to her that the Prime Minister would go that far. Perhaps she had; her disregard for the units had been evident from the start. Her father had told her about the meetings with the Prime Minister and her staff and their general opinion of sharing Earth with robots, as they call them.

That was the only logical conclusion; the Prime Minister ordered the Soldiers to do it. There must have been something that the Prime Minister wanted, or maybe the units just weren't leaving fast enough. The prime minister wanted to make an example of them. "How could she do that to them?" Serene kept saying to herself over and over.

She wasn't sure what her father would do. He didn't like the woman, and he had taken a lot of crap from her, but he hadn't stood up to her just yet. Maybe this would be the last straw. He was due back to Earth today, and she was sure that he wouldn't stand for this from the Prime Minister.

They finally reached the building of the Conformity Council, and immediately MU11 led Serene through the lower halls to the elevator, which would bring them to the council chambers. He remained quiet, and Serene didn't know what he would say, but she could sense the stress within him. They got off the elevator on the top floor and turned left to the chambers. Serene stopped for a moment and read the plaque on the wall in front of the elevators.

"All activities within our community are governed by these four laws. Each day, we must ask ourselves if our actions support these laws. The charter of the Conformity Council is to ensure compliance with these laws. Please support the Conformity Council."

First law - Continue making units.

Second Law - Protect the units already made.

Third law - Expand the knowledge base.

Fourth Law - Maintain variation in thought.

For some reason, reading the laws there in the Conformity Council's building made it clear to Serene that the units were indeed a separate living entity, and they deserved the respect of the arriving humans.

She felt embarrassed as she turned and followed MU11.

He had a good 'head of steam,' as the old human saying goes, and when he got to the door to the Council's chambers, he didn't knock; he just opened it and walked in.

Serene trailed only a few steps behind him, and it was obvious that the council was deep in discussion, and she saw Helen seated at a worktable in front of the council. She suspected that she knew what they were talking about.

"Helen, Adam, Council, I'm sorry for entering without an invitation, but events have occurred that all of you must be made aware of."

"MU11, thank you for coming. I'm sure that you're here because of the incident between ten of our units and the human's soldiers."

"Yes, I am. Serene and I arrived at the scene immediately after it happened. We didn't see anything, but we saw the deactivated units and the three Soldiers. Why did they do it?

"The information that we received is incomplete. It appears that the humans decided that they didn't want any units around the houses that were assigned to them. Those units hadn't vacated their homes yet, and the Soldiers had been given orders to intercept them and force them from the area. When the units were restrained until the Soldiers could escort them from the area, they became confused. They're not used to following orders and being forced to do things. Apparently, the Soldiers felt justified to terminate the units, per the Prime Minister's orders, instead of dealing with the situation in a more predictable manner."

"Helen, Adam, what are you going to do?" MU11 asked.

"We were just discussing that when you entered. We have numerous options that help us remain within the Four Laws. We haven't decided what we'll do. The first thing we'll do is speak with the humans and try to understand why they took those actions, and then we'll work with them to prevent it from happening again."

"But, what if they do it again," asked Serene.

The room was quiet while the Conformity Council and Helen thought. Finally, after some thought, Adam responded, "First, we'll try to prevent that from happening."

"Dad hasn't returned yet?" Serene asked her Mother.

"No, he was expected today, but no one has heard anything."

"Are you worried?"

"Of course, I'm worried. If anything happened, we have no way to know. They're building other ships, but the next one won't be ready for a while. Without communication from

Horizon, it would kill me if we have to wait until HSV#5 is built to get any news."

"I'm sure he is okay," said Serene providing as much comfort as she could.

"Let's hope so," responded her mother.

"I'm going away again today."

"Where are you going all the time? You're never around here? So, you help for a little while, then when we have things under control, you disappear."

"I've met someone," was all she needed to say to stop her mother in her tracks.

"You've met someone?" she said, half asking and half stating. "Do I know him?"

Serene didn't know how to answer that. "I'm not ready for you to meet him. Dad has met him a couple of times."

"And he hasn't said anything to me?"

"I can't explain that, anyway. I'll finish helping, then I'll leave," she said as she turned and left the room, leaving her mother to deal with the information.

When Serene finished helping, she left the house without saying anything to her mother. She knew that her mother would have had a long list of questions if she said goodbye, and Serene wasn't ready for that. So, she made her way to the bridge, she was scheduled to meet MU11 there, and she was late.

When she saw the bridge, MU11 was standing on the other side, and she waved and ran onto the bridge. He waved back, and she smiled, knowing how much he had changed since she met him and how much of an influence she had on him.

They met and held hands, walking up the river towards his village. Today was a special day; MU11 was going to introduce her to MU1 and FU1 and the others in his community. It was true that Serene had already met his parents and sister, but meeting them again, along with the others, put her in a different position. It put Serene in a relationship with him.

MU11 was most excited about sharing the archive with her and demonstrating some key information that he had come across in his research. Since he met Serene, MU11 needed to understand humans, their history, thoughts, and everything about them. He wanted to know more about her. He asked the archives many questions, and it seemed like the archive was asking him questions. He didn't understand why or how the archive was changing, but it definitely was.

Walking into the village, Serene was impressed. The houses were very similar to the homes they were provided. She thought it was funny that everyone called it a village. The people there noticed her and said hello; many smiled towards MU11 and made small talk about the day's business.

"This is my home and where my ...parents live," MU11 said as he stopped and pointed out the structure to Serene.

"You called them your parents," Serene said with a smile, sensing that he had never used the word before.

"Yes, I found the term in the archives."

"What have you called them before?"

"I called them MU1 and FU1; that is their names. We use the term family to include all members, but we never used the word parents. I like it, and I'm going to tell everyone what it means."

They walked in, and MU1 and FU1 met them at the front door. "Welcome into our home," FU1 said as she hugged Serene. Immediately Serene felt welcomed and comfortable with the two older people.

The tension of a first meeting with the parents of a special friend died down quickly. Within a short time, they talked freely, laughing, and telling stories about living on Earth and Serene about living on Horizon. The time together passed quickly, then MU1 took a breath and asked a difficult question.

"We heard about what happened between the Soldiers and the units. MU11 told us that you arrived right after it happened."

"Yes, we did. I'm sorry that it happened. I can't explain why they had those orders, but I'm sure they came from the Prime Minister. My Dad didn't know what was going to happen. If he did, he would have stopped it," said Serene with the immediate feeling to defend her father even though he wasn't there.

"That was very unfortunate. For the Us to be terminated like that violates everything they believe in. I'm concerned that other problems will occur," said FU1.

"Yes, we all are," responded Serene.

To break the sullen mood, MU1 changed the subject, "Serene, we have been looking for information from the archives that will help us understand how you humans think. Hopefully, we might understand you better and prevent this from happening again. But to be honest, the issues are complex."

She felt the need to respond to the comment and offered the best explanation she could, "You're right, the issue is complex, and if I may point out, we are all human, and we share the same thoughts and feelings," said Serene.

MU1, FU1, and MU11 were a little taken aback by the blunt statement. Finally, after a long and uncomfortable pause, FU1 spoke, "You're absolutely right. We are all the same kind, and I don't know if that is supposed to make understanding each other easier or harder."

"Well put," responded MU1. "Regardless, we are in the middle."

Serene sat for a moment, then a small smile crept over her lips, "There are many of us that don't like how the Prime Minister is handling things; you're not alone in the middle."

Each one's circumstance was clear to everyone in the room, and to break the stress, MU1 said, "Does anyone want something to drink?"

Knowing what he was trying to do, they smiled, and each nodded, indicating that they were thirsty. As he walked to the food preparation area, he commented over his shoulder, "We've asked MU11 to help us interact with the archive. He was eager because he wanted to understand our visitors also. Now apparently, we understand why."

They all smiled, and Serene felt a little embarrassed.

After a light meal where the talk was easy and open, Serene didn't know what the foods were, but most of them were fruits, and they tasted amazing. She was confident that she could eat them all, and she enjoyed the opportunity. When they were done, MU11 explained to his parents, "I want to show Serene the archive room. I've told her about it, and I want to show it to her. It has been changing more, and I think she'll find it interesting."

"Changing more?" MU1 questioned.

"Yes, each time I interact with it, it responds differently. I'm finding its responses to be interactive and surprisingly human."

"That is interesting," FU1 responded. "It will be interesting to see what Serene thinks about it."

It was a short walk, and the sun had already set. Serene enjoyed the smells and cool breezes of her new home. When they entered the archive room, Serene was surprised at how simple it was. She expected some large computer interface device, or, at least, a control panel, but there was only a sphere on a pedestal in the middle of the room.

"Where is it," Serene asked, wondering if he would lead her to another room.

"This is it; that is the interface," MU11 said as he pointed at the sphere. "Go ahead and touch it and see if it responds to you."

"Responds to me?"

"Yes, that is how we initiate the contact. If it senses you, it will let you know, and you'll be able to interact with it."

Serene didn't exactly know how to handle that. Maybe it would recognize her, and maybe it would blow her handoff. "I guess I'll give it a shot," she responded as she gave MU11 a little smile and walked towards the sphere. When she reached it, she hesitated, smiled slowly again at MU11, then said, "here goes."

Serene slowly moved her hand towards the sphere, and she could feel the energy emanating from it. But when she finally touched it, nothing happened. There was no music, no brilliant revelations, and no mind-blowing electricity flowing through her body. She looked at MU11 and shrugged her shoulders, "Nothing."

MU11 was a little surprised. He didn't know what to expect, but nothing happening surprised him. She was human, and all the humans could interact with the archive. She was human, and it should have responded. "I'm not sure why it won't connect; it does for everyone here. Here let me try it."

MU11 casually walked across the room like he was approaching an old friend. He stopped next to Serene and placed his hand on the sphere while he looked into her eyes.

What he felt was unlike any interaction he had ever felt before. His mind exploded with senses and information. Instead of being a passive source, the sphere was active and filled him with information.

Serene saw an immediate change in MU11, and while she looked at his face, his eyes rolled back in his head, and he collapsed on the floor. All Serene could do was scream for someone to help. Within a few minutes, word got to MU1 and FU1, and they rushed to his side.

"What happened," MU1 yelled as he rushed to his son's aid.

"I don't know. He had me touch the sphere first to see if I could connect, and nothing happened. Then he touched it and collapsed. Has this ever happened to anyone before?"

MU1 and FU1 looked at each other, and FU1 said, "No, this has never happened before. The archive has been our library, and we seek information through it. It has never harmed anyone. We can't understand it."

"Where did this thing come from?" Serene asked hoping for an answer that would help her understand.

"The archive has always been. When Helen introduced it to us, we needed some way to communicate with it. Helen and her kind communicate naturally over certain frequencies, but we couldn't. Helen and MU11 devised this sphere, and we've used it ever since. We thought it worked in the same way that Helen communicates," said MU1.

MU1 slowly approached the sphere.

"What are you doing?" asked FU1.

"I've got to figure out what happened. Maybe it is malfunctioning," he said.

Slowly MU1 put his hand on the sphere and stood motionless. He slowly turned and faced FU1. "It is functioning, but … it has changed."

"Changed; what do you mean," asked FU1, still holding MU11, who was starting to stir.

"I can't explain it, but it has motion. Before, it was like reading a page, but now it is in motion. I can't explain it beyond that."

MU1, FU1, and Serene were able to get MU11 to his feet and help him back to his parent's home. He didn't say much except one statement that surprised everyone, "My eyes are open."

After that 'enlightening' statement, MU11 fell fast asleep, and FU1 felt they should let him sleep and recover. MU1 offered to walk Serene to a point nearer to her home, and she readily accepted. It would be a great way to talk with MU11's father.

While they walked, Serene enjoyed the quiet time with him. "MU1, I hope that MU11 is ok. I hope I didn't do anything to cause that to happen."

"I can't imagine that it was due to you touching it. The archive has always been here, and it is connected to thousands of times per day. You, touching it, should have had no effect. I'm sure we'll figure out what happened. I'll ask Helen tomorrow; perhaps she will have an explanation."

While they walked, Serene had many questions she needed answers to. "My father told me that you were the first person created from the DNA that Helen found?"

"Yes, that is true. I was the first, and FU1 was the second. Helen continued until she created 10 individuals from the DNA that she found."

"What was it like to be brought up by Helen?"

"I don't remember being brought up by her. She realized that the archives were missing a great deal of information about rearing a young human. She sought support from our organic friends that live in that part of the village," he said as he pointed to the settlement that was behind some trees.

Serene looked in the direction that he pointed, and she saw a grouping of smaller huts, but she couldn't see anything living there. However, the thought that other organic creatures were living there intrigued her, and she asked, "Can I see them?"

"No, I suggest not. They're simple creatures and prefer to live by themselves. They aren't comfortable around Helen and her kind even though they have spent much time together. Some of them interact with Helen and us frequently, but many of them don't understand, and we don't want to put pressure on them."

"I understand; you said that Helen sought their help when you were young?"

"Yes, as I said, the archives were incomplete, and Helen was able to work out a plan with our neighbors to bring us up as their young and Helen and her team helped. As we grew and learned from the archives, we also helped, and when we were old enough, we built our own village. Then over time, we had our own children, but we continued to live next to them and to share our lives with them. They are comfortable around us, but I suspect they would be very suspicious of you."

Serene nodded her head and took another step, then the world around them exploded with the same sounds that she and MU11 had heard earlier. MU1 had never heard the sound, but Serene knew what it was immediately. Then she realized that the sound was coming from the village where the organics lived, and she knew something horrible was happening.

"MU1, that is the same sound that MU11 and I heard yesterday. Someone is firing their weapons in the organic's village.

It took a second for the distress to build on MU1's face, then he turned and ran at full speed towards the village of smaller huts. He quickly left Serene in his trail, although she did a good job keeping up with him. He burst into the village and was horrified to see many of his friends lying on the ground around the common area. He looked up and searched around the common area, trying to understand what was happening, and he saw five men in uniform walking out of the far side of the village.

Serene caught up with MU1 just as the Soldiers were leaving the village. She immediately knew what had happened, and it made her furious. MU1 was still a little confused and walked slowly to the nearest creature on the ground and tentatively bent over, trying to comfort it.

Serene barely slowed down and sprinted across the open area screaming at the soldiers. "What have you done?" she yelled as they turned. One of them hesitantly began to raise his weapon, and a man next to him put his hand out to stop it as he realized that it was a human female who was screaming at them.

She reached them and again screamed, "What have you done?"

"Ma'am, we defended ourselves," the soldier in front said in a monotone voice.

"Defended yourself; they're unarmed and less than half your size?"

"We came into this village to check it out, and they started running around. We thought they were going to attack us."

"They're harmless; why did you shoot them?"

"Better safe than sorry," he said as he turned and indicated to his men to leave. He turned his back on Serene, and they left the village.

Serene just stood there watching them walk away, acting as if they had just stepped on a bug in the grass. She was horrified, embarrassed and she almost threw up. She turned and saw MU1 sitting on the ground, cradling one of the fallen creatures.

Serene walked slowly across the opening, watching MU1 cradling the fallen creature. When she reached him, all she heard was him repeating, "Lital…Lital."

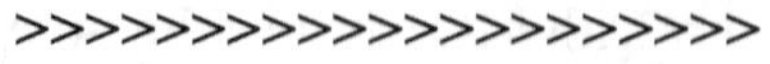

Commander Harnesy paced back and forth in the station. Waiting for HSV#4 to get fixed was driving him crazy. He was not comfortable leaving his wife and two daughters on Earth while he went back to Horizon. Not only uncomfortable leaving them there, but the fact that he also left the Prime Minister. He knew that she would do something that he would have to fix somehow when he got back.

He listened to the comm traffic as he paced, hoping to hear that his ship was fixed. But listening to the familiar traffic helped to keep his mind occupied. The comm traffic was pretty typical until he heard a phrase that was out of place, "This is HMSV#1 ready for a test flight." Harnesy turned towards the person handling the comm system and listened for the response, "HMSV#1, you're cleared for a test flight."

It was tue that Commander Harnesy focused on building HSV#2, 3, and 4 for the last couple of years. He would be the first person to see Earth, so many of the day-to-day operations around him were kept away so he could focus on his mission. But once he heard the call sign "HMSV," he realized that he had missed something major. He had never heard that designation before, and something about it worried him. For his ship and its predecessors, HSV stood for Horizon Space Vehicle. HMSV could mean many things following the same naming convention, but the meaning that bothered him was the M in the lettering. The designation might stand for Horizon Military Space Vehicle.

If he made it obvious and asked, the people around him they would realize that he didn't know about the ship, and they would likely freeze up and not answer his questions. His obvious plan was to act nonchalant, acting like he knew everything."

"I see; HMSV is ready to go; I didn't think it would be ready so fast."

"Yes, sir, we didn't either. After the PM heard about your first trip to Earth, she really pushed hard. It was a real challenge to get her ready and still keep your ship and HSV#5 on schedule."

"Ya I'm sure it was. I'm sure the PM will be very happy when she hears that HMSV is ready."

"She sure will be, and you'll get the chance to tell her that her pet project will arrive about 24 hours after you get back."

Commander Harnesy was doing his best not to be surprised and acting like he knew everything about HMSV. "I'm glad that I'll be the one to give her the good news."

Commander Harnesy was thinking quickly. If HMSV was to carry people, he would have been told. If he wasn't told, then his fear about the 'M' designation was accurate. So, he had to stick his neck out and confirm his worst fears. "She's going to be real happy when she sees what the HMSV has in store for the robots on Earth."

"Yes, sir, it's going to be a big surprise for them when that thing goes off. Stand by, Sir, we've got to monitor HMSV's test flight. I enjoyed talking with you. I think HSV#4 is about ready. You can take a transport to her and get her ready for departure."

"Great, I'm looking forward to getting back," was the only assuring thing he could think of saying. Looking busy and don't look like you care is the best way to stay out of trouble.

Harnesy took the first shuttle to his ship and went immediately to the bridge. The entire time that the passengers were loading, he sat in his command chair thinking about the repercussions of what he had learned. He wanted to get back to Earth; he needed to get back to Earth.

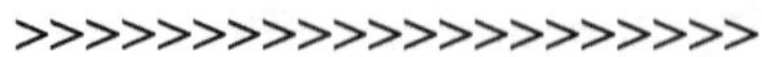

Helen felt like she was spending all her time with the Conformity Council. There were too many issues, and concerns and each of them needed discussion.

"Council, after 10 of our units were terminated, we had another incident yesterday. I know that you're aware of the attack on the organic village. I recognize that many of us feel the organics are of little concern to us, but my concern comes from a different direction. If the Visitors react so quickly and terminate 10 of our units, then follow that with a quick termination of a group of the organics, I suspect they will continue doing what they want with little regard for us. I propose that we prepare our defensive weapon for use," Adam stated to the council.

That statement got Helen's attention. Earlier, she heard they were considering a weapon, but she didn't know anything about its abilities. Regardless, the use of weapons had been disastrous so far, and she thought that any future use would only make things worse.

Even though she was reluctant to hear the answer, Helen asked, "Adam, can you tell me more about this defensive weapon?"

"Yes, I agree it is now time to tell you about it and how we plan to use it."

Helen felt as if the world had just spun out of control around her.

Serene was helping her mother and doing her best not to hint at her relationship with MU11. Serene was able to deflect the questions her mother threw in her direction. Her mother didn't need to know yet, and she would let her father in on the secret first.

The homes that were given to the returning humans weren't all that great. They provided cover, but that was about it. There were separate rooms that could be set up as bedrooms, but there were limitations. The previous residents didn't have personal needs like the humans. There weren't any bathrooms, and even though there was a limited water supply, it wasn't adequate. Besides all of that, they were boring. They were laid out in the same pattern and colors with no yards to speak of. Serene hadn't met anyone that thought the houses were great.

"So, Mom, the PM is still going to build our real houses, isn't she," Serene asked her mother as they unpacked some of their clothing.

"I think so. These won't be fun to live in for a long time. I'm getting tired of walking down the street to take a shower or go the bathroom," her mother responded.

"Sure is a pain. Mom, did you hear about the incident between some of our Soldiers and the local resident robots?" Serene asked, feeling out her mother and needing to hear her opinions.

"Yes, there have been some rumors. I'm not sure what happened, but the Soldiers took care of it."

"From what I heard the robots weren't doing anything wrong. They were just too near and weren't doing what the Soldiers told them. You know, Mom, these robots are pretty sophisticated, and they have their own society. After we abandoned them a long time ago, they've changed, and they're not like the mobile units that we're used to."

"I know; I've heard what your Father has told us. I don't know what to think. I suppose they deserve to be left alone."

"What do you think about the humans that have been brought back with the DNA that was left here?"

"Now, that is a complicated question. I know they aren't robots, but I also know they aren't like us," her mother responded as if she didn't take the question too seriously.

Serene hesitated for a minute, knowing that she was getting into dangerous ground, "What do you mean they aren't like us?"

Her mother also sensed a hidden part to the question, and she turned to face her daughter, "I know they aren't like clones. Our society went through a 'clone' phase a long ago, and no one was comfortable with them. They didn't fit in. Who wants to deal with a copy when they can deal with the original? From what your Dad said, apparently, someone left samples of our DNA when they left Earth. We'll never know why they did that, but they did. I supposed that puts them in a different category than clones. They aren't copies; they're more like cousins. Perhaps, cousins, we aren't comfortable dealing with," she said with a little smile. "I'm not going to get into the whole religious thing; that's way too complicated to figure out. I guess we can categorize them as distant relatives and leave it at that."

"Mom, I've heard rumors of some other incidents."

"Really, what?"

"There are other creatures that live on the other side of the river. They aren't like the humans, they aren't as intelligent, but they live in huts and have a village. I heard that some soldiers went into the village and killed a group of them."

"That sounds too bad, but I'm sure they had a good reason. Let's just finish unpacking those boxes over there; I'm looking for some things."

Serene wasn't satisfied with her answer, but it would be best to let it lie for the moment.

Serene exhaled, hoping to dispel the tension between her and her mother. But, on her next breath, Serene picked up a distinct odor, "Mom, do you smell that?"

"Yes, I do. It smells like smoke. We better go outside and see what's going on."

They rushed out of the house and saw black smoke coming from other homes on another block. There was a ton of smoke, and the problem was obvious.

"Mom, there's a fire."

Bea yelled back into the house, "Bethany, stay in the house, there's a fire on the other street, and we're going to help."

Serene and her mother ran down the street and crossed over to the other side, then around the corner and up the other street. They were shocked to see four houses burning. The local residents were doing their best to get the people out from the adjoining buildings and fight the fire, but they weren't prepared. There was little water and no fire trucks.

"Mom, we can't fight this," Serene shouted to her mother.

"I know, when we came back to Earth, we didn't plan on structure fires. We didn't bring firefighting gear; I think that was planned for later shipments. So, all we can do is get the people out and do our best."

While they were talking, two other homes burst into flames. Serene heard from someone over the chaos, "Oh my God, they're all going to burn."

The street was full of people running back and forth, trying to save what they could and warning other people in the area to get out of their homes and help. The entire scene was full of movement, shouting, and pointing. People were screaming that there were still three people not accounted for.

It seemed that the fire was winning for the longest time, one by one, another home was engulfed, and it seemed to grow.

Serene saw some movement out of the corner of her eye and saw a line of huge vehicles approaching. She turned and was faced with a long line of tankers and robots loaded on transport trucks, "Mother look!" was all she could say before the convoy sped past them. The others on the street just parted and let them through, not knowing what to expect.

The scene developed quickly; the robots on the transport trucks unloaded and pulled hoses from the tanker trucks. The robots on the ground had different shapes; about half were low strung and walked on four legs. A set of large, more stable robots handled the hoses, and smaller bipedal robots seemed to lead the group.

With no hesitation, the smaller robots entered the burning buildings and moved through the structures; after a short time, three of them came out carrying people draped over their backs. The people around them immediately cheered and ran to check on them. The smaller robots searched all the burning structures while the larger ones aimed hoses and quickly brought the conflagration under control.

The people standing around were dumbfounded. Then, without warning, a team of fire-fighting robots had swooped in, rescued three people, and put the fires out in a short time. Then, just as the fires were coming under control, Bea saw the Prime Minister and her chief of staff, Jaled Tern drive up in a small ground transport. When she pulled to stop, she yelled: "What's happening? What are these robots doing here?"

Someone near her yelled back, "They put out the fire and saved three people!" Which seemed to quiet the Prime Minister for a minute.

As Bea watched one of the bipedal robots that appeared to be leading the others, approached a group of people clustered around the Prime Minister. Bea and Serene walked over to hear what was said.

"What are you doing?" the PM said with an indignant sound to her voice.

"We are assigned to this area to control any fires that occur so that we can comply with the Second Law."

The Prime Minister just stood there glaring at the robot that talked to her, and her Chief of Staff Jaled interceded and asked, "Did someone call you and ask for you to help?"

"No, we have sensors, and we respond when needed. We have recovered three of your units, and it appears they need immediate attention. You should see to their repair. Our job is complete now; some of the units will remain in the area to make sure that the fire is out."

With that concluding statement, the bipedal robot turned, and at the same time, about 75% of the other fire-fighting units also turned and began to load on the transport trucks.

Bea looked around and saw everyone just standing and watching, and it was clear they had been surprised by the sudden support from the resident robots. She looked around, trying to find Serene, who had walked away when the robots started to load. She wanted to make sure that Serene was okay. It took a few minutes to locate her in all the chaos and smoke, and when she did see her, she was standing at the end of the street with an interesting-looking young man. Bea wasn't too concerned, even though she didn't recognize him, "he must be from the last group that came down," she thought.

"MU11, what are you doing here? How are you feeling?" Serene asked as she rushed up to him.

"I saw the smoke, and I was worried. So, I came to make sure that you and your family were all right. I feel okay, although I do feel different."

Serene looked at him and didn't know how to respond, so she stayed on the current topic, "I'm glad you came. As you can see, some robots came and took care of the fire. I was surprised to see them, particularly after what happened."

"Serene, your people have been designated units, and the Second Law is to protect all units previously made."

"We never thought about fires when we moved into these homes. When we planned on coming back to Earth, we brought supplies to build new buildings we didn't think would move into existing ones. I know we have firefighting equipment planned for later. We were fortunate that the robots came; this could have been a real mess if they didn't. I think this will change the opinions of some of my people."

"Is that your mother over there?"

"Yes, but I'm not ready to have you meet her. I'm working on her slowly, there has been a lot of changes in her life, and I don't want to add to it."

"I understand."

"Did your father tell you what happened in the organic village?"

"Yes, he did. He was struck hard by what happened. Some of the organics that were brought down were contemporaries of him growing up. There were like family. He is confused and doesn't know how to react. Right now, he, FU1, and other humans are in the village trying to comfort them."

After a few difficult moments, he asked, "When is your father due back?"

"We don't know; he should have been here by now. We don't know if there was a problem. We have no communications with Horizon, we can send ships, but we can't find a way to communicate. So, I'm getting a little worried."

She hesitated before going back to the 'other' sensitive subject.

"So, what happened to you when you tried to connect to the archive?"

"It is difficult to explain. The archive is just there, we ask questions or form thoughts, and it reacts. It is like a large picture drawn in the dirt. You can look at sections of it, but you can't see all of it. When I touched the sphere, I suddenly saw everything, and I felt different. It was like looking at a picture in motion. I still feel different; I think it changed me."

"What do you mean, you feel different?"

"It is difficult to explain. Without going into a lot of detail, it's like I've been looking through a dirty window, and finally, it has been cleaned. As a result, I see things differently."

That was a pretty heavy statement to digest all at once, so Serene let it lie. "You better go; my Mom just saw me, and she'll find a way to wonder over here to check you out."

Commander Harnesy pressed the Distortion Button, and HSV#4 performed as advertised. There was a little shutter in the 3D star image, and they found themselves back in Earth's solar system.

"Sir, we are 89,342 miles from Earth. Shall we proceed into orbit?"

"Yes, proceed. 89 thousand, well, the calculations are pretty good. A couple more trips, and we might just be able to hit the orbit point."

"Contact Earth and let them know we made it back."

"Aye aye, sir."

"Earth, this is HSV#4 approaching Earth's orbit."

"HSV#4, it's great to have you back. We were starting to get a little worried. Did you have any problems?"

"Yes, we had some minor equipment failures before departure. It took a little time to get repairs, but we're here now and ready to download a bunch of anxious people."

"Looking forward to welcoming them. As soon as you're in orbit, we'll send up some shuttles, and you can start sending yours down."

"Acknowledged."

"Sir, I'm running some sensors on the planet, and I've noticed some damage within our housing area. It appears that eight of the structures have burned down."

"After we get into orbit, get the details."

"Yes, sir."

Commander Harnesy sat and felt like putting his head in his hands. "I hope she didn't do something that I'll regret," he mumbled as he thought about the PM.

"Patch me through to my family; maybe I can get some good news from them. I suspect I'm going to need some."

"Yes, sir."

Part 13 A Quiet Day

Serene and MU11 met at the same place on the same bridge where they had met each day. The day was another beautiful day on the planet Earth. The sky was blue, and there was a gentle breeze. The air was still comfortable, and the sun wasn't so strong that a person couldn't stay out all day and enjoy its warmth.

"MU11, I'm glad the firefighters came and helped put out the fire. If they hadn't come, I don't know how many of the homes we would have lost."

"Yes, it was fortunate, and I'm glad that you and your family weren't hurt."

With that statement, he turned and faced her and held both her hands before he said: "I was worried, and when I saw you, I felt better."

She smiled at him, and he leaned in and kissed her. For her, it was pleasant, and she accepted and enjoyed the sensation. Then as they parted, she saw a strange look on MU11's face.

"What's the matter?" She asked.

MU11 hesitated, then with a lump in his throat, he said, "That was my first kiss. I've read about it, and we do it with close relatives. But that was my first kiss with another."

Wow, Serene thought. She hadn't had that many herself, but this must have been some kind of event in his life.

"Did you enjoy it?" She asked, hoping for a positive answer.

"Yes, I enjoyed it much more than I thought I would."

"MU11?"

"Yes."

"Can you tell me more about what happened to you when you touched the Archive Sphere?"

MU11 was quiet as he put his thoughts together.

"I'm not sure. Like I told you before, the archive was a source of information. I would form a thought, and it would present relevant information. Beyond that, it was static. When I connected to it, it became active. I saw movement, I felt the energy, I felt chaos all around, and it was asking me to control it. I saw many images that I didn't understand, but they were different than what I expected. When I look at the world around me, I see it through my eyes. The images I saw in the archive were from a different perspective, as if I was everywhere looking back. It's just so hard to explain."

"Sounds like it. MU11, did I do anything to cause it to happen? Maybe I shouldn't have touched it."

"No, in fact, I got the impression that it was you touching it that changed it. It's like you opened a door and allowed the archive to become what it was destined to become."

MU11 took a deep breath, and Serene sensed he was going to make a major statement.

"I think it was waiting for you," MU11 said with an exhale like he had just said everything.

"Waiting for me? Are you kidding me?"

MU11 wasn't sure how to answer that, "What does kidding me mean?"

Serene looked at him, smiled then realized something.

"MU11, nothing major happened when I touched the sphere, but there has been a feeling growing with me. I feel like there is something that isn't complete. I get a subtle feeling that I need to go back to the archive for some reason. But I can't explain it."

They sat on a log near the bridge for a while. Both of them had a lot of information to digest and understand. Then MU11 had more to say.

"We have found a lot of information in the archive about the people that may have given us our Four Laws. We've also found much about the people that may have planted the DNA for us to find. I think there may have been a plan where they wanted you to come home, and when you did, something would be unlocked. I think our peoples were intended to come together again; we're both ready for the next step. Beyond that, I don't know. I might be totally wrong, but those are some of the impressions that I got."

"Wow," was the only word Serene could utter.

After some more intimate moments of holding hands and thinking, Serene commented, "We just heard that my father is back. He is entering orbit and should be on the ground in a few hours. He talked to my mother, and I think she covered some of the major events a little, but we need to tell him what happened before the Prime Minister confronts him."

"I agree; he is probably the best connection between her and Helen's robots. Perhaps we should talk to him together?" MU11 suggested.

Serene thought for a moment before responding, "Yes, we should. I'll let you know as soon as he lands."

After the shuttle separated from HSV#4, Commander Harnesy had a few quiet moments. The pilot was flying the craft, and he was just a passenger sitting in the back of the flight deck.

He loved those quiet moments when someone else was responsible, and he was by himself. He had the details of the fires that destroyed so many homes, but he knew a lot was going on behind the facts. He also knew that he would be dragged into it before he was ready. All he could do was prepare in some way so he could help. He knew one thing; he would avoid the Prime Minister until she demanded his presence. He needed to go home and spend a few hours with his family. Being with them was where he could clear his thoughts. Besides, the fire was near his home, and he wanted to see the damage, and maybe Bea or his daughters had more information about what happened.

Traveling to his home continued the Commander's quiet time. He had changed clothes, so he wasn't in his uniform, and he was able to blend in with the first load of new immigrants to Earth. He found the ground transportation near the landing site reserved for his crew while they were on Earth. He went directly to his home, avoiding the burned area. He wanted to walk to it so he could see it firsthand and not just drive by it.

"Bea, I'm home," he said as he entered the house.

"Hi," his wife said as she came to the door and gave him a big hug.

"What happened? We expected you to be back last week?" she asked.

"We had some equipment failures, and it took a while to fix, but we made it okay. I saw the reports on the fire. How are you doing?" he asked with a slight emphasis on the word you.

"Okay, the fire really scared us. We have no firefighting ability, and it caught us completely unprepared. We were lucky the robot firefighters came to help."

"Robot firefighters?" he asked, being a little confused.

"Yes, a whole brigade came and pretty much put out the fire, and they saved three people that were trapped. Without them, we would have had a disaster. Didn't the report mention them?"

"Apparently, not fully. It said there was a fire, and some people were saved, and I think one sentence said something about 'locals providing help. But, beyond that, it didn't mention how much help was provided."

"They saved us," was all Bea needed to say.

"Is Serene home? I wanted to see if she wanted to walk to the burn site with me. I want to see it firsthand."

"No, I expect her any minute. She usually comes home down the street near the fire. If you walk over there, you might run into her. She hasn't been around much. I think she has a boyfriend."

"Oh?" he smiled a little, then said, "Okay, honey. I'll be back in a while."

It was easy to find the burned area, between the smell of smoke and the foot traffic. After a short walk, he turned the corner and saw Serene walking towards him. She was holding hands with MU11.

He slowed a little, waiting for his daughter to see him. She was concentrating too much on the boy with her and didn't see her father until she was almost in front of him.

"Serene," was all he needed to say, and she stopped in her tracks, looked at MU11, looked at her father, then dropped MU11's hand.

"Dad, you're … here; already?"

"Yes, I just got back, and I wanted to see the fire. Do you two want to walk over there with me?" He asked, avoiding the other question.

There was silence until they got to the site of the fire. Then he knew that he needed to break the silence acting like nothing was noticed.

"What a mess. I'm glad we didn't lose anyone. This could have gotten way out of control and taken out most of our houses."

"We were lucky; if the robot firefighters didn't come, it would have been much worse," said Serene.

"Yes, your mother told me. She says they saved three people and put out the fire? I should mention that the role the robots played wasn't clear in official reports that I got."

For the first time, MU11 spoke up, "Commander, the robot community has numerous fire-fighting units around the city. They have units designed to enter burning buildings and remove any trapped units. They also have uniquely designed units for the other elements of firefighting, like handling hoses and cleanup. They are very adept at what they do."

"After the last incident with our Soldiers, I was surprised that they helped," Harnesy pointed out.

"Sir, you have been designated as 'units,' so you'll fall under the Four Laws," pointed out MU11.

"Dad, other things have happened," Serene said.

Commander Harnesy surely didn't like the sound of that.

"What?"

Serene took a few minutes and filled him about the encounter between the soldiers and the 10 units, then she mentioned the time with MU11's parents and the attack on the organic village. She failed to mention the encounter with the archive.

"Interesting," was all the Commander could muster, and he was considering the implication when his comm unit came alive.

"Commander Harnesy, this Jaled Tern, the Chief of Staff of the Prime Minister. She would like to speak with you at your earliest convenience. I have sent a ground transport vehicle to your location. Please acknowledge."

"Yes, tell the Prime Minister I'll be there."

"Maybe the two of you should come with me. I suspect this will be an interesting meeting."

The ground transport vehicle turned the corner, and Commander Harnesy, Serene, and MU11 got in the vehicle. While they traveled, they updated each other on current news. Commander Harnesy avoided mentioning HMSV#1.

The vehicle stopped in front of three homes that the prime minister set up as the leadership area. Reluctantly the Commander got out and led the way into the center house, which had a large sign in front which said, PRIME MINISTER BILLINGS.

The front door was open and Harnesy walked in, followed by Serene and MU11. The main room was clearly the PM's office and when she saw the commander, she said. "Commander, I'm glad you were available. Please be seated."

"Ma'am, I don't know if you remember my daughter; this is Serene."

"Of course, I remember you. Nice to see you again."

"Ma'am, this is MU11. He is one of the resident humans here on Earth."

To say the silence was uncomfortable was an understatement.

The Prime Minister's glare rapidly turned to a politician's smile. "Nice to meet you, and this is my Chief of Staff, Jaled Tern; please be seated. Commander, … I didn't expect guests?"

"Ma'am, my daughter is aware of all the challenges that I've encountered, and I think her generation needs to be involved. After all, it will be more their Earth than ours. I invited MU11 because he has lived here his entire life and he knows Helen and Adam. Therefore, he can provide a significant source of information."

The PM sat for a minute, weighing her options.

"Okay, Commander. They can stay.

"Commander, are you aware of what's been happening since you left?"

"I know about the fire … and about how the local robotic fire-fighting brigade saved everyone. I've also heard of some other incidents."

She hesitated before responding, "Yes, … they provided some support. And we appreciate it, but that's not important. We have needs. 5,000 more people are unloading as we speak, including 100 more Soldiers. That along with losing 8 of our houses because of the fire. Our people need more places to live, and I want more of those construction workers to make our houses livable. They are pretty Spartan, and I'm not satisfied."

"Ms. Prime Minister, I'm not sure why you're telling me this. I'm the Commander of HSV#4."

"Well, Commander, you have the most experience with these …robot things … so now you're my ambassador. I'm relieving you of duty on HSV#4; I'm sure one of your crew members can handle the shuttling back and forth. I want to get those houses and construction workers working for me."

"Ma'am, those houses around our settlement are occupied," said the Commander.

"I'm aware of that, but whatever is living in them can move somewhere else. We need those houses."

As Commander, now Ambassador Harnesy was taking a deep breath, Serene spoke up, "Ma'am, those houses are occupied by the Us, and why should they move?"

"Us, what are you talking about?"

"If I'm allowed to contribute, I can clarify that,' pointed out MU11.

The Prime Minister just glared at him, and she didn't say no, so he continued.

"The robots, as you call them, developed a culture on their own, and from their perspective, they were everything. When Helen found our DNA and propagated MU1, Helen and the other robots became Us, and those who were humans became Them. That is how we refer to each other. From their perspective, it makes perfect sense. From your perspective, they are merely robots, but from their perspective, they are a living and thriving race of individuals."

The PM absorbed the last of what MU11 said, shook her head a little, and said, "Okay, they call themselves 'Us,' I don't care what they call themselves; I want those houses. If you can't get them, then I'll use any resources I have available. Is that clear?"

The room fell under an uncomfortable silence for a moment, then Ambassador Harnesy spoke, "What is HMSV#1?"

"How do you know about that ship?" The PM said with coldness in her voice.

"What I heard isn't as important as the fact that I heard it. That is a military vehicle, and it is enroute to Earth. What are you planning to do with it?"

Again, the room was silent. No one moved; hardly anyone breathed. Finally, after a pause that made everyone uneasy, Jaled coughed gently in the corner.

"Ambassador, I have responsibilities, and I plan to satisfy them. That is all that you need to know. Now set up a meeting with this Adam and Helen and get me those houses. You are dismissed."

Faster than anyone expected, Ambassador Harnesy rose, turned, and walked to the door. Serene and MU11 were forced to stand quickly and follow him.

"Ma'am, I'll make sure they set up the meeting," said Jaled.

"Yes, do what you need to, just make sure that he gets me those houses," the PM said with a dismissive voice and flick of her hand.

Jaled followed MU11 as he left the room and caught the door before it closed. He slipped through and followed them down the hallway. He slipped past MU11 and Serene and grabbed Harnesy's elbow when they got to the next door. "We need to talk," was all he could say as he dragged the newly appointed Ambassador to a small room by the door.

"Jaled, please, I want to get out of here. I hope you don't expect to deliver another message from the PM. I really don't want to hear anything else from her."

"Just listen to me for a minute. HMSV#1 is something we all need to be concerned about."

Now, he had everyone's attention.

"Go on," directed Harnesy with more than a little aggravation in his voice.

"HMSV#1 is a military vehicle with a powerful weapon that she plans to use against the robots, or the Us as they call themselves. First, it will destroy the robots, and then PM Billings will have the entire planet."

"What is the weapon?" Serene asked.

"It takes the Light Distortion Engine and can focus the distortion. It has a limited range, but it is strong enough to wreak havoc on the robotic population. It was tested on some of our mobile units on Horizon, and from orbit, it could fry their circuits."

"Why are you telling me this?" Harnesy.

Jaled stood firm and looked into his eyes. "Because we aren't all happy with the way we've come back to Earth. The Prime Minister is making decisions…that make some of us uncomfortable."

"Again, why are you telling me this?"

"We have to find a solution that all of us can live with. I thought you needed to know everything before you talk to the robot leadership."

"Thanks, but I don't know what I'm going to do with that information," then in a gentler voice, he said, "thanks for telling me. Now I must set up a meeting and see what can be done."

Once in their ground transport vehicle, Ambassador Harnesy called his ship, "this is Commander Harnesy."

"Yes, sir."

"I wanted to check in with you and give you a heads up. Apparently, the Prime Minister has changed my assignment, and I'm now the Ambassador between the returning humans and the others on Earth."

"Yes, sir, we were just told. The Prime Minister, herself, called and told us that another Commander would be assigned, and you were no longer the Commander of HSV#4. Judging by the sound of her voice, it didn't sound like a promotion. On the contrary, she sounded pretty angry."

"You read her pretty well, but don't worry about it. Can you still connect me with Adam at the Conformity Council?"

"Sir, she didn't tell us that we couldn't. Stand bye."

Ambassador Harnesy looked at his daughter and her 'guest' and said, "I want both of you to attend the meeting with Helen and Adam. I think we all will need the best people available to resolve this."

"Sir, the connection is made. Go ahead."

"Thanks. Adam, this is Leopold Harnesy."

"Yes, Commander Harnesy. It is a pleasure to talk with you again."

"Adam, my job has changed. I'm no longer the Commander of HSV#4. Instead, Prime Minister Billings appointed me as the Ambassador between our two peoples."

"Ambassador. I appreciate that change. We acknowledge what you have done, and I'm sure you are the best to interface with us. Is that the only reason why you have called?"

"I would like to have a meeting with you as soon as possible; there are a couple of topics that we need to discuss."

"Certainly, Ambassador. Perhaps we can meet at 8:00 in the morning."

Ambassador Harnesy was uneasy waiting that long, but he didn't want to press too hard.

"That is acceptable, and I expect Helen to be in attendance?"

"Yes, she will be."

"For your information, I'll be bringing Serene, my daughter, and MU11, who is one of the humanoids from your village."

"That is acceptable; I know MU11 well. I will see you at 8:00."

"HSV#4, please terminate the connection."

"Disconnected."

"MU11, are you comfortable being there?"

"Yes, I have been working closely with MU1 and FU1 and doing research within the archives. I have participated in discussions with Adam and the council. I think I can be a valued source of information for both sides of the discussion."

"Great, I think we'll need all the help that we can get. We'll meet you there then?"

"Yes,"

Ambassador Harnesy and Serene waited outside of the Conformity Council Chambers until MU11 arrived. When they were ready, the unit near the front door opened it for them, and they entered and sat down.

"Good morning Adam, Helen. I'm glad that we'll be able to talk. Adam, I'd like to discuss a couple of things. First off, you're aware that I brought another 5,000 humans and an additional 100 Soldiers with me from Horizon?"

"Yes, I am."

"I'm sure that you're aware of the fire that we had in our residential area?"

"Yes, I am aware of that also. It was fortunate that our firefighters were able to respond and save three of your units."

"It was indeed, and we are grateful."

He Ambassador took a long breath before broaching the next subject, "Our Prime Minister would like more of the homes in our area to support our new arrivals and also to replace the ones that were damaged. She is also requesting more support from your construction units so that the houses we have currently can be modified, so they are more suited to our needs."

It was Adam's turn to sit quietly.

"Ambassador, you must be aware that will be a difficult request to satisfy. We were able to find housing for the first of your units. We had to displace our units to accommodate you. It will be more difficult to continue moving them as the area you occupy expands. If we were able, it would still take a long time for us to build houses for our units. I'm afraid that we can't satisfy your request in any reasonable amount of time."

"Adam, I expected that answer. I am the one speaking with you, but I am not the human making the request. I'm afraid that any answer that doesn't satisfy the Prime Minister will be difficult for her to deal with. She has 300 Soldiers who she may use to get what she wants. I'd hate to have another confrontation between the Soldiers and your units."

"Ambassador, that last incident resulted in the loss of units which violates our Second Law and is not an acceptable solution."

"Adam, I understand your adherence to the Second Law. I'm also obligated to warn you that the Prime Minister will use any weapon at her disposal to get what she wants. I also must tell you about a weapon that might become available to her. A weapon that she might use."

"Ambassador, 3:42 minutes ago, a ship similar to HSV#4 arrived in our solar system and will enter orbit in 2:42 minutes. Is that the weapon that you are suggesting?"

"I'm not sure, but I suspect that it might be. I don't know what it is capable of, but I do know that the Prime Minister developed it in secrecy after she heard of you living on Earth."

"Ambassador, we have …," and Adam stopped mid-sentence.

"Adam? Helen, is there something wrong?" Asked MU11.

The pause lingered for another couple of minutes, then Adam spoke, "Apparently, the Prime Minister has decided to take action. We are receiving reports that her Soldiers are forcibly removing units from homes around your area. Some of them have been rendered inoperable, which is a violation of our Second Law."

Harnesy was dumbfounded and angry. The Prime Minister made him the interface with Adam, then she started the action without telling him and putting him in a horrible position? She set him up. That was a thought that burst into his mind.

"Ambassador, this meeting has ended. Helen and I are going to the site of the confrontation, and there is an event that I must initiate," it was obvious that he was transmitting a message. When he was done, he stated, "you may come with us."

With that statement, Adam and Helen stood and walked from the room. Ambassador Harnesy, Serene, and MU11 had no choice but to follow them.

Coming out of the elevator on the bottom floor, MU11 pulled Serene aside and said, "I've got to tell MU1 and FU1 and the others. If we aren't involved now, I think we will be soon enough." He turned and left without waiting for a response from Serene. All she could do was turn and follow her father, who was, in turn, following Adam and Helen. They exited the building, and Adams' ground transport was already parked and waiting.

Suddenly Helen stopped, and Adam stopped with her. It was an abrupt stop, and Ambassador Harnesy suspected that something else had happened. When he and Serene caught up to them, it was almost as if Adam was comforting Helen. He touched her arm, and after a moment, she moved again, and they got in the car. Serene and her father climbed in behind them.

When they were settled, Harnesy asked, "Do you have an update on what's happening?"

Adam turned slightly and said, "Yes, the Soldiers are moving our units out of their homes. Many of the units don't know where to go and are hesitating. The Soldiers perceive that as resistance, and in many cases, they have used their weapons. Many of our units are now offline. Unfortunately, Helen's partner Lorenzo appears to be one of the units that have stopped transmitting."

Adam made that announcement in a very matter-of-fact tone, and the ambassador took a few moments to grasp what he was saying. They looked at each other and didn't know how to act. "Helen's spouse may have been caught up in this?" Harnesy whispered to his daughter. "I never thought they actually had spouses," He added.

Serene touched her dad's hand and whispered back, "There is a lot that you don't know about them. They bond for life, and they have children, sort of."

"Where is MU11," Harnesy asked, for the first time noticing that he wasn't with them.

"He went to his people. He wanted them to know about what was happening. They are really caught in the middle. Do you think the Prime Minister did this on purpose?"

"Absolutely, I really don't know why, but I think she set me up. I do know that she considers the robots on Earth to be an inconvenience to her plans."

The ride was only a few more minutes, and as they got close to the conflict area, the foot traffic on the streets seemed to be going in one direction: away from the conflict.

"What's happening now?" Harnesy asked.

"We are transmitting to the units on the periphery of the conflict that they are to leave the area. Unfortunately, your transmitters in the center of the conflict interfere with our communications, and many of our units are getting incomplete or conflicting information. Apparently, your Soldiers are continuing to force our units out of their houses, and if the Us don't comply immediately, they are fired upon," responded Helen.

"Dad, what do we do?" Serene asked with noticeable stress in her eyes. Her father was caught in the middle. He was representing a leader that couldn't be trusted, one that had disregarded all his recommendations and who had ordered the Soldiers to 'kill' innocent robots. Suddenly he felt that he finally understood the situation. Clearly, the Prime Minister had indeed set him up and directed the Soldiers to clear out the robots. Every ounce of his leadership and command skills shouted in his brain that they didn't deserve to be killed; they were a living civilization.

As they got closer to the center of conflict, the streets were more chaotic. Robots that understood what was happening were trying to get away. Some of them were staggering, which implied they had been wounded. They turned the last corner and approached a large square where four large roads came together, and three groups were immediately evident. On the side they were approaching were about 100 robotic units, and they were acting confused, likely from the radio traffic of the military units nearby. About 50 meters away were about 25 Soldiers moving on the robotic units. Behind the Soldiers were about 100 of the Horizon returnees that seemed to be following the Soldiers. Not in a way to force them, but just to follow, likely because they didn't understand what was happening.

Ambassador Harnesy sensed comm traffic coming to him through his personal communicator. He hated the distraction but sensed that he should make the connection and mentally accept the call.

"Sir, this is Ensign Muinez on HSV#4."

"Ensign, what is it? I have a problem down here""

"There is something unusual happening," said the Earth Survey Engineer, who was seated to the Commander's right on the bridge.

"What is it?"

"I'm picking up a massive increase in power concentrated in an area, about 50 Kilometers from the Capital. It's coming from beneath a mountain.

"Sir, the power characteristics are those of a weapon. Beneath the mountain, there is either a circular energy storage container or spherical; I can't tell which. It is huge, and I think that it's getting ready to be released. The energy pattern is below the ground. If I look in the center, I can see a stronger concentration. Sir, the amount of energy is massive. From this perspective, I can't tell if it is a sphere or circle, so it's not clear what the total volume is."

"Standby, I think something is going to happen," the engineer said.

At the same instant, the engineer completed his sentence, the center of the pattern flashed, and HSV#4's alarms all went off at once.

Harnesy could hear the alarms in the background and yelled, "What happened?"

Even though he asked the question, he didn't get an immediate response. Harnesy's former crew was frantically trying to put the puzzle pieces together to form an answer. Then the Core Sustainment Engineer responded to the Ambassador, "Sir, both cores are deteriorating rapidly. We've lost 29% of our energy material, and the decay is slowing but continuing."

"What, that's impossible."

"There was a massive disruption in the magnetic containment fields, and in the time it took them to stabilize, almost 30 % of our Sun Material deteriorated into stable Helium."

"Has the magnetic field stabilized?" he yelled to be heard over the chaos in the streets around him.

"Yes, sir. The variation lasted only a moment, but it was long enough for the material to decay 30%. Unfortunately, we don't have enough power to go back to Horizon."

The ambassador's eyes were large, and his breaths were deep. As long as the magnetic fields had stabilized, the integrity of the ship was assured. But the loss of energy was a crisis. Now he had to control this other deteriorating situation before it got out of hand, and many lives would be lost.

"Stop the car," Ambassador Harnesy yelled. When it slowed, he was out of it and running to a point between the fleeing, confused robots, and the Soldiers. When Serene saw what her father was doing, she bailed out of the other car door and quickly caught up with him.

It took only a minute for them to sprint to a point between the advancing Soldiers and confused robotic units.

"Stop this," he shouted as he put up his hands and faced the Soldiers. "This is not right; you know who I am. I brought you here; you listen to me."

The lead Soldier responded by increasing the volume on his helmet speaker, and he said, "Sir, we are under direct orders from the Prime Minister. She has directed us to clear this area."

"Lieutenant listen to me. Your communicators are interfering with the robot's communications, and that's why they aren't complying. They are confused, and you are causing it. Stop firing on them and turn off your gear."

"Sorry, sir, but we need to communicate with each other and our commanders. The Prime Minister just restated her orders a few minutes ago, and we have been directed to continue."

During the discussion, the humans behind the Soldiers had caught up to them, and they were only a few meters behind them and listening. Then, just as the Soldiers began to advance and raise their weapons, Serene noticed movement to her left. To her surprise and horror, MU11 was in front, followed by MU1 and FU1 and the entire group of humans. They raced across the open area and joined with Serene and the Ambassador.

The Soldiers stopped and immediately recognized the new participants as being human. Once the humans behind them saw the group that was forming between the Soldiers and robotic units, one of them shouted, "They saved our lives and our homes; we can't take away any more of theirs."

With that statement, many of the humans behind the Soldiers either sifted through the Soldier's lines or ran around it and joined the growing group in the middle.

That put the Soldier leadership in a quandary. Their communication traffic increased, which caused more confusion among the cornered robots. Finally, the Soldiers had no choice but to stop their advance. They stood in a group waiting for direction from their leadership.

Ambassador Harnesy saw the front row of Soldiers part, and Jaled Tern, the Prime Minister's Chief of Staff, walked through. He stood for a moment looking at the situation, then he walked briskly towards Harnesy and the mixed group of people behind him.

"Ambassador, we seem to have a situation here."

"Yes, we do," replied the Ambassador. "What are you going to do about it?"

Tern was visibly uncomfortable and shifted from one foot to another before speaking, "The Prime Minister gave these Soldiers specific orders, and you're preventing them from carrying them out."

"Tern, do you know what is happening here? These units have just as much of a right to their homes as we would if our homes were taken from us. They may be robots from our perspective, but they are in charge of their lives, and they have created a viable civilization."

It appeared that Tern was thinking as he looked at the group in front of him, and he seemed to focus on MU11 and his group of humans."

Ambassador Harnesy followed his eyes and felt the need to speak up and hit that issue, once and for all."

"Tern, these people standing beside me are human beings. They are just as much a human as you or I. The first generation was created from DNA, which was left by our ancestors. Their subsequent generations are just like us. They have a place here, and they deserve to be respected."

Tern actually walked in a circle thinking and trying to come up with a solution.

"I'm going to point out one other fact," Harnesy added, "These robots that your Soldiers have 'killed' were confused because the Soldiers' comm equipment was interfering with their internal communication abilities. They were waiting for information from their kind. All they knew was, they were being removed from their homes, and they elected not to follow directions. So, your Soldiers killed them. They are lost and will not contribute to their society; their essence has been lost from their civilization. I was meeting with their leadership, per the PM's direction, to resolve this. But, unfortunately, she acted unilaterally and started this conflict. Is that the kind of leadership you can stand behind?"

Tern continued to pace, glancing towards the Ambassador, and looking around the group.

"Jaled, we have a complicated problem, and it won't be solved with this kind of action. I propose that you and I go to the Prime Minister, explain what has happened, and try to find a way to work this out."

Finally, Tern looked like he was making a decision, "Okay, Ambassador, I agree. Let's meet with the PM and try to find a way out of this."

Jaled walked to the Lieutenant commanding the Soldiers and talked to him, "Lieutenant I am the Deputy Prime Minister; under my authority, you are directed to remain in position and do nothing to put any of these human beings or 'units' in jeopardy. Do you understand me?"

"Yes, sir."

The stress in the group around the Ambassador seemed to lessen, and Harnesy turned briefly, indicating for Helen, Adam, Serene, and MU11 to come with him. Helen and Adam began to follow, but Serene and MU11 stood motionless, holding hands.

"Aren't you coming? I need you with me."

Serene looked at MU11, then her father, and said, "Dad, we have somewhere else to go, a place where we can contribute."

"I need you with me," he pleaded.

"Dad, you won't understand, but trust me. This isn't over, and we'll be more effective doing what we need to do."

That was the first time that Leopold Harney's daughter had stood her ground so firmly, and the Ambassador had no choice but to respect her decision.

"Okay, do what you must. I'll find you after this is over, and we'll talk," he said in a manner that showed respect for what she needed to do, even though he didn't understand her actions.

"MU1, FU1, can you come? I need you to be there."

"Yes, we'd be happy to go with you," FU1 responded.

Once they got in the transport vehicle, the Ambassador said, "Jaled, you need to know that as a result of this incident, a weapon has been fired upon HSV#4, and the power supply has dropped by 30%. That means that we don't have enough power to return to Horizon. So, we are either isolated here until HSV#5 arrives, or we take a high stakes gamble and go to the local sun to refuel."

Ambassador Harnesy had stated the facts for those in the vehicle and specifically for Adam and Helen. He knew they had fired the weapon, and they needed to know the impacts.

"Ambassador, you may assume that I directed the use of that weapon," said Adam. The vehicle was silent for a second even though it continued moving to the Prime Minister's location.

"It is my job and that of the Conformity Council to follow our Four Laws. The termination of units had to cease, and your Prime Minister had to be encouraged to go down a different path. The weapon was intended as a demonstration of resolve that your leadership would recognize. We were unsure of its effects on your ship, but we expected a significant result, and we are glad that there was no loss of units."

After that explanation, there was little to add, so the ambassador made an announcement "Jaled, it is time that you meet these 'other' residents of Earth. First, this is Adam, who is the leader of the Conformity Council. The Conformity Council is chartered with adhering to their Four Laws of Conformity. Second, this is Helen, she was the unit that discovered the hidden DNA, and she was able to create the first generation of humans on Earth in over a thousand years. Finally, this is MU1 and FU1, who were the first two humans created, and they were the first of their generation."

Jaled took a deep breath and shook each of their hands. It wasn't a huge sign, but definitely the action of a man who has just accepted other equal partners in solving a problem.

"Okay, tell me about Earth," was all he said, and it opened up a good discussion that brought them together.

Serene and MU11 made their way quickly to the human Village. They knew where they were going, they knew they had changed, and they knew they would contribute to a larger solution for everyone. They knew that the Earth of the future would be above and beyond what anyone could foresee. They knew that a power was emerging, and they realized that it was larger than either of them. They were just the door through which the changes would emerge.

Ambassador Harnesy, Jaled, and the vehicle containing Helen, Adam, MU1, and FU1 stopped at the communications center for the humans, and they got out looking for the PM. They knew she would be there telling the Soldiers to act in other parts of the city. Besides the Soldiers they encountered, other actions were occurring, and she needed to be in the lead. Other Us were dying.

"Where is the PM?" Jaled yelled to the first person he saw. He got a quick wave indicating that the PM was inside. They rushed in and saw her in a room set aside for radio traffic, and she was talking over the comm system. Jaled gave a hand signal to his subordinate, the leader of the Military, who reported to him, indicating to him to follow them.

The Ambassador, Jaled, and the military commander walked in on her last sentence. "I don't care, Commander. That was a direct order."

"Prime Minister Billings, we need to talk. The situation in the city is changing, and I don't think we're doing the right thing."

"Too late, the problem will be solved in a few minutes," she responded.

"What do you mean?" Harnesy said with an edge in his voice.

"Who are these others… and why are they here?" She said with indignation in her voice.

Adam spoke first, "I am Adam, and I speak for the Us on this planet. Your military is killing our units in a violation of our Second Law. You must stop."

"And who are you?" she directed to Helen.

"I am Helen, and I discovered the DNA," which the PM acknowledged with an un-impressed head nod.

"I know who you are and what you think you are," she said, looking at MU1 and FU1.

"What do you mean the problem will be solved," yelled Ambassador Harnesy.

"I just directed the Commander of HMSV#1 to use his weapon on the capital. That weapon will solve all our problems."

"You mean it will solve your problems," Harnesy responded.

"What will this weapon do," Adam asked.

"It may disrupt your processor circuits," responded Harnesy with a nod from Jaled, "It will kill your units."

Jaled jumped in, "Prime Minister Billings, your actions are not in line with our laws, and I will direct the military to cease all aggressive actions until we can work through these problems."

"Go ahead," she responded. They aren't the ones you need to worry about.

"What do you mean," asked MU1.

"HMSV#1 is what she means," responded Jaled.

"Colonel, get the Commander on the radio. I am taking over for the Prime Minister, and we are stopping all actions."

"Sir, I'm sorry. But the PM gave the Commander orders to turn off his radio until after his mission was complete."

Serene and MU11 ran into the village and went directly to the Archive Sphere. They knew why they were there. They didn't know what they would do, but they knew they had access to a tool that could be much more powerful than any other player.

They stood on opposite sides of the sphere, looked at each other, and then put their hands on it.

Suddenly they saw, they didn't use their eyes, yet they saw everything and heard everything. They were no longer in the archive room, but they were everywhere. They saw the group confronting the Prime Minister, they saw HMSV#1 in orbit, they saw what the Commander was preparing to do, and they even saw the people on Horizon waiting excitedly for their turn to travel to Earth. The solution was simple.

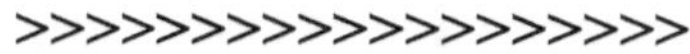

HMSV#1 was no longer in orbit around Earth; it was in deep space 52.7 light-years away. The crew didn't feel anything; they didn't notice anything until the Earth vanished. The Commander didn't know what happened, how it happened, or why it happened. He also knew that it would take many weeks of calculations to find a way to return to either Earth's orbit or Horizon. Their mathematics wasn't written for a long jump from that position in space, so they had a lot of work to do.

Everyone in the Prime Minister's room knew immediately that HMSV#1 was gone. They didn't know where it went or how it got there; they only knew it was no longer in orbit.

"Ms. Billings, I don't know how I know it, but HMSV#1 is no longer an issue," said the Ambassador to a room of confused people and robots, yet they all understood. "We all need to talk."

"Ambassador, you work for me. I'm taking steps to protect Earth from these…robots…and what they created. You will do what I tell you."

Ambassador Harnesy looked at Jaled and made a simple statement, "Please remove her."

There was only a moment's hesitation before Jaled nodded to the Soldier at his side, and the ex-Prime Minister was escorted from the room, despite her screaming.

The first discussion took only an hour. The only agreement was that they needed to slow down and work together to find a solution. Prime Minister Harnesy led the discussion, and all actions against the robots were stopped.

"Now that we have to wait for HSV#5 to be finished and come here, we have time to figure out the best solution for all of us," he announced.

Serene and MU11 smiled. They knew what they had done; they knew what was happening. They knew what Leopold Harnesy was saying, and they knew when HSV#5 would enter orbit. But they also knew they had time to solve the problems that the people from Horizon brought to Earth.

Helen went to her home. Approaching her neighborhood, she slowed, and she approached the residence that she had shared with Lorenzo and Thomas. She didn't know what she would find, but it would be difficult. What she was feeling wasn't normal for creatures of her kind. She had feelings that were new to her, and they were very uncomfortable.

Helen turned the corner and saw the front of her home and the shape of her partner on the grass in front. She slowed her vehicle, never taking her eyes off Lorenzo's form. Parking the transport vehicle seemed to take more concentration than normal, but she accomplished it. She got out of the vehicle and turned to approach the motionless form of Lorenzo. She had no concept of how to deal with the loss. All she could think of was to remember all their time together and save the memories so they would be uploaded to the archive when her time came.

####

The End

Ray Jay Perreault Free Book

Ray Jay Perreault has an Award-Winning Science Fiction Novel available – no strings attached; follow this link, and you'll be able to get a FREE copy of "Virus-72 Hours to Live." Winner of the 2016 Apple Literary Award as the summer's best Science Fiction.

By joining my reader's club, you'll also have the opportunity to get other books of his FREE or discounted as well as having the option to Alpha/Beta Read his new novels before they're released.

Link to Join my Reader's Club

I often run campaigns for the other eBooks and Audible books. So, you'll have the chance to get major discounts and other FREE opportunities.

Epilogue

Thank you for reading this book. "Progeny" and "Circle is Closed" were originally written as short stories. However, they complimented each other and covered two points of time in a larger story. After I wrote them, I saw the potential of creating an interesting moral dilemma. So, I combined the stories and expanded the back story.

With this release, I've separated the story into a two-part story and boxset. That will allow readers that bought "Progeny" to continue the story without having to buy boxset "Progeny's Children."

This story allowed me to explore another type of evil. Unfortunately, evil is usually depicted in a simplistic form in most Science Fiction literature. For example, the antagonist is an evil computer or evil corporation or just an evil creature, but the author just leaves it. I like stories that take the evil in different directions, and I hope this book does that.

Evil is always in the eyes of one side of the conflict but not the other. In this book, humanity was put in a difficult position, and some of their options could easily be seen as evil. But from their perspective, some of them didn't think so.

I hope you think about evil in literature, and possibly reading this book will give you something else to think about.

Ray Jay Perreault

http://rayjayperreaultcom

rayjayperreault.com

About the Author

Ray was born in New Hampshire, received his Bachelor of Science in Aeronautical Engineering at Arizona State University. Now retired from an influential, multi-decade career in aerospace.

Bringing a new voice to science fiction writing, Ray realized a niche was calling him as he began to write deeper characters and create more sophisticated stories and realistic situations for Sci-Fi fans to relate to.

Initially attracted to heroic characters with powerful weapons taking on hundreds of aliens, Ray began his literary career with a desire to extrapolate Sci-Fi stories with a touch of everyday reality that most of us experience in work and our everyday lives.

His literary work is thoughtfully enriched by his decade-long experience in the US Air Force, where he flew C-130s on missions to 27 countries and T-38s while training the best pilots in the world and the first female US Air Force pilots.

During his 28 years at Northrup Grumman, Ray worked on some of the most top-secret military aircraft projects globally, including the F-23, F-35, B-2, Global Hawk, and many more that can't be named.

He is grateful to his wife, Charlene, and his two daughters, Christine and Robynn, for their support on this new journey.

Books by Ray Jay Perreault

<u>eBooks</u>

SIMPOC Bk1 – The Thinking Computer - Amazon
SIMPOC Bk2 – Human Remnants - Amazon

Virus – 72 Hours to Live (Bk1) - Amazon
Virus – Earth's Last Battle (Bk2) - Amazon
Earth II -You Have No Honor (Bk3) - Amazon
Earth II – Rebirth (Bk4) - Amazon
Earth II – Julius the First (Bk5) - Amazon
Earth II – Emergence (Bk6) - Amazon
Earth II – (Bk7) IN WORK 2021

Gemini - Amazon
Progeny's Children-Amazon
SIMPOC Box Set (Bks 1 & 2) - Amazon
Survivors - Amazon
Fermi's Pair of Socks - Amazon

Short Stories

Progeny - Amazon
The Greatest Host - Amazon
Circle is Closed - Amazon
Good Morning... - Amazon...
Red Dots - Amazon
Science Fiction Anthology Vol. 1 Ed 2 - Amazon

Contact the Author

I love to get any comments from you. So please drop me and let me know your thoughts.

mailto:rayjaywriter@yahoo.com

Wordpress.com

Facebook.com

yahoo.com

tumblr.com

twitter.com

google.com